Two Pumps
for the **Body**
Man

Two Pumps
for the Body
Man

B. A. East

NEW PULP PRESS

Published by New Pulp Press, LLC, 926 Truman Avenue, Key West, Florida 33040, USA.

For information contact:
Publisher@NewPulpPress.com

ISBN-13:978-0692668443 (New Pulp Press)
ISBN-10: 0692668446

For S.A. East, Jr.

In '43 he sailed west to Pearl, then onward through the Pacific: Tinian, Saipan, Iwo. He was a U.S. Army sharpshooter, an MP guarding Japanese prisoners of war. In '45, weapons at rest, he traveled back east by train. He worked as a plasterer at the White House. His clearance gave them fits: his fingers, worn smooth by labor, refused to yield prints.

And to the memory of five friends whose stones ring a grassy plot beyond reach of the inhospitable Arabian desert: Imad, Basheer, Romeo, Ali bin Taleb, Jaufar Sadik.

Two Pumps
for the **Body**
Man

... does that Star-spangled banner yet wave
o'er the Land of the Free, and the Home of the Brave?

- U.S. National Anthem

PART I

Chapter 1

Shouts and sirens drowned the urgent chatter on Jeff Mutton's two-way. The diplomatic security agent shut his catalogue – women's footwear – and grabbed the phone. "What is it?" he demanded of the Marine standing post.

"National Guard up and down the street. I got zero visibility at Alpha gate."

"What's the problem?"

"Saudi troop transport parked in front of the camera."

The radio blasted static. More chatter. Mutton didn't understand the Arabic, not even after two years in the Kingdom. But he understood his crawling nerves and the prickling hairs on the back of his neck. He turned down the radio and paced like a bulldog, restrained by the phone's short leash. Squat, muscular, square-shouldered, Mutton resembled a bulldog: no neck, a glower, a crewcut.

"Lock us down now!" he ordered. "No one in or out. I want everyone under a desk." Everyone meant scores of souls at the American Consulate, a bitch of a situation in the bald desert heat, Saudi militants all around. "I'll get Hassan to work the truck. Give me one minute, then hit the duck and cover."

More sirens as Mutton dialed. Popping: gunfire. "What do you make of it?" he asked his deputy.

"Interior Ministry," said the cool Yemeni. "Going after their fifty most wanted."

"Where?"

"Hajrayn."

Mutton knew the neighborhood. A maze of old buildings opposite his compound. "Can you reach Ghani? His truck's blocking our view at Alpha gate. We need –"

– the hi-low alarm wailed, obliterating all other sound. "Dammit!" he shouted. "Meet me at Post One!"

Mutton crouched behind his desk and locked the footwear catalogue in a drawer with his Bible. He spider-crawled to the Mosler safe and grabbed his Sig Sauer P229. He eyed the shotgun rack, decided he was going outside, and grabbed his short-barreled Colt. He slid a polished black holster onto his belt and locked an 11-round clip in the Sig. He took his Kevlar vest off a peg and shouldered in.

Mutton pushed through the heavy door to the lobby. There stood Hassan, the big Yemeni majestic in his floor-length thobe. No Kevlar. Cool.

Mutton signaled and Decker released the locks on the heavy ballistic doors. Mutton pushed out. Shouts and sirens filled the afternoon. The heat pressed down as Mutton crouched along toward the gate. Hassan moved beside him, erect and unaffected.

"Not a drill," Mutton told the guards in the control room. He looked out the ballistic door separating his secure environment from the threat outside. National Guard lorry in front. Squad cars at either end of the street. Masked soldiers guarding an empty prison wagon. Up and down the street goons from Interior carried themselves like cops anywhere: glowering and severe, thick black mustaches drooping like frowns, sharp noses and heavy foreheads over thick-lidded eyes. They gathered in clusters and spoke into radios, handguns in black leather holsters, straps crossing at the back of their white thobes.

"What do you make of it?" he asked Hassan, stalling, unwilling to go out.

"Standard round up."

Mutton looked again. Up the street to the left the mosque, minaret peering over his wall. Behind the mosque the Kingdom Hospital, it's glass façade rising twenty stories above his 40-acre compound. Mutton looked for Ghani.

"There!" A Filipino guard pointed with his radio.

A line of bearded men, bound at wrist and ankle, marched toward the prison wagon. They wore short, dirty thobes. They walked in a hobbled line.

"Terrorists," Mutton said, unconvinced.

Hassan Ali lifted his chin. "Ghani."

Mutton saw the handsome commander emerge from Hajrayn. He moved fluidly, a man most at ease raiding terrorist safe houses.

Mutton radioed Post One to kill the alarm and unlock the door. An eerie silence settled. Ghani stepped in and the Marine locked it back down.

"My friend," Ghani said. He hadn't broken a sweat. "You like it?"

"Not in my front yard, no."

"Not to worry, my good friend. It is protection. To keep our best allies safe." Ghani's eyes twinkled. Stubble darkened his cheeks.

Mutton hated having to trust Ghani. "What's going on?"

"We had a tip."

"You couldn't warn me?"

Ghani shook his head. "I am sorry. Eyes and ears everywhere."

Mutton understood. He also eavesdropped. "What have you found besides prisoners?"

"My good friend. We will do forensics on the crime scene."

"Weapons? Explosives? Maps? Any leads on what they were watching?"

"We will persuade them to talk."

"The consulate?"

"As yet, I do not know. You can't rule it out."

"Commander Ghani, the truck –"

– Loud pops erupted. POP POP POP. Ministry agents rushed in packs toward the intersection, toward the gunfire. POP POP POP. Ghani whirled and pushed the door but it didn't budge. He pushed until Mutton pulled him back. Both men watched through the blast-resistant glass – agents rushing into Hajrayn, weapons drawn.

Mutton lost his breath before he heard the blast. They all hit the deck. On the street now agents ran from the intersection. A cloud of dust and smoke, then a thick plume, pushed out from the maze and up over the buildings opposite the consulate.

Chapter 2

Jeff Mutton was summoned to the Consul General's office. Vanna Lavinia waved him onto a sofa in the sitting area, where heavy furniture stood on rich Persian carpets. She joined him, eager to get away from the pile of diplomatic cables sandbagged on top of her desk. She had no stomach for that kind of reading. A fit and leggy blonde, Vanna had very little stomach at all.

"I want facts, Mr. Mutton. Not theories." Displeased, she was going straight to it. "Tell me why you insist on keeping us closed."

"Fact. Interior Ministry raided three terrorist safe houses across from our front gate."

Vanna smirked. "That was yesterday. And Interior arrested the culprits." She spoke with confidence, her blond bob and pert little nose the very window dressing of her certainty.

"Fact: Interior encountered heavy resistance. Fact: terrorists blew up a fourth building. Fact: a bunch of cops and Interior agents were killed in the operation."

Vanna shook her head. "Question: how many terrorists? Question: was it a bomb, or merely construction in Hajrayn? Question: how many Ministry casualties?"

Mutton looked away. Straight-backed in her armchair, the athletic, porcelain-skinned CG towered over Mutton. He sank lower and lower on the burgundy sofa until he'd sagged to the level of her coffee table. Down there he caught sight of her ankles and felt weak. She made him hot. She made him bothered. She made him wish to be imprisoned beneath the high, narrow arch of her peek-toe shoes! He could barely stand the way she made him feel, which was why he loved her so much. Exactly how he'd felt during his short marriage, which he'd survived by getting a divorce. 'Fact,' he thought, 'You're hot.'

Vanna sought to put Mutton at ease and passed a crystal bowl of chocolates. "Go ahead, Mr. Mutton. They do nothing for my figure."

Mutton reached for a chocolate with stubby fingers, ignoring the opportunity to flatter.

"Now, why don't you tell me your concerns?"

"It concerns me that Ghani didn't share intel on terrorists in our neighborhood."

"It's their city, Mr. Mutton. Your jurisdiction ends at our front gate."

"As a courtesy – "

"Did the terrorists attack us?"

"Not this time."

"Because our allies took the hit. Our allies protected us. We should be grateful."

"I don't trust Ghani. I don't trust any of them." Mutton stopped, conscious of how bad it sounded. He took in the office, sensitive to the kind of diplomat he was dealing with. Scores of photos hung like trophies on dark paneling: here Vanna had conquered a shriveled Yasser Arafat; there she smiled beside Moammar Gadaffi; her broad grin beamed between the scowling faces of Robert Mugabe and Dr. Hastings Kamuzu Banda. Covering the walls were photos of herself with Fidel Castro, Daniel Ortega, Hugo Chavez, Idi Amin, Jerry Rawlings, and a black man in a leopard-skin pillbox hat. Mobutu Sese Seko.

"Listen," Mutton said. "Interior Ministry's conducting the interrogations. We'll never know the truth."

"So you have no facts. So I am ordering us to re-open."

"The fact is, torture produces unreliable results."

"Mr. Mutton, you are talking about our allies."

Mutton lowered his eyes and kept mum. Vanna

decided she'd got him in a corner and changed her approach.

"I understand your distrust of Commander Ghani. So why not ask someone you *can* trust?"

"Who would that be?"

"Sheikh al Bafarti."

"Al Bafarti? But isn't he a –" Mutton stopped. Accusing the sheikh of financing terror would pit him openly against Vanna. Poker talk suggested passion between her and the small, brown Arab, and Mutton was afraid – with Vanna Mutton was always afraid – that she'd read his accusation as sexual jealousy. That was another front in another war he had neither the will nor the weapons to fight: Bafarti's role as a terrorist financier Mutton could deal with, but smutty images of a voluptuous Vanna sprawled on her back beneath a hawk-nosed midget, pumping away ... this erotic scene sent boiling blood straight to his head where it paralyzed him with rage.

"He's in construction, Mr. Mutton. Or what else did you have in mind?" She fixed her angry blue eyes on him. "Sheikh al Bafarti handles 90% of the construction in Hajrayn. That puts him in a position to know a thing or two about terrorist safe houses there. Don't you think it would be in his interest to know a thing like that? Certainly a man only measures up to that kind of wealth from a lifetime of knowing every angle."

"Ma'am, with due respect. I'm responsible for security at this Mission. I insist we remain closed until we finish the security upgrades recommended months ago."

"Mr. Mutton, you are in charge of *security*. I am in charge of the Mission, which includes security. And so much more. I will not allow us to be kept closed. It sends the wrong message to our allies and emboldens the enemy. Closing this mission runs counter to our strict orders from

Fourth Branch to maintain solidarity with the Royal Family. Am I clear?"

"Did you say Fourth Branch?"

Vanna backpedaled. "We have strict orders to show solidarity with the Royals."

Mutton tightened his lips and set his jaw. His face reddened. He took the short stub of pencil from his ear and rolled it between his palms. "We need barbed wire," he said. "Jersey barriers. Shotguns. We need sandbags, towers, a new drop arm. I need training for my guards. Any day now the enemy's going to jump that wall, storm that gate, bomb that gas depot. They're watching from the hospital. Diplomatic Security authorized two-point-five million months ago, yet we haven't started a single project."

"D.S. authorized it. Did Congress approve it? And just listen to yourself. Barbed wire? Jersey barriers? Shotguns? Are you building a prison? You're using threats and terror to dig us in. That's what the terrorists want: to drive a wedge between ourselves and the Royals."

"Let me install new wheels on the gate. Just that."

"You said we can't repair the gate without causing major traffic delays. We are *not* going to be bad guests in the Kingdom by tying up traffic."

"If the gate doesn't close faster –"

"Have you tried a little WD-40?"

"WD-40? The problem's much bigger than WD-40."

"Because sometimes I find a little WD-40 can help these things."

"This isn't something for WD-40."

"And if not a little WD-40, then a lot of it. A *LOT*."

"But, ma'am ..." Mutton wasn't getting through.

"WD-40. It's a lubricant. A marvelous lubricant." She spoke the word lasciviously, her lips puckering, the soft 'ooh' pushing out the slightest hot breath before catching on the 'b' and bringing her lips back into a smile.

Mutton stared, wondering what lubricated fantasy the word brought to her mind, then snapped out of his trance. "Ma'am, the entire mechanism needs replacing. We can do it in a week. Give me one week."

"We are *not* disrupting traffic. You can start another project, but you'll need to balance the negative image with some positive diplomacy."

"Diplomacy and security don't always work together."

"Make them work together. Or do I need to remind you of your little performance in my closet?"

Mutton froze. It was the first time she'd mentioned it since his humiliation.

His submission emboldened her and Vanna leaned in. She hadn't had a man in such a long time. Not that she wanted a man. Not this kind of man, anyway, not a cop. A man of wealth perhaps, someone to raise her above her white-trash Texas roots. But it looked more and more as if she'd spend her life alone. That made an ambassadorship so vital to her. She could maintain her independence *and* have the kind of luxury she deserved.

"Open us up," she said. "Lift the security directives. Let the Facilities and Recreational Services Association host a party."

"FARSA is free to entertain at the beach house."

"I want parties *here*. Real parties. Diplomatic parties, with hundreds of guests."

Mutton was silent. He could never go against her wishes as long as she held that humiliation over him. How much more did she hold on the others? On No Lips, he already knew. On Storp? Belvedere? The Junior offices?

"We have an agreement?" Vanna prodded.

"I fix the gate. You host a party."

"Not the gate. Something else. But work with Potts in Public Affairs. Now that parties are allowed, we have only two months before the Fourth of July. We have a big reception to plan. If you see Miss Wellstone, tell her to draw up a guest list. We're having a party here this weekend."

Chapter 3

The heat pressed down, low and suffocating. Mutton slung off the heavy Titleist golf bag and strapped it to Vanna's golf cart. Hassan set down a big black duffel, a heavy metallic clank ringing forth as it hit the dust.

"This is a golf outing?" Ed Kahn asked. The Pakistani-American had brought the cart around from general services.

Mutton shook his head. "M4," he said, tugging a head-cover off the wide black snout of a rifle barrel.

He hefted the weapon, checked the safety, and aimed at the sky. Construction cranes marked the skyline. Mutton lowered the rifle. An explosion from the construction zone in Hajrayn sent shudders down his spine. Two days earlier explosions in Hajrayn had killed half a dozen of the Kingdom's elite forces. And now, at Vanna's insistence, the consulate had re-opened. Mutton was taking action. He tapped each of the black and white head covers. "Colt SMG 9mm submachine gun. M249 SAW machine gun. M240 belt-fed. And this." Mutton pulled it out. "Shorty. My Remington 870 shotgun."

Ed lifted a pick and spade from the golf bag. "And these?"

"These are for digging."

"Digging? As in, a sand trap?"

"What?"

"I mean, the golf bag. Why are the pick and shovel in your golf bag? What's the connection?"

"That's not my golf bag. I don't play golf."

Ed was confused. The junior officer had been at the consulate for just a week and he didn't want to ask too many questions. He thought he'd try one more. "Are we going golfing, shooting, or digging?" he asked, figuring he'd covered the bases.

"We're keeping them guessing," Mutton said. He nodded toward the hospital.

"Keeping who guessing?" Ed looked. All he saw was the hot sun glaring back at him from the hospital's mirrored façade.

"Let's go," Mutton said. They climbed on and Mutton sped toward Bravo Gate. An iron drop arm and a steel girder made a narrow lane. A lead plate stood at 45-degrees, blocking the entrance. "Delta barrier," Mutton said. "Could stop a tank. But it won't stop attackers on foot. Got a second hand on that watch? Ok – clock it when the gate starts opening."

Mutton took out the M-4. He stepped behind the cart, laid the barrel across the back, and sighted toward the entrance. He radioed the guardhouse. The gate lurched and rolled open on creaking wheels. When the gate had opened half way, the Delta barrier dropped and hit the concrete with a boom. Then the process reversed. The gate rolled shut, the hydraulics ground heavily to raise the plate, Mutton squinting into his sights the whole time.

"Time?"

"Forty-two seconds."

Mutton cursed. "Got any idea what can come through that gate in 42 seconds?"

"Wouldn't our guards – "

"Our guards are unarmed. And the Saudis outside have no ammo. Hop on."

They drove across the 40-acre plot. A dozen buildings squatted on the sand. Bungalows, offices, a workshop and warehouse, Marine barracks, a medical unit, the Consul General's residence, all built along a half-kilometer loop of potholed tarmac. A flag rose from the center of the compound beside the snack bar where Miss Wellstone was preparing to host a disco. Stray cats chased dust devils spinning between the steady waves of heat shimmering off the sand. Looking down on it all, the glaring façade of the Kingdom Hospital.

"Second worst facility in the entire Foreign Service," Mutton said. "Couldn't even get that right."

They drove on.

"Every one of these buildings is a deathtrap. No hard lines. No locks. No blast doors." Mutton stopped the cart. The humidity hit them full and hot. Mutton pointed. "See that?"

"What, the wall?"

"On top of the wall."

"I don't see anything on top of the wall."

"Exactly."

Ed squinted. "I don't see it."

"Razor wire."

Ed saw only high-rise buildings beyond the wall. Construction cranes. Sunlight glimmering off the hospital. "I don't see it," Ed said, squinting.

"Because it isn't there."

Ed looked at Mutton but saw nothing in his face to prove the man had gone mad.

"We need it installed. How long will it take?"

Ed shrugged. What did he know? New to the Foreign Service and even newer to the consulate, he was filling in for the General Services Officer. Tom Cautwauler had asked for a transfer to Iraq where he thought he'd be safer rebuilding that country than working at the consulate in Saudi Arabia. Ed recited the bureaucratic language he'd learned from Cautwauler.

"Procurement procedures have to follow the regulations set forth in the Foreign Affairs Manual, Book Two —"

Mutton cut him. "Don't talk like Cautwauler. Don't

13

think like Storp. Think like someone whose life depends on this." Mutton had sorted Ed out fast: quiet, smart, malleable. Not likely to cause trouble. Just another soul to be protected, and Mutton wanted to set him straight. "Your life depends on it."

Ed's stomach stirred, a common ailment since reporting for duty in the Kingdom. Back in Washington they'd patted him on the back and congratulated his bravery. They'd told him he was serving on the front line of the war on terror. But the backpatting there didn't comfort him here, and Ed had been forced to seek help at the health unit. Yet Dr. Meddler could find nothing wrong.

"You feel symptoms, but you have no illness?" the bald, bespectacled doctor said. "Sounds like hypochondria. Very common in the WOT."

"The what?"

"The WOT."

"I'm sorry. I –"

"The war on terror. You'll be ok. It's nothing."

"It feels like I have *something*. I feel nervous and sick."

"That's the war on terror. Here, take this to Nurse." The doc handed him a slip. "She'll sort you out."

Ed brought the prescription to the FARSA warehouse where he was given a bottle each of vodka, gin, rum, and scotch.

"But I'm a Muslim," he told Miss Wellstone. The FARSA manager promised to keep his secret to herself.

"It's not a secret," Ed said, but Miss Wellstone sent him away with a merry wave.

Remembering this now – the diagnosis, the flawed prescription – Ed gripped his stomach and told Mutton he'd help secure the compound.

"Now you're talking. Let's go." Mutton drove to the north wall. He handed the pick and spade to Ed and unstrapped the black duffel. The bag clanked as Mutton hoisted it over his shoulder. At the wall Mutton set down the M4 and took the pick. He swung and grit his teeth, jarring his arms up to the elbows. Ed scraped the surface gingerly with his shovel. A thin film of dust covered hard corral.

"What are we doing?"

"Planting decoys."

"By hand? But this is coral. You know they're using dynamite to blast this stuff over in Hajrayn." As if to prove it, another explosion ripped the afternoon. Mutton shuddered. Ed gripped his shovel with one hand and rubbed his stomach with the other. Mutton went back to work, already sweating, jarring his arms against the coral.

Ed said, "We can hire an army of foreign workers to do this cheap."

Mutton shook his head, grit his teeth. "Non-cleared personnel can't know what we're dropping in."

"What're we dropping in?"

Mutton kicked the duffel. "Ordnance."

"Ordnance?"

"Dud ordnance," Mutton said, and went back to swinging his pick. "But it's enough to fool them."

"Fool who?" Ed asked, but Mutton didn't answer.

They worked until the radio crackled. Hassan, warning that Vanna was on her way back. "Good enough for now."

Ed was glad to stop, his lawyer's hands raw.

"I'll do more tonight," Mutton said. "Just needed them to see us dig. Throw them off."

"Throw who off? Throw who off what?"

Mutton didn't answer. He strapped the duffel to the cart and drove toward the chancery. They passed the marine house where Corporal Hunker crouched smoking on the stoop, waiting with his slingshot for the crows to arrive. Mutton stopped at the Health Unit. "Take the cart back around front," he told Ed. "I'll radio Hassan and have him meet you. He'll return the bags to the locker. I've got an appointment with the Doc."

Chapter 4

Mutton shrugged and drew down his head like a turtle. The explosion rumbled. Dr. Meddler didn't flinch. "Stress," the psychiatrist said. "From duty on the front line."

"The front line?"

"Of the WOT."

"Of course," said Mutton. Meddler jotted a note. Mutton ducked as another explosion rumbled. Meddler's lips were moving. When the vibrations slowed and the rumbling ceased Mutton heard Meddler reading from his notes.

"... Jumpy, tense, overwork ... Inability to sleep at night ... General malaise ... Anxiety .... Anything else?"

"Can you give me something for a strained back?"

"How did you strain your back?"

"Pushing a loveseat against the door of my villa."

"Why were you pushing a loveseat against the door of your villa?"

"In case the *jihadis* stormed my compound."

"What made you think *jihadis* would storm your compound?"

Mutton mentioned the Interior Ministry agents killed in Hajrayn. "And 40 dead from the truck bomb in Riyadh."

"That was two weeks ago."

Two weeks earlier a dozen fanatics had driven dump trucks onto four residential compounds in the capital shouting, "God is great!" To prove it they killed 40 foreigners – Christian, Muslim, Hindu – with their truck bombs, and wounded 150 others. They held scores of hostages. The U.S. announced the immediate departure of half its staff from Saudi Arabia and the Royal Family dispatched troops, Humvees, jersey barriers, and 50 mm cannon throughout the country. The war on terror had taken an ugly turn, and Diplomatic Security Agent Jeff Mutton found himself on the front line with blue half-moons cradling his eyes.

"They still have hostages, chafing at ropes binding their wrists."

"Fewer hostages, I'm told..."

"Because they're being killed!"

An explosion rumbled in the distance.

"It's these daily warnings from the Embassy," Mutton said. "Against living and working in the Kingdom. But they won't give me an assignment out of here."

"You could take a job in Baghdad."

"You think I'm crazy?"

Meddler shook his ostrich-egg head and jotted. He wore wire-rimmed glasses with round, smudged lenses. "Just testing," he said, and handed two slips to Mutton. "Give these to Nurse. And have her send in the next one."

Mutton hesitated. He wasn't well. He had the jitters, as much from the fear of his own death as from the fear of being blamed for the death of others. He wanted to talk about Vanna, but the last time brought her up with Meddler, the doctor went on and on about the CG's feet and shoes and closet. How much did Meddler know?

"Anything else I can do for you?" Meddler checked his watch and Mutton saw there would be no help for him.

In the waiting room he found three junior officers. Clements and Pudge from consular sat on either side of the political officer, Martin Tinker. An explosion interrupted and Tinker threw himself to the floor. The health unit vibrated. Tinker scrambled on hands and knees to get beneath the coffee table. Clements and Pudge didn't move.

"Table won't help," Pudge told Tinker.

"Glass surface," added Clements, the sharp, fierce JO in charge of visa operations.

Mutton handed his slips to Nurse. "Do you feel all these explosions out here?" he asked.

"Every one of them," Nurse said, chipper as ever.

"I don't feel a thing inside the chancery."

When no alarm sounded, Tinker picked himself up off the floor. The skinny JO slapped the knees of his expensive navy suit.

"Doc said to send in the next one," Mutton told Nurse.

"No rush," said the old British expat with saggy cheeks and long teeth. "There's no cure for what he's got."

"Tinker told you what he's got?"

Nurse shook her head. Tinker's illness defied naming. Because he believed his work was Top Secret, the JO was unable to tell Dr. Meddler his problem. If the information hadn't been classified TS, Tinker could have at least given the doctor a clue. But Tinker believed the information was so Top Secret that he himself couldn't say what was making him ill. Clements and Pudge had easily diagnosed Tinker's condition as self-delusion, but since they were only junior officers, their diagnoses didn't count.

"He thinks he's an undercover agent," said Pudge, approaching Mutton at Nurse's counter.

Tinker moaned on the sofa behind them.

"He thinks he's got secrets."

"Top Secrets," added Clements.

Tinker moaned louder.

"His case really is important to us," Clements said. "He's the embodiment of all our trouble."

"I thought the CG was the embodiment of all your trouble," said Mutton.

"She is," said Clements. "And Tinker's her errand boy."

"To be made Ambassador, Vanna needs to please Fourth Branch."

"Fourth Branch?" Mutton asked, certain he'd heard that before.

Tinker moaned and picked himself up off the sofa. He crossed the carpet and locked himself in the bathroom.

"They want intel to support the invasion of Iraq."

"And to justify the war on terror."

"But there isn't any."

"So Tinker improvises."

"He plagiarizes from *Newsweek* for his cables to Fourth Branch."

"What's Fourth Branch?" Mutton and Nurse asked together.

Clements and Pudge withdrew. "Can't tell you," they said.

"Beyond Top Secret," explained Pudge.

"Beyond SDDTS?" asked Mutton. He'd created that powerful new classification himself for local use.

"Fourth Branch is more secretive than anything you've never heard of."

"And more powerful than the president."

"We've already said too much."

"The enemy is everywhere, and he is listening."

A powerful rumble shook the afternoon.

Chapter 5

Vanna Lavinia felt the weight of her unread cables with the force of a migraine. She had stacks of reading to do, starting with the flashing red messages from Jeff Mutton. The presence of so much unread information mocked her. Hadn't she perfected the fine art of delegation? Why was Mutton sending security concerns to her when it should have been the other way around?

Her system of delegation worked as follows: visa issues she sent to Belvedere, who forwarded them to Marshall Clements, and political issues went to DB, whose out-of-office reply reminded her that Martin Tinker was covering for the senior political officer. Media inquiries went to Phil Potts in public affairs, who spent hours blowing into that ridiculous Sousaphone of his in preparation for a parade that would never happen. Management issues she forwarded to Storp who added them to a three-inch stack of printer paper, and intelligence, what there was of it, went to No Lips in the office that wasn't there. So that now, having undone Mutton and his security anxiety, such delegation should have left Vanna free to practice the high art of diplomacy: deciding whom to invite and whom to snub for the glorious re-opening of the Club Soda disco on Thursday night. But how could she concentrate on important things like that with security issues threatening to ruin it all?

A call from Pervis Mayflower interrupted. "Sheikh al Bafarti, line one," the secretary said, and hung up before Vanna could have her take a message. Calls from Sheikh al Bafarti had become a game of cat and mouse. Pervis would tell her the sheikh was on the line, but when Vanna picked up, a smooth-voiced secretary at *The Green Truth* would ask her to please hold.

Not acceptable!

Sheikh al Bafarti was an important contact, yes, with interests in banking, politics, construction, security, and the news. But Vanna Lavinia was *the* Representative in her assigned Province of *the* Representative in the Holy Kingdom of *the* President of the United States. Vanna was *the* Consul General! Vanna had made it clear to Pervis that she held the line for no one. Yet every time Pervis forwarded a call from Sheikh al Bafarti's office, a smooth-voiced young man instructed Vanna to please hold.

She stared at the phone, afraid to touch it. She watched the line flash, despising that little red light. How she dreaded being put on hold! Finally she punched line two and ordered Pervis to take a message from the caller on line one. "This afternoon, get the sheikh on the line before putting the call through."

"The sheikh's on line one," Pervis said.

"He is not on line one."

"Which line is he on?"

"He's not on any line."

"Oh. What did he want?"

"I don't know what he wanted."

"Why didn't you ask him?"

Vanna exhaled heavily. "Look, I think I know what he wanted. Just make sure he's on the line to ask for it before you put the call through."

Sheikh Mohammed al Bafarti wanted what dozens of her other best contacts wanted: a visa. The sheikh's request was a source of great interest for Vanna because Al Bafarti could be a formidable foe. Board member for a dozen important enterprises and Director General of *The Green Truth* – the Kingdom's most widely read newspaper – the Sheikh could raise the rabble against the United States. His singular voice could ruin her efforts to win hearts and minds and impress her masters in Washington. More importantly, resolving al Bafarti's visa situation was key to her own invitation to join the Saudi entourage in Crawford, where she could flatter and schmooze the kind of people with the power to make her an Ambassador.

Vanna hadn't risen to the top of the American diplomatic corps by ignoring detail. She paid attention to the little things, especially the perceived slights of her colleagues. These she registered in a thick ledger stored beside her desk in the sturdy Mosler safe intended for classified material. The ledger was a record of all the obstacles she faced as a ravishing young female climbing the ladder of a traditionally male world. Vanna hunched over the ancient book, hidden by the piles of unread cables stacked on her desk, and flipped through the pages recalling the weaknesses of her staff.

The ledger included entries against senior aides like Gary Storp and insignificant JOs like Marshall Clements. Storp's history of zero insubordination, she reasoned, suggested the Management Officer had something to hide. And by denying visas to top-level contacts, the impudent Clements threatened the very social ladder up which Vanna intended to climb. He was jeopardizing her ticket to Crawford, which in turn jeopardized her Ambassadorship to Oman!

Colonel Windsock she gunned down for hiding details as he staffed up the Office of Overseas Predator Strikes, and No Lips she dinged for total secrecy on his intelligence activities. Martin Tinker in Political was written off as bumbling and inept, while DB's impeccable service was damned by his absence. Vanna interpreted Pervis' presence as a sign that someone in DC was out to sabotage her, and speaking of Washington she certainly hadn't forgotten Larry Porcas, the lowly IT troll in orange Harley-

Davidson suspenders who'd shorted out the international phone line during a conference call with important people at Fourth Branch! How she boiled to know she'd never lay eyes on Dr. Meddler's notes, damn his confidentiality. What a ledger he must have! What she wouldn't give for a glimpse of its pages!

Speaking of pages, where were the media reports highlighting her grandeur? It was nothing but negative press for her. Look at the coverage of her fashion show, which the media portrayed as an infidel attempt to corrupt Saudi feminine virtues. The Commission for the Promotion of Virtue and the Prevention of Vice had lodged a formal complaint! The Ministry of Foreign Affairs had threatened to declare her Persona Non-Grata! The list of infractions for Phil Potts was lengthy by comparison to the list of his successes, which she didn't bother to track. Too bad Mr. Potts was an old-timer with a long history promoting democracy in dangerous places, and an even longer list of friends back in DC. There was little she could do to destroy him as he spent his time puckering and blowing into that ridiculous Sousaphone of his.

One officer she would have the pleasure of destroying, however, was Jeff Mutton. All his noise about security, his insistence on installing barbaric protective measures, razor wire, sand bags, jersey barriers; security, security, security, all of it threatening to make the U.S. government look bad. And if the U.S. government looked bad, she looked bad. And one thing Vanna Lavinia could not tolerate was looking bad. In the ledger Mutton took it on the chin for every damaged petal of every damaged flower sent by her contacts and run through his screening apparatus before they reached her. Oh, yes. Vanna meant to reign in Mutton's security concerns, or see the man destroyed.

But first she had these bothersome cables from the

Department to read. The cable Mutton flagged about the Hajrayn bombing troubled her most of all, because it carried major implications for security. Job security. Were she to lose an employee to an act of terrorism before she'd taken action, she could kiss goodbye any hopes of making Ambassador. Desperate to convene a Full Emergency Action Response meeting, she punched four digits on her speakerphone and tapped her nails impatiently waiting for Pervis to answer.

"Consul General's office," the secretary said.

"Pervis!"

"Can I help you?"

"Pervis, it's me."

"I'm sorry, you'll have to speak up."

"Pervis!" Vanna yelled. "Convene the FEAR. ASAP!"

"I'm sorry, but this connection seems to be very bad – "

Vanna cursed and yanked the phone from the cradle.

"Sorry. But that kind of language is not appropriate for a call to the American Consul General's office," Pervis said, and clicked off.

Burning with desire to convene the FEAR Committee before her career went up in flames, Vanna rose quickly, crossed yards of Persian carpeting, and yanked open the door.

"Pervis!"

"Yes, ma'am?"

"We need to convene the FEAR."

"The what?"

"The Full Emergency Action Response Committee."

"Oh, dear," Pervis said. "Just a moment." She began clicking around and squinting at her screen.

"Never mind," Vanna said. "Never mind." She turned on a heel, stormed into her office, and sent a quick e-mail insisting that Pervis convene the FEAR. That would cover her should anyone be killed by a terrorist attack before the committee could meet.

Having taken this decisive action Vanna drove her golf cart past the cats to her residence where she slipped along the walkway, cursing the crow guano underfoot, and tangling her shoe in a pothole. She sat down to a lunch of broccoli soup, diced cucumbers, and a glass of white wine. Over lunch she added the names and crossed out the names of people she wanted and didn't want to attend the reopening of the Club Soda and other parties she planned to enjoy. She rang the bell and her Yemeni houseboy, Ahmed, brought out a no-flour cake. Two hours later Vanna returned from her working lunch to find that the committee still had not been convened.

"But you said, 'never mind,'" Pervis said.

"That was *before* my email requesting the meeting. B*efore.*"

"So you've changed your mind?"

"No, I did *not* change my mind. I never ... Please, just set up the meeting."

"When would you like to have it?"

"ASAP."

"Let me see." Pervis clicked around, her arthritic old hands moving interminably slowly. "You have the American Ladies at 3:00; hair appointment at 4:30; Atkins Zen at seven. Tomorrow it's the Butter Without Bread club meeting and a conference call in the morning, lunch with the al Razaks – you depart at noon. The afternoon is marked 'personal time'."

Vanna sighed. She was forever being called upon to make personal sacrifice in service to her country. "Move the hair back to six and cancel the meditation. Convene a mandatory FEAR Committee at four pm sharp."

"That gives them just over an hour."

Vanna relaxed. In one hour, the FEAR Committee would hear the recommendations of the Diplomatic Security Officer, and any failure by her staff to stay alive would fall squarely on Jeff Mutton's shoulders.

Chapter 6

The group, nearly a dozen men, got to their feet on Vanna's arrival. She took her place at the head of the table, smiled at them all, and invited them to be seated.

"Good afternoon," she said, pleasantly as if it was the most fun any of them had ever had.

"Good afternoon, ma'am," mumbled the downtrodden Management Officer at the foot of the table and the military-correct Colonel Windsock in the middle. The rest – Mutton, Potts, Pervis, Clements, Meddler, No Lips, a few others – merely rhubarbed.

"I'm sure we're all familiar with the Department's latest Emergency cable." She grinned at each and stopped only when her eyes reached the gloomy, flat-faced Mutton to her left. "Pervis, dear. Let the minutes show that all here present are aware of the cable, and that I started this meeting by reiterating my emphasis on the need for strong security."

Pervis stopped doodling and sat up straight. She checked to see if Storp had written it down. Indeed the dear, balding middle-aged management officer had dutifully taken dictation and Pervis returned to her doodling.

"Mr. Mutton," Vanna said. "Now I've stated my position, may we have an assessment from you?"

Eyes on his hands, voice a low growl, Mutton said, "We all know what happened across the street the other day. What we don't know is whether the Saudis got everything they were looking for. Surveillance detection reports suggest threats remain. There is a high probability of continued efforts to strike U.S. interests in the Kingdom, and each of us is responsible for our personal security. Remember: in the war on terror, we have to be right 100% of the time. The terrorists have to be right only once." Mutton sat back and took his pencil from his ear. "Security is everyone's responsibility."

Vanna smirked and shook her head. "And as Security Officer, are you not prepared to offer recommendations that will increase our chances of success?"

Mutton had been trained in many tactics for protecting diplomats. He could build strong barricades and make high-speed J-turns. He was an expert with pistols, shotguns, rocket launchers, and flamethrowers. His deadpan gaze hid an overwhelming vitality and will to wrestle, fight, punch, kick, cut, stab, throw, shoot, and kill. He'd survived chemical weapons, hand grenades, car bombs, carjackings, high-speed chases, and numerous threats from criminal elements, soldiers, and enemy combatants. But Jeff Mutton's instinct for survival told him that the threat he faced now dwarfed all these killers combined.

"An agent in the field faces no greater threat to his security," Mutton was told as a Special Agent recruit, "than liability for a diplomat's safety. In high-threat situations, you DS Officers have only one surefire weapon: the Security Directive."

Security Directives, the training officer explained, absolve DSOs of culpability in the event of injury, death, or diplomatic mishap. "You can write a directive for as many scenarios as you can imagine, and I encourage you to do so. A good security officer will draft so many directives that a diplomat can't walk, ride, or chew pink bubblegum without a violation, absolving you, the DSO, of responsibility. That's why I liked working in Jakarta, where diplomats couldn't breathe the polluted air without breaching some part of Security Directives three, eight, eleven, forty-five, and seventy-two."

Mutton cleared his throat. "I'm instituting new directives. I'll reissue the bulletin of existing directives after the meeting and for the sake of brevity I'll stick to an overview of the new ones. SD-35 doubles the number of duck and cover drills we conduct each week. I want everyone to know how to react in the event of an attack. SD-36 mandates all movements from the consulate be made in fully armored vehicles, and 37 requires all officers to vary routes, times, and vehicles while commuting to work – "

"You can't do that," the Management Officer challenged.

"Do what?" Mutton asked Storp.

"Implement a directive that requires ownership of more than one vehicle."

"Who's requiring officers to own more than one vehicle?"

"SD-37 requires officers to vary vehicles while commuting to work," Storp said. "That would require ownership of more than one vehicle. I won't sign off on it."

"Feel free not to," Mutton said. "But then you'll be the one responsible for each and every officer during their commute to work."

Storp saved face by deferring to Vanna.

"You can't ask officers to own more than one vehicle," Vanna said.

"I'm not asking," Mutton said.

"Mr. Mutton, I will stand up for my people."

"Feel free to contradict the recommended directive. You are free to take responsibility for your people as they commute to work."

Vanna realized that she had little to gain by fighting SD-37. SD-37 had no impact on her own commute, a mere golf cart ride around the compound. If she fought SD-37, on the other hand, Vanna would be responsible for injuries, deaths, and other mishaps that befell her officers. But it wasn't until Vanna conceived an actual benefit to herself from implementing the directive that she threw her full support behind it. "Implement the directive," she told Mutton. "And Mr. Storp, have motor pool make the Caddy ready. SD-37 means I get to use the Ambassador's Coup DeVille."

"You already use the Coup DeVille."

"Yes, but now I *have* to use it."

Colonel Windsock ran his fingers through his curly black hair. Pervis doodled hearts into her steno book. No Lips stared straight ahead and concentrated on not being there as Mutton continued his list. "... SD-53 requires all officers to participate in the weekly radio check at 7:30 each Monday morning."

"Sorry Mutton," Clements said. "I have to leave before 7:00 in order to get the visa shop opened. Can I be excused from the radio check?"

"No can do. We need to be sure we can contact you by radio when the shit goes down."

"Why not call me on the phone?"

"We need a Plan-B in case the phones are cut."

"My cel phone can be Plan-B."

"Not if the network is jammed. We need a Plan-C if the phones are out and the network is jammed."

"How about I use the mobile antenna on my way in?" Clements suggested.

"We have to be sure we can reach you at home."

"What's so good about the radios, anyway? Maybe the radios are down. What then?"

"Then we'll just call you on the telephone."

Clements went silent at the futility. Mutton continued his list. Vanna nodded along in agreement. As she saw it, Mutton's directives would bring her staff closer, flocking to her for safety. She would be seen as a leader in difficult times, remembered as more than a Consul General. She would be remembered as a General Indeed on the front line in the war on terror.

But Mutton had other ideas. Now that he'd gotten what he wanted most from Vanna – a start to his security upgrades – he was going to publicly prohibit social gatherings on the compound. He didn't worry about reneging on their agreement. He was paid to save lives, and hosting large gatherings at the consulate would only make them a bigger target. Better to deceive the CG, Mutton thought, than condemn innocent people to death by *jihad*. "... Finally," he said, "SD-57 hereby restricts all after-hours activities on the compound. No Club Soda events. No Marine parties. No cocktail hours whatsoever ..."

Vanna tapped her pen against the table, a dry smirk on her lips. "Thank you, Mr. Mutton," she said. "Your recommendations are a reminder of the dangers we face here. We need to weigh your suggestions."

She paused and put on her reading glasses, hoping to appear more intelligent. She studied the papers before her. "But this cable also stipulates that embassies and consulates throughout the region should improve the American brand by increasing public outreach. Mr. Mutton, restricting use of the compound limits our safest venue for public diplomacy."

Mutton's eyes narrowed. He looked at his hands. "The CG has my recommendations."

"And you have my support. But you also have the Department's cable. Where do you suggest we host our public events?"

"The cable directs us to curtail large gatherings in hostile environments."

"Pervis, dear. Stop taking notes." The secretary stopped doodling and looked up again, puzzled. "Jeffrey, off the record, I respect your assessment. We will implement all your recommendations. But we do have morale to consider. And the cable clearly states that in order to win the war on terror we must first win the battle for hearts and minds. How can we win hearts and minds if we have low morale?"

"The cable directs us to lower our profile."

"It says the United States is committed to dialogue."

"The cable warns that tyranny breeds hopelessness."

Vanna glared at Mutton.

Mutton said, "Increased surveillance. A pattern consistent with pre-attack activity against others in the region. I recommend no after hours activity on the compound. I'm not even confident we should be open for business as usual."

"Mr. Mutton, you've begun stringing razor wire. Hasn't that helped? Have you forgotten our agreement? This cable instructs us to continue the Diplomacy of Deeds. If this compound is not the safest place to carry out the Diplomacy of Deeds, then clearly DS is not doing its job."

Mutton's face reddened. He gripped his pencil between thumbs and forefingers. Only by concentrating on this short stub of wood was he able to keep from bursting, until the steam that reddened his face boiled back down to the point where he could ask: "Diplomacy of Deeds? Diplomacy of Deeds?! Can somebody please explain to me what is meant by Diplomacy of Deeds?!"

Vanna raised her eyebrows coolly and looked at Phil Potts, the red-faced, white-bearded, overweight academic. "Perhaps our Public Diplomacy Officer can answer that. Mr. Potts?"

Potts had no idea what was meant by Diplomacy of Deeds, so he gave it a familiar short form. "It's what we call D.O.D."

"D.O.D.?" Vanna asked.

"Diplomacy of Deeds."

"But D.O.D. is the Department of Defense."

"That's right," said Colonel Windsock. "D.O.D. *is* the Department of Defense."

"Then what is the Diplomacy of Deeds?" Vanna asked.

"It's also D.O.D.," Potts said, too far into his lie to back out now.

"Can't we call it something else?"

"Which?" Potts asked.

"Whichever didn't come first."

Colonel Windsock said, "I think Department of Defense came first."

"Then change Diplomacy of Deeds," said Vanna.

"We can't, ma'am. The Undersecretary for Public Diplomacy invented it." Potts left it unsaid that Vanna didn't outrank the Undersecretary. "Appointee," he concluded, by way of explaining a concept that didn't make sense.

"Well, we don't need two D.O.D.s," Vanna said.

"And we can't have the Department of Defense running Public Diplomacy," said Potts. "Maybe we can call the Department of Defense by the old name. The War Department. Then we can call it the W.D."

"W.D. is too close to W.M.D. And I don't think we have the authority to change the name of an entire Department."

"You can't change the name," Windsock said, though he wasn't sure.

"How about PD, ma'am?" said Potts.

"PD? What's that?"

"Public Diplomacy."

"I know that. But what *is* Public Diplomacy?"

Potts decided it was better to tell the truth rather than prolong the meeting by inventing explanations. "I have no idea, ma'am."

"Perfect. PD it is." Vanna smiled at the committee, pleased with the accomplishment. "Where were we?"

Storp consulted a stack of papers before him and reminded her.

"Yes. Security. Clearly, we must continue with the Diplomacy of Deeds, and this compound should be the safest place to do so, or the security officer isn't doing his job. Wouldn't you agree?"

Mutton was silent.

"I'll take your silence for consent. After all, I'm the decider. Mr. Storp, we are hosting guests in two days. I would appreciate it if they could arrive without slip-sliding away on crow guano. Where are we on that?"

Storp consulted his stack. "The poison Tom used was ineffective against the crows."

The skeletal, pockmarked No Lips perked up at the mention of poison. "What was he using?" he asked.

Storp consulted his stack of paper. "KK-VR?"

No Lips shook his head. "Tell Tom to give us a call. The KK-VR is out. He wants the KK-VX. You didn't hear it from me."

Storp made a note on the top page of his stack. No Lips cleared his throat. Storp stopped writing and scratched his pen across the page. "I'll have Tom give you a call," he said.

Chapter 7

Mutton watched the black and white images on the monitor: cab stops beside the wall; driver ducks below the dash; Saudi soldier, AK-47 dangling from his neck, shouts and gestures for the car to move. He waves, appears to shout, approaches the cab; traffic re-starts, four lanes thick; cabbie opens the passenger door and scoots to the sidewalk.

Next to Mutton's wall.

The soldier approaches quickly. The bearded cabbie in dirty blue thobe closes the passenger door, opens the rear door. Approaching soldier steps back. Mutton's bowels go tight.

The driver reaches into the back seat.

The soldier shouts, crouches in a firing position. Mutton knows: no ammo.

The driver pulls out a three-gallon gas can.

The soldier shouts, gestures fiercely.

The cabbie turns and yells, gesturing frantically, palms open. He shouts and gestures toward car and gas can.

Mutton showed the tape. No reaction from Ghani. He sat opposite Mutton, chewing a twig of miswak. "This is where your guy helps fuel a potential bomb," Mutton said.

Ghani snorted.

"That driver should've been on the ground," Mutton yelled. "Heels kicked apart. Elbows chicken armed. Three men on top of him." He could yell at the commander in the privacy of his office. No subordinates to see.

Ghani, cool as ever, "Why does this worry you?"

"Your guards did nothing to stop that car."

"My guard approached the driver."

"He had time to pour three gallons of accelerant next to our fuel depot."

Ghani smiled, relaxed, an awful contrast to Mutton's hysteria. "No explosion."

"That's how you measure success? No explosion? You know they probe our security. Now they've found something to exploit."

Ghani shrugged. "It is nothing. My men are there."

Ghani's composure angered Mutton. "Just the other day you lost half a dozen men in Hajrayn."

"Two more succumbed today." Ghani spoke matter-of-fact.

"You've told me squat about the raid."

"We are interrogating."

Mutton stayed on the offensive. "We have a potential vehicle bomb parked outside my fuel dump. We have a stranger close enough to jump my wall. We have – "

"Why do you worry about that?" Ghani showed the first sign he was losing cool. "I see you are putting up the razor." The razor, proof that Mutton lacked faith, offended Ghani.

Mutton was getting his razor wire, spool upon spool of it topping the foot-thick blast walls, but it wasn't enough. Surveillance reports listed cars circling the compound; erratic driving and unusual stops; activity in Hajrayn, eyes from the hospital. "Your men are slow," he said. "We need a better deterrent."

"My men are trained and staged to protect you. The razor is an insult to them and me."

"Your men have no ammo."

Ghani shook his head, disappointed in Mutton's lack of faith. "You have the razor."

Mutton chose to test Ghani. "Let me show you something."

Mutton drove the cart, stopping beside freshly dug

earth and piles of broken coral. Ghani looked Mutton in the eye. "Booby traps?"

"Anyone comes over that wall loses a leg."

Ghani nodded.

"Can you keep it quiet?"

Ghani sucked on the miswak and nodded. Mutton wanted Ghani to spread it around. Both men looked up when an explosion in Hajrayn rocked the afternoon.

"There's more," Mutton said.

Mutton drove further along the wall, stopping where the carpenters were hammering a tall wooden structure. "Guard towers," Mutton said. "One on each wall; two at each entrance."

"How are you manning them?"

"Local guard force. They're being trained to handle weapons."

"Trained where?"

"On compound."

Ghani sucked his miswak.

"Keep that under your hat?"

"Why are you showing me this?"

It was Mutton's turn to shrug. "Because I trust you," he said.

"You hear explosions," Dr. Meddler said. "What do you see?"

"You told me to close my eyes," Mutton said. "I see nothing."

"This is an exercise. Please cooperate. You hear explosions. What do you see?"

"I see smoke, and helicopters circling."

"What color is the smoke?"

"White."

"How do you feel about the smoke?"

"It makes me uneasy."

Dr. Meddler's pencil scratched the paper. "And the

helicopters?"

"They worry me."

Meddler's pencil scratched the paper. Mutton kept his eyes closed.

"You hear the call to prayer. What do you see?"

"Beards."

"How do they make you feel?"

"They make me nervous. The prayer call and the beards make me nervous."

"Why is that?"

"They shout it across rooftops, and hordes of bearded men gather at the sound."

"What else do you hear?"

"I hear banging."

"That's the carpenters, building the towers."

"I hear gunshots."

"Those are the contractors fastening barbed wire to your walls. Do you see a pattern here?"

"No. That's why I came to see you."

"You fear your own creations, even those things intended to protect. The helicopter. The smoke. The call to prayer."

"The smoke and the call to prayer are to protect me?"

"Smoke is a warning against fire. Prayer unites men in peace."

"I don't see it that way."

"But you are not a credible judge. You are being treated for insecurity from service on the front line of the war on terror."

Another explosion ripped the afternoon. Meddler's pencil scratched across the paper. "You need to unwind. I hope I'll see you at the Club Soda this weekend."

Chapter 8

When Phil Potts saw Marshall Clements in the corridor, the heavyset old Public Affairs Officer asked the JO how he'd gotten out of his cage. "Don't you have visas to refuse?"

"Vanna wants a consular officer."

Potts smacked his thigh and sucked his lips.

"You've been summoned too?" Clements said.

"I've been duped. If you're involved, she wants to talk visas. If it's visas, it's Sheikh al Bafarti."

"The terrorist?"

"You'll have to be more diplomatic than that."

"How can I behave diplomatically in this environment?" Clements slowed his pace to match Potts'. They moved through the mold-covered chancery, a damp stink rising from the carpets. Broken, crooked ceiling tiles dangled overhead. The coughing, wheezing air conditioners made a lukewarm 75 degrees. Rats had chewed holes in the gypsum walls.

Clements pushed open the heavy lobby door. Behind the blast-resistant window of Post One Corporal Hunker bent under the weight of his helmet, goggles, and flak jacket. Hunker released the lock, a loud clunk, admitting Potts and Clements to the hushed classified corridor.

At the front office they found Pervis Mayflower digging among the open drawers of the Moslers. The safes dwarfed the wrinkled wisp of a woman. She wore a dark, flowered dress and her hose unrolled toward black, square-toed shoes. She hunted among the classified documents with cherry-red Top Secret coversheets buried in the morgue-like drawers.

Clements approached the secretary, who noticed him

there only when he coughed. Pervis straightened, covering her heart with a wrinkled hand. She turned her head on a stiff neck and brought thick glasses onto her nose.

"Dear me," she said. "All these alarms have me jumping out of my skin." She stared at Clements as if she'd never seen him before. In a shaky timbre she asked, "Aren't you the young man in general services?"

"That's Ed Khan."

"Where's my ergonomic furniture?"

Potts said, "We're here to see Vanna."

"I have sciatica, you know. I have a doctor's note."

"Have you talked to Nurse?" Clements asked

"I don't need a nurse. I need my furniture."

Potts said, "We're here to see the CG."

"That awful man in General Services. Mr. Cautwauler, he promised new furniture."

"You should talk to Ed," said Clements. "He's Acting General Services Officer."

"Acting? This isn't make-believe! I need ergonomic furniture for my sciatica."

"We're here to see Vanna," Potts insisted.

Pervis squinted at him. "You'll have to come later. She's meeting with Belvedere and Potts right now."

"I'm Potts," Potts said. "And Clements is here for Belvedere."

"Oh, dear. Just a moment." Pervis limped over to her desk and picked up the phone. When she hung up she said, "The CG will see you now."

Neither was eager to enter. Clements recognized his vulnerability to her beauty, and Potts just wanted to mark his days before retirement with tributes to John Phillips Sousa and the grandeur of Old Glory. Pervis had to shoo them in, and when she did Vanna rose from behind the pile of cables stacked on her desk. She approached slowly, grandly, and took her usual place, erect in a plush

40

armchair. Potts' large body sank lower and lower into the burgundy sofa. Clements sat in a wing chair at the far end, staring at Vanna's calves and ankles.

"Young Clements," Vanna said. "I've been receiving an inordinate number of phone calls lately. I do hope the Royals are getting appropriate service from you."

Clements assured her it was so, and waited for her to continue.

"These callers, young Clements, seek visas. For their families. Royal families."

"I give the royals a special time to appear for nterviews. But they want visas without interviews."

"Can you do it?"

"Not according to the 9/11 Commission."

Vanna slumped a notch. She bounced a dangling pump on the tips of her toes. Clements stared at her thighs, watched the muscles alternate from taught to slack, taught to slack. "I'll let you both in on a little secret. Why this is so important to me. The Crown Prince is planning a trip. To Crawford. I'm to accompany the sheikh in the entourage."

She let the news sink in.

"So, where do we stand on his visa?"

"Bafarti's name's still on the terrorist watch list."

"What for?"

"Financing terror, mostly. And new entries keep popping up."

"*Our* Sheikh al Bafarti? It can't be the same. It's preposterous, this frivolous attention to the watch list. Don't you know how names are added to that list?"

Clements mentioned the men whose work took place in the shadows, behind crates marked "diplomatic" and stacked floor-to-ceiling along the classified corridor. "No Lips? Liston? The intel guys in back?"

"It's hardly intelligence. Our friends hiding behind

doors behind doors behind doors add names to those lists to justify their existence. And now their self-justification is getting in the way of my visit to Crawford."

"I thought the visit was postponed. On account of Iraq. The invasion."

"The Saudis are not so faithless as you in our efforts to help Iraq. The Saudis are in the vanguard. By the time we stand up a Democracy there, the whole Middle East will want to visit Crawford. Mr. Potts, can't you help? The Sheikh *is* a Public Affairs contact, after all."

"Public Affairs doesn't work with that kind of information. We're just here to fix it when mistakes go public."

"Well this is a mistake, and it threatens to hurt us, to hurt *me,* publicly. Need I remind you that the Sheikh controls the media in this country? We're celebrating the Fourth of July in two months, and I expect good coverage. I don't want to open *The Green Truth* on July 5th and find articles about American arrogance accompanied by terrible photographs of myself sweating in the spotlights."

Vanna looked from Potts to Clements. Potts' knees pressed together as he sank deeper into the upholstery. Vanna towered over him. She smoothed her skirt along her thighs. Clements watched eagerly. She met his eyes and her face relaxed. Her eyes softened and the tension evaporated. "This reminds me, Mr. Potts. We need softer lights. Talk to Cautwauler. I don't want to be shiny."

"Shiny?" Potts asked.

"I want to glow."

"Glow," Potts said, nodding thoughtfully.

"I was so *shiny* last year. In my Fourth of July photos. It was the lighting."

Potts pretended to write. He made emphatic underlines and circles with his pen, but he kept his mouth shut. Agreeing that she appeared shiny would get him in trouble for saying she was shiny; disagreeing would get him in trouble for disagreeing.

"Public Affairs, of all sections, should be concerned about this. When I look bad, America looks bad."

"You never look bad, ma'am."

Vanna accepted the compliment with a nod. "This is the other reason I called you both in here. Where do we stand with the Fourth of July reception?"

"I thought it was cancelled," Potts said. "I thought Mutton – "

"Mutton! He's turning this place into a prison. Concertina wire on the walls. Barricades on the streets. Guard towers. He wants to train the local guards to shoot! You should thank me, Mr. Potts. You know what his plan would do to our image here?"

"But the cables – "

"Don't talk to me about cables. Do I have time to read cables?" Vanna craned her neck toward her desk. "Look at that pile – " She stopped herself, smoothing her skirt as she smoothed her voice. "Perhaps some Consuls General are satisfied to sit behind their desks all day reading reports about what's going on outside their doors. But I believe in diplomacy. I spend my days *engaged* in diplomacy. Now, tell me. Which dignitary can you get to sign the Pledge?"

This caught Potts off guard. He thought she'd let go of her scheme to have a Saudi prince join her in signing a Pledge of Allegiance to the War on Terror. Potts stalled. "Maybe we should wait until after the anniversary of 9/11 to do the pledge."

"I don't want our Fourth of July celebration getting mixed up with our 9/11 celebration."

"Nine-eleven celebration?"

"Well, you *did* mention 9/11. Have you developed a plan for the anniversary?"

"I suspect we'll be asked to play it down. For security reasons."

"Play it down? At the height of the war on terror!? Nine-eleven is the signature event!"

"But with the focus now on Iraq ..."

"Washington would love to see a link between 9/11 and Iraq. I want a celebration."

"Do you mean 'commemoration'?"

"Call it what you want. The point will be to mark the anniversary with a party."

"I'm not sure a party is the best way to mark 9/11."

"It doesn't have to be a big party. Something to show our friends in the Kingdom that we stand beside them in the war on terror."

"We could do a memorial service for members of staff."

"Maybe. But nothing somber. Our contacts might not like it."

"I wasn't thinking about our contacts. I was thinking of a memorial service for the staff."

"There's no point in a service for staff. We need *Public Diplomacy*. Fourth Branch wants us to reach out publicly."

"Fourth Branch?" Potts asked.

"Look," Vanna said. "My point is that this should be a celebration. If we invite our contacts to some morbid event about 9/11 we'll lose a lot of the good will we have right now."

"It's a somber day."

"Somber? It's Patriot Day! The president will issue a proclamation! Last year he launched the Freedom Corps. Maybe this year we could have members of staff sign up to the Freedom Corps."

"Freedom Corps?" Potts asked. "What's the Freedom Corps?"

"I don't know. Look into it."

44

"I would suggest we make sure nobody on our staff lost anyone on 9/11."

"*Do.* Do make sure. We can have them give the toast."

"The toast?"

"Champagne. None of that cheap sparkling wine, please. We'll invite our closest contacts, drink to their health and the continued friendship of our countries. I'll make a speech. Write me something about how both our nations have suffered in this war on terror. I don't want to seem insensitive. Even citizens of the Kingdom have lost loved ones in the WOT."

"Mainly terrorists," Potts said.

"People's sons lost to war," she said dreamily.

"I don't think we should make a connection between the Kingdom's youth committing suicide in Iraq to the deaths of civilians in terrorist attacks."

"A celebration will give a positive spin when announcing our concerns about more attacks. It'll boost our profile in announcing these warnings. You know how badly our image suffers when we predict a bombing!"

"That's something I wanted to bring up with you," Potts said. "My media contacts tell me the terrorists draw strength from our attention."

"Well, the terrorists certainly know public diplomacy as well as we do. Maybe better. Shame on you, Mr. Potts – "

– the hi-low alarm, like a European police siren blared before Potts could speak. "All these alarms," Vanna shouted. "Which one is that?"

"Duck and cover," shouted Clements.

"Where we crawl beneath furniture?"

"Yes, ma'am."

"Despicable. How can we do diplomacy in this environment, crouched beneath our desks? Run along, you two. I'm sure Pervis will find a place for you to hide."

Chapter 9

Clements took his place on the couch in Meddler's clean, cold office. Behind him Meddler sat straight-backed, legs crossed at the knees. The rumbling explosions came and went. Wednesday afternoon. An increase in explosions before the weekend ban. Clements didn't flinch.

"You're doing much better," the psychiatrist said. "How do you like the treatments?"

"I enjoy them very much. I just worry that drinking on the job will affect my security clearance."

"No. Mr. Mutton understands. He has his own reasons for understanding." Meddler paused as the rumble of another explosion chased itself off into the distance. He cleared his throat. "The last time we spoke, you talked about nursery rhymes."

"The butcher, the baker, the candle stick maker," Clements said. He recalled their faces, the three visa applicants – the barber, the cook, the custodian – standing opposite him beyond the ballistic glass of window number seven. "Short thobes and beards. The mark of the zealot."

"Go on."

"And their eyes. So dark. So sharp. So ... piercing. I don't know. Good or evil, right or wrong? The intensity itself was a rebuke."

"A rebuke?"

"To my ... lack of faith. I felt unclean by comparison – " A rumbling explosion disrupted.

"Why do you think you felt that way?" Meddler asked.

"I'm a bureaucrat. With a stamp. Following regulations in the 9FAM. An errand boy sent by grocery clerks to collect the bill. The fanatics, on the other hand, act on behalf of God."

"So what did you do, with the butcher, the baker, the candle-stick maker?"

"What could I do? They were Vanna's referrals."

"But you felt that issuing visas to them would be wrong?"

"Yes."

"And you had no choice because of Vanna?"

"Yes."

"Then why not go to Mutton? Why not bring it to Diplomatic Security?"

Clements felt Meddler should have been the one on the couch: clearly he was not well. Did he not see that Vanna had mastered them all? A chancery full of men biting their palms in desire. No other female stimulation, none of the ordinary sights and sounds and smells of them, the Kingdom's women draped in black abaya, moving like blobs under the hot desert sun. Vanna had even beaten Mutton, the man with the guns. Mutton was her biggest conquest! Clements said, "There must be some skeleton in Mutton's closet."

Meddler cleared his throat. "I never – I almost never discuss other clients. Let me just say that Mr. Mutton would be very happy to investigate an abuse of office. Especially where Vanna is concerned. It would be enormously helpful to him."

This interested Clements, until he heard another rumble and remembered all the banging and hammering of security upgrades around the compound. "Mutton's busy with security upgrades. The last thing I want is to distract him from that."

Meddler agreed. "Back to your zealots. Tell me about them."

"I started with the barber. I issued the visa out of respect for Islamic grooming. Maybe the Prince really did need a barber in his entourage. And, he wasn't listed in

ACHOO. At least, not at the time."

"ACHOO is, again?"

"America's Consolidated Homeland Observation Outlet. Our master watch list."

"So then you interviewed the cook? Didn't it seem odd that a prince would require a cook while staying at the Ritz Beverly Hills?"

"He said his role was to dial room service. And since there's no way a Saudi Prince would dial for himself, I issued. And he was Vanna's referral, and he wasn't in ACHOO."

"What about the candle-stick maker?"

"Actually, he listed himself as 'Custodian'."

"That reminds me. Have you heard my joke about King Fahd?" Clements had heard it many times, but he didn't expect that to stop the doctor. "If King Fahd is the Custodian of the Two Holy Mosques, does he report to work with a mop? It's funny because it's impossible."

"It's also sacrilege, and could get you killed."

Meddler stopped laughing. He said, "So you issued a visa to the custodian in spite of his short thobe, his beard, and his piercing eyes?"

"Yes. I looked at the application, but the document gave me nothing I could use to defend a refusal. All I needed to know stood beyond the glass: the beard, the thobe, eyes that said: 'You can refuse, but through me runs the will of God. For you there is no hope. It is only a matter of time.'" Clements shivered on the couch.

"Tell me. Did you get any advice before issuing?"

"I asked Pudge what he thought. He said I should issue. Said I *had to* issue."

"Did you ask him why he thought a prince might need a barber, cook, and cleaner at the Ritz Beverly Hills?"

"Pudge told me not to use logic. 'Try explaining it as if I were Vanna,' he said."

"And so you issued."

"I was new on the line. Who was I to argue? Next thing I know, the department sends a cable telling us all three had been added to ACHOO."

"What did Vanna say?"

"According to her, there is little more behind it than a clerk, paid by the keystroke, to enter names from a list of reports."

"And according to you?"

"I think Washington thinks there's a reason to worry."

"So what did you do, when the cable came in?"

Clements had gone to the filing cabinets and pulled the applications. He looked closely at the photos with the sharp, piercing eyes. "I couldn't believe I had issued to those guys."

"You said they were referrals from Vanna."

"When the shit goes down, the system will show that I issued visas – not one, but *three* – to these guys. With those eyes and those beards. It will show that I let three terrorists talk me into visas. Knowing what I know! About this country!! All of them bad, the barber, the cook, the cleaner. The butcher, the baker, the candlestick maker. It's a nursery rhyme. A fairy tale."

"If it's a fairy tale," Meddler said, "it isn't real. If it isn't real, you have nothing to worry about. What did you do next?"

"We sent letters requesting that they come see us, so we could revoke the visas. They haven't come."

"Did you tell the Prince he might have terrorists on his staff?"

"Vanna said there was no way she would accuse a Saudi prince of employing terrorists. She said she knew better than Washington, and described the clerk in the basement paid by the keystroke entering names from reports."

"So these guys can travel?"

"These guys can travel."

"And now the sleepless nights?"

"I wonder which morning I'll wake up to news about a major attack in New York committed by the handful of nursery rhyme characters that slipped past my window."

In the distance, a longer, rolling explosion told Clements and Meddler that another building had come down in Hajrayn. Clements didn't flinch.

"You really are doing much better. I think the party will be just the thing for you. Will I see you there tomorrow night?"

"Have enough to drink and you'll be seeing two of me."

Chapter 10

For Clements, visa interviews had become little more than an exchange of lies. Applicants lied to him about their reasons for wanting to travel, and he lied to them about his reasons for denying a visa. Clements' work had turned the thoughtful former Religious Studies doctoral candidate into a cynical bureaucrat with a taste for booze and a love of his cheap plastic refusal stamp, which he hammered against every passport he could until he and Pudge and Ed and one of the Pierce Pierces each averaged a 75% visa refusal rate. But the day before FARSA opened its first disco in months, Belvedere delivered the bad news. "Deputy Chief of Mission wants a refusal rate no higher than 10% for citizens of the Kingdom."

"They're the worst offenders!"

"Fifteen on 9/11!" Pudge said.

"Consider yourselves lucky. Vanna despises the DCM. She's willing to accept a 50% issuance rate overall." Then Belvedere dismissed his officers by returning his attention to the schedule he was drafting for the week that had just come to an end.

"To make that happen, we'd have to issue visas to unqualified candidates," Clements protested. "Like al Bafarti."

"Fifty percent," Belvedere said without looking. "And make sure one of those 50% *is* Sheikh al Bafarti. Vanna said she doesn't want any more phone calls. That's the order."

"Is it an order to issue visas to unqualified candidates?" Pudge asked.

"You'll have to adjust your sense of what it means to be qualified."

"I'm pretty sure the Foreign Affairs Manual prohibits issuing visas to terrorists."

"Vanna prohibits refusing more than half your applicants."

"Tell her we're keeping it under 50%. Just don't tell her that's the issuance rate."

Belvedere looked up from his schedule and put his arms over his head, resting them on the back of his swivel chair. "Have I told you about my management style?"

Belvedere' management style was to avoid conflict with his superiors by agreeing with everything they said, and to guide his subordinates along the same tranquil path of non-resistance. Belvedere found that he managed best by managing least and by keeping a busy schedule. To prove that he had a busy schedule Belvedere filled his hours by drafting his schedule, which had the benefit of keeping him away from the consular windows overlooking the front line of the war on terror. Drafting schedules also freed him from implementing the ill-conceived plans of the sexy and beguiling superior he was too weak in the knees to stand up to, and left that unhappy job to his subordinates. So long as Clements fed Belvedere the proper data, they were free to adjudicate visas as they wished. "That's why my management style works," he said. "I let my younger officers implement the solutions."

"He also forgets to back us up when our solutions are called into question," Pudge said.

Clements' solution was to hold firmly to regulation 214(b) of the Immigration and Nationality Act. INA Regulation 214(b) stated that applicants were eligible for a visa only if they could prove their intention not to immigrate to the United States. In other words, they had to prove a negative. This made adjudication a subjective matter, and gave Clements, Pudge, Ed and Pierce broad

"Have a seat," Storp said, indicating a chair covered in plastic green padding. "Ed, right? Have you had a chance to see the compound?"

"No, I – "

"Second worst facility in the entire Foreign Service. Couldn't even get that right. Finished behind Ndjamena, wherever in hell that is. We've got a facility here that's over fifty years old. Fifteen-hundred-meter perimeter. Forty acres. Requires lots of maintenance. From the potholes in the road to the cats and crows running amok out there. Our GSO's a junior officer, just like you. You meet Tom? No? I suggest you meet him next. I've already settled it with Belvedere: You're being seconded to GSO so Tom can join the mission in Iraq."

"Sir, I – "

"Don Storp. Retired Army. No need to call me sir."

Storp ticked the top sheet, licked his thumb, and shuffled the sheet to the bottom. He didn't seem to hear Ed introduce himself.

"Next. Leave policy. This post has two kinds of officer. Junior offices, and everybody else. With few exceptions, the JOs are young, single guys, just like yourself. Everyone else is married, children – some have four children, if you can believe that. Officers without family will not be granted leave during summer or holidays in order to allow officers with family to travel during those times."

"Sir, I – "

"Let me get through this. Questions later." Storp marked the top sheet and moved it to the bottom. "Third. You will be assigned responsibilities in addition to your official assignment, which now includes Acting GSO. You've been assigned Post Language Officer. You'll liaise with Maimouna, our language instructor. Very popular young lady. When you see her, you'll understand why. I suggest you meet with her next."

Storp leaned forward with a sheet. Ed signed without reading and handed it back to Storp, who put it at the bottom of the stack and squared the edges.

"My fourth point: duty. Every two months you'll be assigned duty. Duty means that on Tuesday you come to my secretary's office, collect the duty bag, and forward all duty calls to your mobile phone. It's your job to be familiar with the duty binder: hospitals, emergency services, airlines, et cetera. Priority attention goes to requests from Washington. Washington never sleeps, and neither do we. You're expected to keep the duty phone turned on and by your side at all times. Some weeks the duty officer escorts the mail pouch from the airport. Larry Porcas can fill you in on details – I suggest you meet with him next."

Storp ticked the page, licked his thumb, and shuffled the page to the bottom. "Number five. The Facilities and Recreational Services Association. FARSA. Responsible for booze. Tea. Medicine. Call it what you will. I never touch the stuff. Miss Wellstone will go over all this with you, but as Management Officer I want to make it clear that strict rules govern the purchase, consumption, and disposal of alcohol in the Kingdom. You can join the association for a nominal fee, and I suggest you do so – after all, FARSA is us and we are FARSA. Miss Wellstone is the manager. I suggest you meet her next."

Storp ticked the sheet and shuffled it to the bottom. "Six. Duck and cover alarms. This is a high threat post. We have duck and cover alarms every day. When you hear the alarm, get under your desk and stay there until you get the all clear. Jeff Mutton's our security officer. I suggest you meet him next."

Storp paused. "Anything else?" He stared at Ed. "What else?" A brief, uncomfortable silence ensued. "No questions? Good." Storp stood abruptly. He reached across the desk to shake Ed's hand. "Welcome to Post."

"Thank you." Ed stood and shouldered his bag. He was woozy from 24 hours of travel and the ten-minute orientation to life at his new post.

"You have something for me to sign? A check-in sheet in your welcome pack? You don't have a welcome pack? Who's your sponsor? Tinker? I suggest you meet with him next. He'll have a check-in sheet for you. You're not really here until I get that. Which brings me to my final point: decisions, agreements, discussions held within this office are only valid if they're backed up by emails sent by me, or by documents signed by me. The general policy should be 'It isn't real if it's not in my stack.' What else?"

Ed had nothing to add.

"Get your check-in sheet. We're shorthanded here. I'd like you to get started in GSO this afternoon. Have you met Belvedere? No? I suggest you meet him next."

"Good for you," Belvedere said when Ed told him about his additional assignment. "Having somebody in GSO gives us an inside track on work orders. Storp thinks he pulled a fast one on me. He thinks I'm an idiot. But when my work orders start getting processed faster than his work orders, we'll see who the real idiot is."

"Belvedere's a real idiot," Clements said when Ed told him that Belvedere supported his assignment to GSO. "He actually bought Storp's line about faster service?"

"I really don't have a problem working in both sections," Ed said. "If the Consular section needs help getting work orders done, I'm happy to do it."

"Suit yourself," Clements said. "But don't mix it up. Approve work orders. Refuse visas."

Ed refused visas in window number four, beside Clements in window number seven, Pudge in window number six, and Pierce Pierce on Ed's immediate left in window number five. In window number two a local staffer took in applications, and in the first window a mumbling Indian cashier collected a hundred bucks from every person applying for a visa.

"Number 4475, please come to window four," Ed called over the PA. "Four four seven five, window four."

A man in a floor-length white thobe and a red and white checked khafiyeh emerged from the seated crowd. He looked at his ticket, then looked across the room toward the windows. The applicant gathered his large family and waded through the crowd.

"Good morning, sir," Ed said.

"I want to talk to an American."

"Excuse me?"

"I want to talk to an American."

"I am an American."

"I want to talk to a real American. Like that one." He pointed in the direction of window seven. "Or the blond one," he said. "Blond American."

Ed wasn't shocked when applicants compared him against light-skinned, blue-eyed, fair-haired colleagues like Pudge. Born Mohammed Amr Khan to Pakistani parents, his father a successful Detroit doctor, his mother a vocal community activist, Ed had been allowed to choose his own path. "You are an American, Mohammed," his father said. "Born in the greatest country on earth. This life is yours to follow your calling. That is the American Dream." To his father's silent dismay Ed's American Dream was to follow no calling at all. He spent four years studying American Literature, joined the Peace Corps to teach English in Africa, and eventually graduated law school before joining the Foreign Service.

"I am an American," Ed told the applicant. "An interview with me is as good as an interview with any other officer."

Ed didn't really believe this. Ed believed that an

interview with him was better than an interview with any other officer. Clements, Pudge, and Pierce were easily offended and could be spiteful and cruel. Clements refused by bureaucratic recitation: "I regret to inform you that you are ineligible for a Non-Immigrant Visa, based on section 214(b) of the INA, which states that all applicants must prove they have a residence abroad which they don't intend to abandon. You have not demonstrated this. Good day." After which he hammered down his plastic self-inking refusal stamp on the last page of the applicant's passport and slid it roughly through the slot at the bottom of his explosion resistant window. For him the stamp was the chief weapon on that particular front of the war on terror.

The stamp was a simple device. It noted the date and the place where an individual had applied for a visa and been, after an interview and due consideration, denied a visa. Punched with a satisfying "Ka-CHUNG!" against the last page of a passport, the stamp left poignant notice: "APPLICATION RECEIVED." It advised officers all over the world that the bearer of the document had been found, on such a date and in such a place, ineligible for a U.S. visa. Clements and Pudge had raised the significance of the stamp to ritual:

"This is your stamp," Clements told Ed, handing him the cheap plastic thing.

"There are many like it," Pudge added. "But this one is *yours.*"

"Your stamp without you," said Pierce, "is useless."

"Without your stamp, *you* are useless," Clements said, and they continued in order.

"You must stamp your stamp true."

"You must stamp the passports of your enemy, who is trying to kill you."

"You must stamp his passport before he leaves the

window. He or she."

"What counts in the WOT are the refusals you make. You will refuse."

"You will learn your stamp's weaknesses, which mainly include that the ink dries up and that it is a cheap plastic thing made in China that does little to neutralize your enemy in any permanent, meaningful way."

"You will learn its strengths, which include its simplicity, and the fact that it identifies the enemy to other consular officers at consulates around the world."

"You and your stamp will become part of each other, you will."

In solemn conclusion, the three together spoke the final line of the Consular Officers' Credo: "Your stamp and yourself are defenders of our country." With this ceremonious handover of the stamp, Clements, Pudge, and Pierce had nearly concluded Ed's training in visa adjudication in Saudi Arabia. But there was one final point.

"Under the INA, applicants are not required to prove the intention not to commit terrorist acts," Clements began.

"So we refuse suspected terrorists under 214(b)."

"We will settle for their inability not to prove they do not intend to immigrate to the U.S."

Ed accepted their advice, though he took issue with the way they handled Vanna's referrals. "If these are people she knows," Ed said, "why wouldn't we issue? Her judgment must count for something."

Clements shook his head and told Ed that was his penis talking. "Vanna's hot. I get it. But you can't be like Mutton and Storp, Meddler and No Lips. No jerking off, like Belvedere. You don't have to be a eunuch, like Potts, but it gets you nowhere to be gallant, like Colonel Windsock in OOPS."

"OOPS?"

"He's setting up the Office of Overseas Predator Strikes. Strictly design stage. But it leaves him a lot of free time to swoon over Vanna, who quite frankly wants only one thing."

"What's that?"

"An ambassadorship. And you can't get it for her. There's no point in respecting her referrals. The most she'll do for you is stand over you and let the piss rain down all over your head."

"Oh, God," Pudge said, his face turning red.

"Never mind him. Just remember what I told you about the butcher, the baker, and the candlestick maker. They haven't responded to the revocation letters. I'm up half the night worried about terrorists storming my compound, and the other half worried about the next attack on the Homeland, courtesy of those three bearded fanatics. Don't let it happen to you."

"Every applicant we refuse is one less potential terrorist who can enter the U.S.," Pudge said.

"Better to sacrifice the innocent than issue to the guilty," Clements said.

Ed saw it, then. No applicant would ever be free from the ghosts of the fanatics whose visas, issued from these very windows, had allowed them to be in the U.S. on 9/11. The ballistic glass held their indelible impressions. Clements, Pudge, and Pierce took great pride in their refusals as an expression of their personalities.

Pudge refused by baffling the enemy. "Your failure to possess the intent not to abandon a residence abroad has resulted in a 214(b) denial of this request for a Non-Immigrant Visa."

"I'm sorry, sir. I am not getting you."

"I can't issue the visa."

"Why not?"

"You're not eligible."

"How do I become eligible?"

"By demonstrating ties to the Kingdom."

"What ties? How do I demonstrate these ties?"

"You cannot."

"Why not?"

"Because you don't have them."

"How do I get them?"

"You cannot."

"Why not?"

"Because the laws of the Kingdom forbid foreign nationals from buying or owning property, and from establishing a home he or she does not intend to abandon."

"But my family has lived here for generations."

"And are they citizens?"

"They are not."

"Exactly."

"So no visa?"

"Correct." Ka-CHUNG! "NEXT!"

Pierce Pierce adjudicated and refused by painting black the grey areas: "Are you trying to insult me? Are you trying to trick the United States Government? I am an officer of the U.S. Government charged with protecting the Homeland. You have been found attempting to defraud this office." Bam! His stamp resounded like a gunshot against the applicants' passports.

Except between 10:30 and 11:30 on Wednesdays and Saturdays, when the flight crews from the Kingdom's airline arrived as a group. A score of young Thai, Filipina, Bangladeshi, Moroccan, Egyptian, and Lebanese ladies, with names like Miffy and Muffy and Kitten and Please, all of them unescorted, came in a gaggle of giggles and gossip, with big pouty lips and long curly hair and collars thrown open, eyelashes flashing around their big almond eyes, their perfume wafting across the waiting room and through the slot at the bottom of the explosion resistant glass. The sight and the smell and the sound of them made Pierce weak in the knees. Their perfumed passports smelled of nirvana. They teased and they titillated and Pierce flexed and he flirted. Then he said yes, yes, yes, and he issued many visas and he scheduled many dates. The ladies' lips smiled and they batted their eyes and Pierce leaned toward the glass like a man in a trance. They fished through their purses with delicate fingers and Pierce leaned forward for a glimpse at their world. They were respite from the ugly front line of the war on terror, these divine visitations, the cream of the crop of the national airline, and Pierce drank them in.

But once they were gone he was back in the zone with his favorite refusal: "I have a duty to defend the Homeland." BAM!

"Do you really believe all that stuff about the Homeland?" Ed asked.

"Oh, yes."

"The WOT?" asked Clements.

"Definitely, yes."

"Bring 'em on?" asked Pudge.

"Yes."

"Mission accomplished?"

"Yes."

"When we're talking about war, we're really talking about peace?"

"Without question. Look. We're being probed here. Every day, another terrorist tests us for weakness. What we do in here to promote security in the Homeland is just as important as what Mutton's doing out there to protect our security in here."

It seemed to Ed that what his colleagues needed more than anything was to unwind. Though he'd never had a drink in his life, he looked forward to the Club Soda the following night, and hoped it would bring some peace to the JOs and others who seemed to be losing their heads on the front line of the war on terror.

Chapter 11

The neat white stack of printer paper, three inches thick and butterfly clipped at the upper left corner, contained every significant promise, agreement, action, decision, conclusion, proposal, quotation, idea, debate, suggestion, concern, and what-have-you that Vanna might ask Gary Storp to update her on. The stack comprised e-mails, schedules, memos, minutes, budgets, calendars, and a duty roster, and was littered with hand-written notes and lengthy passages from the Foreign Affairs Manual, Books One through Nine. The stack was organized topically and indexed thoroughly and it concluded with personnel directories for the consulate, embassy, and Department of State in Washington, D.C. The stack of paper served as the right hand to the man who considered himself the right arm to the woman who called herself the Representative in that particular Province of the Representative in Saudi Arabia of the President of the United States. Management Officer Gary Storp carried the document everywhere he went, including the John, in case of urgent calls from an anxious Vanna wondering when she could expect her new golf cart, *which had better arrive in burgundy, Mr. Storp. Burgundy.* How he loathed the thought of disappointing this sexy creature, a woman who looked young enough to be the daughter he never had and whose shoes he longed to wear, no matter how badly they pinched his toes.

Armed with his formidable ream Storp arrived at the front office suite, prepared to do battle with Pervis in his weekly argument that preceded his weekly meeting with the CG. Storp didn't like arguments. His face grew hot and his whole head reeled. His thoughts became jumbled. His heart pounded and sweat beaded up on his lumpy forehead. Arguments took him off script, and Gary Storp didn't do well unscripted.

"She's extremely busy," Pervis said.

"We have our standing end of week meeting at eleven."

"You'll have to wait. She's just such an extremely busy person."

"Vanna herself scheduled this meeting."

"Vanna does not schedule meetings. That's why I'm here."

"Then you scheduled it. Just look at this calendar."

"Are you telling me how to do my job? Because if you're telling me how to do my job, let me tell that GSO of yours how to do his."

"Tom Cautwauler?"

"He's an awful man. Where's my ergonomic furniture?"

Storp consulted his script. "It's in the warehouse. Just submit a work order and have it delivered."

Just like that Storp's script got him through the door and a good way through the small talk until he made the mistake of leaning back and looking relaxed on the faux-leather sofa.

Vanna led by instilling fear in her subordinates, and Storp's lack of fear represented a clear threat to her leadership. Fortunately she had countless tools with which to correct his poor judgment. Vanna, erect in her armchair, knees crossed and shapely calf bouncing seductively, tapped the tropical turquoise blotch of her fingernail against her temple. She squinted at Storp and considered which dull blade she would use to inflict the pain.

"I'm reminded, Mr. Storp. What is the status of the recreational center?"

Storp straightened. He reached for his script and

hunched over it, knees together, pawing through the pages like a dog after a bone. "FARSA ...," he said. "The board ...." He sifted through the pages until he found the one he wanted: an email from Clements. "The board will meet next Wednesday."

"But whatever is there to meet about?"

Storp read directly from Clements' message. He refused to interpret. He didn't like having other men's words in his mouth. Other men's words were logical, and speaking logically caused Storp to feel like a stranger to himself. It was an out of body experience during which he watched himself in horror, a balding, middle-aged man, slightly overweight in ill-fitting clothes, trying to hold it together. As long as he didn't see this image of himself, Storp maintained control. But as soon as he saw the poor image he cut, Storp became a quivering wreck, flushed and regretful. He read from Clements' message explaining why the employee association preferred to put their money toward a new boat rather than a rec center.

"The only way they're getting that boat in here," Vanna told Storp, "is if they put my name on it."

Storp noted this fact on the top sheet of his stack. "Full name?" he asked.

"*The Vanna Lavinia.*"

"Because maybe we could talk them into calling it *The Vanna.*"

"Do you have any idea how many Vanna's there are in the Foreign Service?"

Storp was sure the fact didn't exist in the stack on his lap, but he dug down deep anyway so as to appear useful.

"Isn't there something in the FAM about naming new property after the Principal Officer? Every post I've served at, I've seen plaques commemorating buildings to past principal officers. I'd like a plaque of my own."

"I can write to Washington."

"Check the FAM, first. Don't want to raise unnecessary attention." Vanna ran a turquoise fingernail along her smooth and shiny thigh, drawing Storp's eyes to the rising line of her hem. Convinced she'd muddled his sad, lumpy mind she struck again with her dull blade, exercising a slow torture that would leave him panting at the prospect of more. "Where are we with the Fourth of July? I've heard nothing from your planning committee."

"Its – They're – We're all pretty busy with the Club Soda re-opening." To distract from the Fourth of July, Storp admired the carpet at his feet, an expensive gift from one contact or another who Vanna barely knew but dearly loved.

"Not because of my position, Mr. Storp. Because of my person. Check the ethics language."

"No need to, ma'am. You're perfectly right."

"Do we need to have the carpet appraised?"

"I wouldn't do that, ma'am."

She looked at the rich, reddish carpet and said, "Probably worth thousands of dollars."

"I didn't hear that, ma'am. My sense of carpets is very bad. I'm sure I would pay several thousand dollars for a carpet worth only hundreds."

Vanna smirked and went for more. "Speaking of ethics. What about your mission with our friends in back? What has No Lips got that I haven't got?"

Storp told Vanna about the leather furniture in No Lips' office.

"If they have leather furniture, I want leather furniture."

"That isn't all – "

Before Storp could continue, the hi-lo alarm pierced his ears, alternating high and low, high and low. Vanna and Storp stared at each other, unsure what to do. Ducking for cover was bad enough when nobody witnessed the act. But Storp felt that cowering on his knees underneath furniture, ass in the air in front of his boss, was a lousy strategy for promotion. And Vanna worried what crawling under her desk would do to her hair.

"Maybe your desk?" Storp asked, regretting the suggestion immediately. It felt like a proposal to park somewhere dark and secretive and spend the night fumbling with zippers, an idea that now gave him an uncomfortable bulge.

"Certainly the desk has room for one of us," Vanna shouted. "But I refuse to be the kind of leader who protects herself and abandons her subordinates."

The intercom crackled to life and Decker announced: *This is the Marine Security Guard. This is a drill. I repeat, this is only a drill. All staff are to remain in the duck and cover position until the conclusion of the drill.*

"You might squeeze behind the potted Fichus by my desk," Vanna suggested. They moved at a crouch, and after they'd repositioned themselves Vanna shouted, "Where were we?"

Storp, on his knees, trembling and cowering behind a potted plant like a cartoon figure, realized he'd left his script behind in the scramble for cover. "I – I – I was about to suggest we requisition new furniture for you," Storp guessed.

"Using what money?"

"Post Improvement Funds?"

Vanna's face grew puffed and red. Her forehead wrinkled, and Vanna hated wrinkles. "Need I remind you that I have ruined a dozen of my favorite shoes, ONE DOZEN, on that strip of tarmac you call a "road" out there? We will not touch one cent of the Post Improvement Funds until I see every pothole repaired."

"Of course," said Storp, ready to agree to anything. It was impossible to concentrate. His ears hurt. Screeee –

Uhhhhhh! Screeee – Uhhhhhh! Screeee – Uhhhhhh! Storp prayed for Decker to end the drill. He muttered promises to join Miss Wellstone and GLASSCOCK in the illicit chapel at the back of the chancery if only the screaming would end.

"Speaking of repairs. When will Mutton's contractors finish installing the razor wire?"

Storp masked his ignorance behind a mumbled response.

"As soon as it's finished, he's sure to insist on more. Don't even let him ask me about the front gate. His security plans would turn this place into a prison. Take care of it. Am I clear? Eliminate it. You're the management officer. How long will it take?"

"Ma'am?"

"To replace Mutton?"

"I – "

"His insecurity threatens my promotion. It threatens your promotion, Mr. Storp."

"Yes, ma'am."

"This place already feels like a prison. The inmates are running the asylum. Do you know what those JOs are up to?"

"No, I – " Amid the blaring of the hi-lo alarm Storp heard: "emergency, Emergency! EMERGENCY!"

"Refusing visas. For my contacts! They're threatening my chances of getting to Crawford. I won't have it!"

"No ma'am."

"Get them under control."

"Yes, ma'am."

"Another thing. Direct orders from Fourth Branch are to make us loved in the Kingdom."

"Fourth Branch?"

"You misheard. Let's just say we need intel to support the invasion of Iraq and the war on terror. Let's send them something to show how much the Kingdom loves it."

"Tinker's working on something."

"Tinker. He's busy drafting the Human Rights Report, the Religious Freedom Report, and the Trafficking in Persons Report. Do you know what those reports will do to our efforts?"

"Yes, ma'am."

"The Crown Prince will be livid when he hears what we say about their human rights record. How can I win hearts and minds with that looming over us?"

"Potts?" Storp guessed.

"Potts! The Sousaphone. Mr. Storp, if you'd like to remain my Management Officer, here are your orders. I want to stop hearing complaints from Mutton about security! I want to control every aspect of this mission, from the furniture in back to the JOs in consular! I want a plan on my desk for the Fourth of July! And I want cables detailing how well I'm doing to promote the war on terror!"

"Yes, ma'am."

Vanna stared cruelly out at Storp from the cave of her desk. "Are we clear?"

"We're clear."

"Any questions?"

"No, ma'am." The siren immediately relented. In the profound silence that ensued Storp lost his thought. He rose slowly to his feet behind the potted fichus, a tortured wreck, lost in the wonder of his own survival. "I'll take care of it," he said, crossing the carpets as quickly as he could.

"Mr. Storp?"

"Yes?"

"Don't forget your stack of papers. God knows I have enough piling up on my own desk."

Chapter 12

The big party Mutton dreaded began with a happy hour that everybody else had looked forward to. Happy hour was an escape from the revolving lights of police cruisers at roadblocks around the city, sandbags outside residential compounds, and hysterical statements from news anchors on TV. It was an escape even from friends back home admonishing them to take care and stay away from terrorists. They were grateful for the advice, but found it impractical. It disheartened them to get messages from home, where a color-coded system warned citizens of danger as they boarded trains, where phantoms lurked in crowds at airports, shopping malls, and large sports stadiums. The war on terror had reshaped the very government of the United States.

"They've achieved near-omnipotence with their campaign of terror," Clements said. He settled back at the poolside tables that Pudge and Ed had pushed together with Liston, Potts, Thorner, and GLASSCOCK. The tables were covered with plastic cups of vodka and gin, far from the dance floor beside the brick wall that bordered the pool outside the snack bar. A green awning kept them out of sight from the Kingdom Hospital. The green awning also protected them from bombardment by the scores of giant crows that wheeled and flapped above in the dusk. Tinker wandered over and, pretending not to, joined them.

"The president's vice outranks the president himself," Pudge said.

"You mean the vice president?" Ed asked.

"I mean the president's vice."

"The anti-president," added Clements.

"Always something new," Ed mused.

"Nothing new," Clements said. "It's in the Constitution. Vice president is exempt from checks on Executive authority because he's in the Legislative Branch. And he's exempt from checks on Legislative authority because he's in the Executive Branch."

"What about the Judicial Branch?" asked Ed.

"They have nothing to say about it whatsoever," said Potts.

The first guests began to arrive, a group of diplomats from the British Consulate. They greeted Miss Wellstone and headed straight for the bar. The DJ started playing on cue.

"So he's all-powerful," Ed realized.

"Took more than two centuries to figure it out," Clements said. "It's a whole new branch of government. Fourth Branch."

Mutton came up behind Pudge, a drink in each hand, and leaned in to ask, "Did you say Fourth Branch?"

"I'm speaking hypothetically," Clements said, and distracted Mutton with his solution to the directive that they issue to 50% of their visa applicants. "We issue visas for other countries."

Thorner stopped watching the Eritrean girls take off their abayas at the entrance. He stopped just long enough to ask Clements what the hell he was talking about.

"Our percentage would be greatly improved if we could issue visas for, say, France. Or Chad." Clements looked over his shoulder. "Eritrea."

The sky had darkened. Fewer of the big wheeling crows squawked and dove. The music had taken over and the DJ's lights splashed color in waves. The tables were empty, but a crowd stood in packs of four and five near the bar at the entrance. The local staff tended bar in white shirts and black bow ties, their formality out of place amid the dust that coated the plastic tables and chairs. Pudge lifted his plastic cup to signal another round.

"Why would you want to issue visas to Eritrea?" Liston asked.

"It doesn't have to be Eritrea. Let's make it France."

"Why would you want to issue visas to France?"

"Because it's not the United States."

"That doesn't make sense," Thorner said. "A better solution would be to stop letting foreigners into the U.S."

"My father was a foreigner," Ed said, without bitterness.

"On what grounds would we issue visas to France?" Liston asked.

"Punishment," said Pudge. "For refusing to be an ally in the WOT."

Thorner said, "If you're not with us, you're with the terrorists."

Simon arrived with a tray of beer. The call to prayer went up from the minaret nearest the consulate, then a second, then a host of voices filled the evening with calls to the faithful. The crows settled and their screeching died away, replaced by the prayer call echoing across the rooftops beyond the perimeter wall. The music didn't stop. The drinking and the laughter grew louder and louder, louder thanks to the silence that fell over the city as the devout gathered to pray.

Liston asked, "Why would the U.S. Government issue visas for any other country?"

"Why wouldn't we?" Clements challenged. "We police the world. Right, Mutton?"

Mutton agreed, though he hadn't been following the conversation. He was busy keeping an eye out for terrorists.

Liston shrugged. "Makes no sense."

"The WOT makes no sense," Clements told Liston.

Sammy Liston attended the party because of the mold

77

devouring his bungalow. Dr. Meddler advised that boozing it up at the Club Soda was better for Liston's health than sitting home alone breathing mold spores. Liston lived on the compound, as did Buzz and Specs, retired Navy communicators, pasty men who dressed in jeans, chain-smoked cigarettes, and worked in an office that winked and churned and whirred and blinked with hi-tech equipment dedicated to hearing things not intended for their ears.

"You know what makes no sense?!" Liston said. "I'm responsible for million-dollar equipment and I can't even requisition a mouse trap!"

"You can requisition all the mouse traps you want," Ed replied.

"Why bother?" Liston said. "Your guys in General Services haven't completed a single request. The mold is ruining my lungs! The rats are destroying my equipment! Equipment's worth more than you are. I'd have to kill you if you knew about it. SDDTS."

Ed had no idea what SDDTS meant. He'd never seen Liston's equipment, and he didn't want to. Liston, Buzz, and Specs did their work in a vault behind an iron portal with wheels and cranks and dials that sealed them in tighter than a submarine crew.

"I'll tell you why it makes no sense to issue visas to other countries," Tinker said. "Foreign Affairs Manual. I had a hard enough time memorizing our own 9 FAM. There's no way I want to learn another one."

"I'm not talking about another country's regulations," Clements said. "Our own FAM should authorize us to issue visas to France."

Tinker shook his head. "Reciprocity. Then we'd have to let France issue visas to the U.S."

"Not with the reciprocal agreement I suggest: we issue visas to France, and France also issues visas to France."

"Then who issues visas to the United States?"

"We do."

"How?"

"It's in the FAM."

Tinker said, "Nobody who wanted a visa to France would apply at the U.S. Consulate."

"Who said anything about people wanting a French visa?"

Liston asked, "Would the visa to France be like a Schengen visa, good for all Europe?"

"No. There are some countries of Europe who are our allies in the war on terror, and we wouldn't want to punish them. Think of Poland. We wouldn't want to punish them after what they've done for us in the WOT."

"You aren't making any sense," Liston said.

"Exactly," Clements said. "We're talking about *war*. On *terror*."

"I'll tell you what makes no sense," Thorner said. "Letting any foreigners at all into the United States."

"What makes no sense," Clements said, "is standing toe to toe with terrorists, armed with nothing but a stamp."

Hearing the word 'terrorist', Mutton grew more attentive.

"Denying visas to an enemy who can see us," said Pudge. "You think I feel comfortable refusing a visa to a terrorist who knows what I look like?"

"Terrorists," Mutton said, glad for a chance to add to the conversation. He enjoyed the one-upsmanship between Clements and Pudge. He enjoyed their conversations enormously. "They kidnap people, cut off their heads, then drag the corpses behind shitty beat up cars."

"You think Pudge wants to be dragged behind a shitty beat up car?" asked Clements.

"You think I want my parents to see my corpse on FOX News being dragged behind some shitty beat up car while these animals shout: *God is Great!*?"

"That would make for great ratings," Thorner said.

"Faced with a terrorist, I don't want to refuse him a visa so he can hang around and kidnap me after work," Clements said. "I want him out of the country. I want him on the next plane to somewhere. Anywhere. France."

"At least they'd think we gave them something for their trouble."

"Maybe we can issue visas to countries that already have terrorists," Clements suggested. "Like Afghanistan."

"The Kingdom has terrorists," Mutton said. With that in mind, he went back to watching the guests, who all seemed like normal people on a normal night looking for a good time. They were diplomats from other consulates, engineers for the oil companies, even used car salesmen. Nurses. Flight attendants. Businessmen from around the world. Yet any one of them might be a terrorist. By that logic, Mutton reasoned, any one of them might not be a terrorist. He saw Vanna come in with a short, dark Arab on her arm. Al Bafarti. Even he seemed fairly ordinary, aside from looking so much shorter next to the tall and elegant Vanna, dressed in high boots and short skirt. Mutton felt jealous stirrings. She made him so hot, so bloody angry with passion. How he wanted to get down on his knees before her and touch her ankles. How he wanted her! How he hated her!

"You don't issue visas to a country that somebody's already entered," said Tinker.

"What about that guy at the airport?" Liston asked. "Conklin."

Emmanuel Conklin, assigned to the consulate as an Economic Officer, remained in the custody of the Kingdom's immigration service. The Kingdom was vague about the charge, but it stemmed from their suspicion that Conklin was a Jew. Conklin's status to the Ministry of Interior was that of extra-terrestrial detainee: he hadn't formally entered the Kingdom, yet he'd been processed out of the United States.

Tinker said, "I think he really is a Jew."

"What difference does *that* make?" Clements asked.

"He could be a spy."

"Who's he spying on?"

"The Kingdom's laws prohibit entry to Jews," Tinker said, as if that settled it.

"Lucky bastard," Thorner said. "Almost makes me wish *I* was a Jew."

"There's no evidence that he's Jewish," Clements said.

"He's in good spirits for a guy who's been held for seven months with no charges and no access to the outside world," Pudge said.

"Is he being tortured?" Ed asked.

"Depends on your definition of torture," Pudge said.

"My definition of torture is living in the Kingdom," said Thorner.

Mutton had a hinky feeling about the crowd, now. They'd grown thick up by the bar. The DJ had turned up the music and quite a few ladies had gone to the dance floor. They looked good dancing, but they weren't terrorists so he tried to stop himself from watching them. Was al Bafarti leading Vanna to the floor?

"None of this is the point," Clements said. "Conklin *had* a visa. I'm talking about issuing visas for terrorists to enter countries they aren't already in."

"Preferably countries that already have terrorists of their own."

"Terrorists want to kill Americans. Let's issue them visas to a place no American wants to go to. Like Njamena."

"Worst posting in the Foreign Service," said Liston.

Pudge sat at the edge of his chair, excited. "We issue visas to Chad. All the terrorists go to Chad. Then we follow up with a *Consular Warning* against traveling to Chad, citing increased terrorist activity. It's perfect. We could even send in GLASSCOCK to blow up a few things and really make it count. Or the Gunny."

The Gunny nodded as he strode past their table to join the Eritrean girls on the dance floor. The plastic tables and chairs under the awning had filled up. The crowd had grown to four-deep by the bar. Liston stood and offered to bring a round of drinks before last call.

Tinker grumbled something about the blond at the entrance, excused himself, and stepped away on lively, spring-loaded toes. At the bar Corporal Hunker was handing a plastic cup to a bleached young woman with fresh white skin bulging up from her low-cut top.

"Who's that?" asked Ed.

"Saraya," Clements said.

"Tinker's nurse," said Pudge.

"Tinker used to hold her purse while she danced."

"With other men."

"Held her purse," Clements said.

"What's the big deal?" Thorner asked. "She's a foreigner."

Pudge said, "It's Hunker. How would you feel if Corproal Hunker stole your chick?"

"Excuse me, gentlemen," Mutton said. He'd heard enough. He was going to cut in and dance with Vanna. But when he stood, he felt wobbly, and headed instead for the door.

"Plenty of women here," Ed said.

"This is nothing," Pudge said. "Nothing compared to the days before the invasion."

"Hasn't been the same since February," Clements said.

In February the U.S. had evacuated hundreds of personnel and families from posts throughout the Middle East, anticipating violence in response to the invasion of Iraq. Before then, hundreds of ex-pats from dozens of countries flocked to the Club Soda and boozy weekend parties at the Marine house. Guests crowded around the bar while half a dozen bartenders poured out the contents of gin and vodka bottles clamped upside down, draining shots of rum and scotch into plastic cups, opening cans of beer, and fast as they could serving another volley of drinkers with tickets for booze. Miss Wellstone greeted hundreds of guests at the door, many of them Westerners who'd lived in the Kingdom for ten and fifteen and twenty years. The consulate offered reprieve from prohibitions on alcohol, pork and moral depravity. By ten o'clock the lines and colors and people blurred and hundreds of guests lined up six rows deep by the bar at the heart of the compound, the darkness softened by strings of colored lights and the bluish watery pool-glow. The dance floor throbbed beneath the heavy, humid air. Bass shook the colors and blurred the lines and the poolside spun with wild revolution. The ladies squeezed into skimpy attire while young bachelors and old perverts sat at the tables lining the pool, dirty old oilmen and geologists and engineers who rode Harley-Davidsons with the Harley Owners Group and chased sexy young nurses and flight attendants from Eritrea, the Philippines, the former Soviet Union. The music played and the drinkers drank and the dancers danced while the sounds of bottles, ice, and laughter filled the soft, humid nights inside the compound beneath the American flag.

Outside the compound lurked the white-robed thugs calling themselves the Commission for the Promotion of Virtue and Prevention of Vice. The Religious Police. The Muttawa. They skulked about with full authority to detain individuals deemed to have broken the Kingdom's moral code, an antiquated set of laws established in the 7th century.

But the glory days had faded after a speech full of errant intelligence at the United Nations in February, the evacuation of diplomats and families from the Middle East, and the invasion of Iraq in March. After the April bombings in the capital, even more diplomats and families were evacuated; Mutton's office of Diplomatic Security instituted a curfew, and events became limited, exclusive affairs before being cancelled altogether. Now a quorum of fun-starved guests jammed the dance floor and danced to Sisqo with Vanna, who'd taken off her shoes and shone under the lights with sweat and happiness. Every now and then she waved toward the table, encouraging her gloomy and sullen officers to join her.

Ed stood up. "I think she wants us to go dance with her."

"Sounds like a job for the FARSA president," Pudge told Clements.

Clements had become FARSA President by being too slow in declining the nomination. The other members of the board – Potts, Cautwauler, Thorner, Buzz, Liston, and Colonel Windsock – were paying attention during Belvedere's self-laudatory speech about his accomplishments as FARSA president during his year at the helm. They were ready when he announced: "All those interested in not serving as FARSA president, raise your hand."

Clements found himself beneath a forest of arms reaching for the moldy ceiling of the conference room. The others filled the room with hoots of mirth, giddy at not being caught as FARSA President.

"Are we quite done?" Vanna demanded, displeased to have Clements as president. He was a JO, yes, and subject to her review. But his mental acuity and retention of complex FAM language also made him a formidable opponent. He already caused endless frustration as visa chief. Now Vanna worried about the trouble he'd cause as she angled to use FARSA profits for her own projects.

"What about Cautwauler?" Clements protested. "Tom didn't raise his hand."

"Tom's not here," Storp said.

"Exactly. He didn't raise his hand."

"Tom's not eligible. As Master GSO he has a conflict of interest."

"What a surprise," said Thorner. "The GSO has a conflict of interest with our morale."

Clements didn't bother fighting it. Rather, he submitted wholly, a zealot in his own right. Clements had no single addiction, no single vice, no single virtue. His singular trait was absorption itself. As an athlete he ran until it was no longer healthy and as a student he memorized the library stacks until he forgot what he'd set out to recall. He quit amateur athletics to study Comparative Religion at Columbia University and gave up on his dissertation to pursue a more tangible mystery at the blackjack table. He quit gambling when he reached his tenth scotch of the night, reveling instead in the free drinks brought to the tables at the seediest casinos in Atlantic City.

Clements quit this self-destruction following a ruinous run at Ceasar's Palace that began on September 9th and ended two days later, when Clements emerged from the tomb for the bus ride home to the Bronx. As he drew near the city he saw great columns of smoke rolling into the sky, the twin towers lit up like birthday candles on a dull, grey cake. When he learned what had happened a patriotic surge thumped in his chest. He forgot his obsession with Atlantic City, the seedy relic of a bygone era, and accepted an offer from the Department of State to join the Foreign Service. Several months later, on a quiet campus in Arlington, Virginia, he gathered with 100 other civic-minded fools inspired to serve a government at war. Clements accepted the FARSA presidency in the same spirit that had gripped him then.

Serving as president wasn't as bad as he'd expected. Miss Wellstone handled the day-to-day operations, an astute manager who kept perfect books and could be trusted with the booze. She treated Clements like a VIP. At the Snowflake Ball in the desert heat of January, when all the tables by the pool were jammed with sweaty guests in tuxedos and gowns, Miss Wellstone set up a table inside the snack bar where Clements ate his filet mignon at a candlelit table in the company of a cute Filipina who called herself Sorbet. He enjoyed the air conditioning, the companionship, and the candlelight, but more importantly he didn't have to scrape and bow before Vanna or endure the brutish bad humor of Larry Porcas's drunken friends in the Harley Owners Group.

Miss Wellstone had made FARSA a profitable machine, and she was paid handsomely for her efforts. "What do you do with all that money?" Clements asked.

She smirked her pretty English lips and said, "Oh, I'm socking it away for a rainy day, don't you know. This good weather can't last forever." She smiled knowingly. "I'll open my own bar some day. I have property on Crete."

FARSA was a six-figure industry that provided booze to consulate staff and to the general public at Club Soda events. There was romance to the operation, a smuggler's joy to defying Saudi prohibition. Clements calculated that when FARSA paid $0.30 for a can of Stella Artois and sold it easily for $5.00 at the Club Soda, where 500 people gathered twice a month and guzzled an average of five drinks apiece, FARSA stood to earn $12,500 minus meager expenses – $750 for the beer; $500 for a DJ; $500 to pay bar staff and for cleaning up.

"We're cleaning up," Clements told Miss Wellstone. She was in her office counting envelopes of cash. "We earn over $10,000 profit per event."

Miss Wellstone nodded discreetly, concentrating on the twenties and fifties and hundreds she seemed to be forever stuffing into brown bank envelopes. She parted her lips and peeled back the filthy bills with her long, slender fingers. "This is nothing," she said.

"Nothing? It's a fortune."

"Compared to my returns. I hope you're in the market, my dear. There's a killing to be made. But it won't last forever. Get in now. Mr. Bush's war on terror will drag on and bleed the market."

She wet her thumb and forefinger on a sponge and counted out another envelope. "Now you're president, you'll have to watch Vanna. Having Belvedere as president was a blessing for FARSA. Ineffective as he is, the CG's plans for a recreational center moved at a snail's pace."

"The what?"

"The rec center. Go-karts, mini golf, a covered playground for the children: see-saw, swings, jungle gym, sandbox – "

"What children? Families are evacuated. Jungle Gym? Sandbox? This whole compound's one giant sandbox!"

"Well, now you're president, you'll see for yourself the plans she has for our profits."

But the invasion of Iraq and the quadruple bombings in the capital drove out more and more Westerners, and FARSA events were no longer profitable. Clements asked, "Do we even have enough money to pay rent at the beach house?"

Miss Wellstone put down her envelope. "Well, we certainly can't pay for the beach house, a new boat, *and* a rec center." Miss Wellstone took another stack of bills and wet her thumb and forefinger. A smirk played along her lips. "Do people with a drinking problem sign up to work in the Kingdom, or does the Kingdom create people with drinking problems?"

Now, with the grand re-opening of the Club Soda disco, Clements had the answer. He could barely keep his tongue inside his mouth as he watched Vanna, glistening with sweat in her short skirt, grinding between Mutton and al Bafarti, shoes tossed carelessly to the edge of the dance floor.

"Is she drowning?" Clements asked.

"I think she's rubbing the whole thing in Mutton's face," Thorner said. "'Look at me,'" he mocked. "'Big party! No attack!'"

"Let's see what the Commission for the Promotion of Virtue and the Prevention of Vice have to say about it when this drunken lot try to depart."

Chapter 13

Blurry with drink, clumsy from a night of smoke and noise, Mutton teetered on the chair where he stood to remove his American flag from the wall. Under normal circumstances he would've called Kippinger to help fold the flag. But under normal circumstances he wouldn't be removing the flag in the first place. There was no reason he could think of for taking it down that wouldn't cause him shame, so he worked alone. Keeping the flag from touching the carpet he made two folds, creating a narrow band of red and white, the starred blue field on top. He pressed his chin against the blue field to hold it to his chest and reached for the corners below.

With the four corners in his hands he stepped down from the chair and laid the flag across his sofa. He folded the triangles, smoothing as he went. The last fold made a neat tri-corner of white stars on a blue field. This triangle he placed in its wooden display case. It had been the flag commemorating his grandfather's service during World War II.

From a plastic bag he pulled the green flag with the white sword and Arabic script. He removed the price tag from an eyelet and stood on the chair. He tried putting the eyelets on the screws but the Kingdom's flag was narrower than the American flag. Mutton ran wire through the eyelets and twisted the wire into loops, like tiny nooses, and hung the loops on the screws.

~ ~ ~

Ed's two-way hissed and crackled. The marine at Post One was communicating with Porcas. Ed shrugged off the chatter and rolled over, feverish. A burst of static rushed through the bedroom. Decker's voice rose and fell among

the airwaves: – *Report of terror – hiss ... – acking oil fac
– sss ... I repeat sss ... – at the sss ... facility in ... sss. –
Ersonnel stand by – sss ...*

Ed thought, *it isn't real. It's a dream. You are acting
GSO.* Acting. *None of this is real.*

His mobile lit up and vibrated across the nightstand.
Ed grabbed it and heard Storp's voice, thick with drink.
"Post One reported an attack just north of us. Staff should
not report in the morning. Activate the cascade system and
instruct your men not to report in the morning."

Ed looked at the clock. "It's Friday," he told Storp.

"Tell them to call you when they've reached the last
person on the list."

"Today is Friday," Ed repeated. "The men don't report
on Friday."

"Tell the contractors *not* to report. The duty driver
should *remain* at the consulate."

It was as if Ed had not spoken at all. Storp clicked off.
Ed lay on his sweaty sheets and closed his eyes. The radio
came to life. Through the static Decker instructed: *all
personnel stand by.*

In the living room Ed dropped into the Lazy Boy
recliner and found a news channel. The ticker on *Sky*
scrolled breaking news: ARMED ASSAILANTS STORM
OIL COMPOUND IN SAUDI ARABIA; GUNFIRE,
EXPLOSIONS REPORTED; KINGDOM ON STATE OF
ALERT AFTER ATTACK AT AMERICAN FACILITY.

Decker shouted into the static: *All personnel stand by.*

~ ~ ~

Through the hiss and static of a bad connection the
caller spoke to the anchor in Hong Kong. The sky was just
starting to lighten outside Potts' window. Potts, hungover,
heard one, then another, then many *Muezzin* calling the
faithful. The televised phone call prattled on. An
eyewitness had escaped the facility and described what

she'd seen. She guessed not fewer than four terrorists had ... and taken hostages and ... killed at least ... American ... *hiss* ...

Potts switched from *CNN* to *Sky* where a reporter read prepared text: gunfire at midnight outside the McDonald's on the oil compound; four attackers, several hostages, two Westerners dead, thought to be American. Witnesses heard the attackers shout, "We are the *mujahideen*. God is greatest!"

The *muezzins* quieted. Potts called the media specialist. "What's the press saying? What do Bafarti's people know?"

"Four terrorists on the compound," Hatem said.

"What's the government doing?"

"Security forces have yet to mount a counter assault."

"Hostages?"

"Yes. And two dead."

"Anything from official sources?"

"Police found a pipe bomb at the international school. A bomb squad is on the scene."

Potts' two-way crackled and farted. A *CNN* correspondent in Tel Aviv waited for news to develop, passing time by responding to leading questions from the anchor about tensions between the United States and the Saudis. The correspondent dissected the significance of the target. Former experts, touted as experts, answered questions. Potts recognized the bald ambassador who'd served in the Kingdom 20 years earlier.

"Does the target show a sign of desperation for the militants?"

"Excellent question. Well I think you're right. It's a soft target. Diplomatic interests, especially Western diplomatic interests in the Kingdom, have reacted to the recent threats by beefing up security. As I mention in my new book ..."

"This is an attack on a major oil refining center which employs hundreds of American and Western contractors, and houses perhaps a thousand of their family members. Mr. Ambassador, what can you tell me about the impact this will have on the Americans living in the Kingdom?"

"Well, as I say in my new book ..."

~ ~ ~

Mutton removed the mattress from the bed in the spare room and stood it against the wall. He disassembled the frame and set the parts beside the closet. He pushed his weight against the empty dresser but it refused to slide across the thick pile carpet. He tipped the dresser over and left it lying below the window.

In the living room he flipped over an orange sofa and slid it along the carpet. He struggled and pushed and finally got it through the bedroom door. He left it upside down against the furthest wall.

From the other bedroom he brought a lamp, a wicker table, a box of old clothes, camping gear, scuba equipment, and a duffel bag full of golf balls. He brought in his golf clubs and looked at the clutter he'd created. The sofa, lying upside down against the wall, looked conspicuous.

He piled cushions and pillows across the overturned sofa. He brought in more junk, unscrewed lampshades, put two lampshades on the sofa and left the others by the closet. He tipped over the box of clothes and spilled the old golf balls across the floor.

Now the sofa was hidden among the clutter.

~ ~ ~

Pudge sobered immediately. A large, naked corpse filled the TV screen, bloated and mottled, blue with old tattoos.

Pudge swigged a tumbler of scotch. No impact. He swigged another. No impact, no change – he still wanted out of the Kingdom. As the officer responsible for services to American citizens, it was Pudge's duty to get out a message assuring the public that the U.S. Government was concerned about the safety of its citizens living in the Kingdom while emphasizing the fact that the U.S.G. was not responsible for the safety of its citizens living in the Kingdom. The message would have to appear helpful while discouraging calls for help. The message would have to be precise. The message would have to be true. Most important of all, the Warden's Message would have to be cleared up the chain of command.

Belvedere was first in line to clear, and he took this responsibility seriously. He was in the midst of tedious calculations about how the attack on an oil facility might effect his investments. The attack could have any of three consequences: his stocks could plummet on fears that the world's oil supply was insecure; his stocks could skyrocket when investors learned that the oil infrastructure had suffered no damage; finally, the attack might cause no change at all in the value of his stocks. Belvedere decided that under such circumstances, the best course would be to call his broker in New York. Since calling New York from home would cost Belvedere more than driving to the consulate where he could place the call without paying, Belvedere went out to start his car, but it was dead from disuse.

"Sir, today is Friday," the Yemeni duty driver told him when he called for a vehicle. "No work today, *al Hamdu Lilla.*"

"I have work to do related to this attack," Belvedere said.

"Very well, sir. But Mr. Mutton has ordered personnel to stay away from work."

"That's ok. I won't actually be doing any real work."

"Very good, sir. I am on my way."

It was only when he got to his office that Belvedere

realized it was too early to call his broker. Full of nervous energy he decided to do some work, after all. As Consular Chief, he would need to clear a Warden's Message assuring the public that the U.S.G. was concerned about the safety of its citizens living in the Kingdom, while emphasizing the fact that the U.S.G. was not responsible for the safety of its citizens living in the Kingdom. He called Pudge and told him to draft a message.

"I've already done it."

"In that case, I clear."

"But you haven't seen it."

"Haven't I told you about my management style? I rely on your judgment. Go ahead and send out what you've got."

"Security instructed all personnel to stand fast. I can't get to the consulate."

"We need to contact the wardens. I authorize you to come in."

Belvedere didn't know how to operate the warden system. He was able to send emails, but there were also faxes and phone calls to make. Phoning and faxing could take all morning, and Belvedere didn't want to be caught at the consulate if it came under attack. He felt stuck in a game of musical chairs. The music could stop at any moment and Belvedere didn't want to serve as the representative dead when the consulate came under attack.

~ ~ ~

Dr. Meddler asked himself how he felt about it.

"Bad," he told himself. "Scared."

"And how does that make you feel?"

"Bad."

"That's interesting."

Dr. Meddler wasn't sure what to say to himself after having told himself that what he said was interesting. He hadn't meant to be interesting. He had meant to express fear.

Dr. Meddler, whose real name was Philip, wrote a poem about his feelings about the war on terror. Then he tore the paper up and set it on fire.

~ ~ ~

Vanna Lavinia hunkered in the corner of the closet that GSO had lined with lead and sealed off with a thick steel door and an electronic Hirsche pad whose code was etched into the soles of her shoes. She locked herself in and hunkered down on the floor among all her many pairs of heels and pumps and peek-toe shoes and sandals and flip-flops and boots. In the dark she reflected on her anger, fear, and confusion. She was angry at the terrorists because after a raid like that against an American target she'd have to do battle again with Mutton and all of Diplomatic Security to be allowed to host a Fourth of July party. As for her fear and confusion, she narrowed those down to one small question: where were those pumps of hers with the security code, and now that she'd locked herself into the vault, how would she get out without them?

~ ~ ~

Well-hidden beneath his sofa, Mutton phoned Hassan. "Have you reached Ghani?"

"This is Ghani," said the voice on the other end.

"Commander Ghani?" Mutton asked, unsure if drink had confused what he heard.

"My good friend Mr. Mutton. How can I help you?"

"What do you know about the Amco attack. Any collateral intel?"

"Yes, is bad news, isn't it? Bad news."

"Any of your men hit?"

"No. Is the bad news. My men and I, we are back here. No fight for us. We are back here, protecting you."

Mutton thought he must still be confused. "Ghani, is there any collateral intel? Other targets? What do you think?"

Ghani sounded bored. "No, my friend. You are safe."

"Safe? How do you know?"

"I am protecting you. And you have your razor. So pretty."

Mutton worried. He thought of the razor wire around his compound, now littered with colorful plastic bags. Pink, red, blue, yellow, and black plastic bags had all blown up out of the sewers and off the streets on the high evening breezes and clung to the razor wire protecting his perimeter. Was Ghani mocking him? Mutton rubbed his head and thought, *the party's over.*

~ ~ ~

Potts' stomach had already turned. Local news aired footage of a naked male corpse lying in the road, ankles and wrists bound, tied with thick rope to the back of an old sedan. A mob of Arab and South Asian workers in filthy clothing crowded around shouting "God is great!" They leered at the corpse with the rubbery skin.

The camera zoomed in. Potts made out the bluish swelling of tattoos. He turned his head and retched into the pail. His throat burned and he felt painfully hollow inside. The emptiness came with a relief at knowing the CG would be forced to call off the Fourth of July reception.

... Security forces stormed the facility in the early hours ... Chased the attackers, killing one immediately ... Three attackers hijacked two vehicles and police gave chase through the port city ...One sedan dragged the dead American through the streets at parade speed ....

~ ~ ~

In the back of the chancery behind doors behind doors behind doors a singer crooned about his inability to find what he was looking for. No Lips debriefed GLASSCOCK.

96

"I want to know what happened up there!"

"It's not our op."

"That isn't the question. The question is, 'What happened up there?'"

"The news is reporting – "

"I've seen the news! I don't need to know what the newsmen know. I need to know what the newsmen don't know."

GLASSCOCK was not an analyst. He was in operations. GLASSCOCK liked to be told what to do, and to do it. He wasn't there to analyze. "There are cells outside our control operating in the Kingdom," GLASSCOCK guessed.

"You damned well better be sure this isn't one of our cells."

"This isn't one of our cells."

"Nothing from Fourth Branch?"

"Nothing from Fourth Branch."

"Then we have another problem out there." No Lips turned away. Through tightened non-lips he whispered, "Terrorists."

After a moment he asked, "Do you have any idea what this does to our media campaign? Our cooperation with the security services? We've got no recent warning we can point to. Fourth Branch will – "

"I can fix it."

"How?"

"Counter-op."

"Stop talking about it and do it."

"Do you want me to clear it, first?"

"This isn't the C-Y-A."

~ ~ ~

From the living room Mutton brought footwear catalogues and a dozen books, including a gold-edged copy of the St. James Bible. He placed a stack of books under each arm of the sofa, lifting it enough to create a gap he could slide through. He practiced several times until he was satisfied he could slip his muscular body through fast. Head first on his belly was quickest. Once in, he could roll onto his back and hug his Bible for solace.

From the box of camping gear he took a Thermarest and two large flashlights. He slid them under the sofa. He added a bed sheet and pillow. Mutton slid underneath and lay there thinking about how long he might have to hide. He got out.

In the kitchen Mutton filled a two-gallon jug from the water cooler. He collected cans of beans and corned-beef hash in a box and added a bowl, a fork, a spoon, and a Swiss army knife. He added a plastic bucket and a roll of toilet paper. He brought all this into the cluttered room. When he entered he saw that the clutter looked natural. He stepped cautiously around the golf balls and placed the box of food and the bucket next to the sofa.

He found two unread novels in the living room and put them underneath the sofa, along with an unopened bottle of Johnnie Walker Black. Then he looked at his camping gear.

~ ~ ~

"You want me to report to the consulate?" Ed asked. He wasn't sure he'd heard Storp correctly.

"Yes," Storp said. "We can't both be there. I'll need to run Management Ops from my residence in the event the compound is hit while you're there."

"What will I be doing?"

"The usual. Standing by. In case we need someone there. You'll be Acting GSO."

~ ~ ~

In addition to informing American Citizens of what the consulate could not do for them, it was Pudge's job to inform Buddy Cringle's wife in Manila of the oil contractor's death.

"Mrs. Cringle? I'm calling from the American Consulate. In Saudi Arabia?"

"Wha'? I can' hear you." The widow shrieked into the bedlam behind her, then spoke into the phone. "Chirren. Wha' you say?"

"I said, I'm calling from Saudi Arabia. I'm an official at the American Consulate. In charge of American Citizen Services."

"I American citizen."

"I'm afraid I have some bad news, Mrs. Cringle."

Pudge paused. He expected Mrs. Cringle to know. The attack had been widely reported by international media and Pudge heard a television in the background.

"Can' talk long," Mrs. Cringle shouted. "Chirren. I already tell you, I American Citizen. Wha' you wan'?"

"It's about your husband, ma'am. Buddy Cringle is your husband, isn't he?"

"Of course. Is how I American citizen."

"I'm afraid I have some bad news. Mr. Cringle-" Pudge paused. Buddy Cringle hadn't merely died. Two attackers had tied him to their sedan with rough hemp rope, jerked him from his feet, and dragged his large, naked body through the streets. The Red Crescent doctor had told Pudge: "The good news is, the fall likely knocked him unconscious before the dragging started."

It wasn't the kind of good news Pudge wanted to pass along. He wanted to be sensitive to the widow. He mumbled in the most sympathetic tone he could muster that Buddy Cringle had met his demise.

"Mister, wha' you say?"

"Ma'am, your husband was killed in a terrorist attack."

There was a pause, then Mrs. Cringle said, "Wha' about settlement?"

"Settlement? Yes, we should talk about settling the

remains."

"Wha you mean 'remains'? I wan' full settlemen'. Full."

"Of the- I mean the remains of your- Your husband's body."

"There is no settlement?"

"Mrs. Cringle? Your husband died this week. In a terrorist attack in Saudi Arabia. As next of kin, it falls to you to take care of the remains."

There was silence.

"Would you like him repatriated?"

Pudge only heard the television in the background.

"I mean, can we send his body home?"

"Home? Yes. Send the settlement home."

~ ~ ~

The terrorist corpses, natives of the Kingdom, did not draw the same crowd as that of Buddy Cringle. Their fate was ambiguous: they were martyrs; they were heretics. Some praised them for avenging the Prophet (Peace Be Upon Him) whose memory had just been desecrated by the disco hosted in the den of American iniquity. Others condemned the terrorists for not targeting the den of iniquity itself. In the Saudi media, however, one thing was clear: the American infidels were to blame for the attack given all the trespasses they'd visited on the land of the Prophet, PBUH.

The Royal Family decreed the four attackers to be members of the Kingdom's most wanted, and *The Green Truth* reported them criminally insane, not fit to be called Muslims. Meanwhile militant websites boasted that the young Lions of Islam had defeated an enemy who'd invaded the Holy Land.

Only one fact was indisputable: two of the charred corpses were found sitting upright behind the melted dashboard of the Cedric sedan stolen for the attack.

Interior Ministry had been thorough when finally given authority to storm the compound. The first volley pierced the Cedric's gas tank and sent a fireball boiling into the afternoon sky.

~ ~ ~

The last thing Mutton did before going to sleep each night in his sofa bunker was check the entrance where he'd hung the green flag with the white sword beneath Arabic script attesting witness to the one God. He looked into his spare bedroom from the lighted hallway. The clutter held an eerie emptiness. But it was a real clutter. There was an escape route to the window. The golf balls would cause unwary intruders to fall. If the *Mujahideen* took control of the compound like they had to the north, Mutton could hide for days, sparing his family the sight of his headless corpse towed through the streets behind some shitty, beat-up jalopy.

He removed the bulbs from the ceiling light and crawled into his bunker. He praised the Almighty God for the recent attack. In all likelihood, it would put an end to Vanna's Fourth of July party. Then Mutton fell asleep clutching the pair of pumps he'd stolen from Vanna's closet, breathing them in deeply until visions of her floated before his tight-shut eyes.

PART II

Chapter 14

Mutton felt in his bones that the Amco attack was a dry run, a test, a prelude to an attack on the consulate. Just a matter of time before they got hit. So when he finally found the courage to crawl out from beneath his sofa-bunker and face reality, he reviewed the progress Ed's contractors had made in securing the compound. Razor wire up. Guard towers built. Jersey barriers outside his walls doubling the offset between a blast on the street and any fixed object on the compound.

All well and good, but his cop's intuition told him the measures weren't enough. The gate still closed too slowly. His guards had made little progress on the range. And Ghani had given him bupkus for intel from the operation across the street.

And attending to these extraordinary measures had caused Mutton to neglect standard internal reviews. Months had passed since he'd investigated violations for mishandling classified material. And in that time he'd become aware of a nagging presence, an ethereal entity, a government body as spectral to him as the terrorists outside his gates who wanted him dead. Fourth Branch.

Mutton saw logic in combining the investigations and thought first of Martin Tinker. Mutton knew Tinker plagiarized from *Newsweek* and other magazines to draft his Top Secret cables. Why plagiarize? He doubted the JO knew enough to fear stepping outside to get his own reporting. Could it be the mysterious Fourth Branch, seeking intel to promote the war on terror, had ordered him to find sensationalized reporting? Wouldn't that explain the need to write cables that seemed to be drawn straight out of popular news?

"I get it," Mutton told Tinker, probing the aberration by feigning sympathy. "Why expose yourself to danger by leaving the consulate, right? Just as easy to sit behind your desk and copy the work of journalists who are better paid and better trained to do the same thing. But you should know: it's a violation. As I'm sure you learned in high school, plagiarism is never ok. It could be grounds for citation."

Mutton paused and let that sink in. Nothing from Tinker.

"Unless," Mutton said, "you have a directive. Orders from above? To collect your intel this way?"

"I don't know what you're talking about," Tinker said.

"You may think that nobody else around here still reads *Newsweek*. But I do."

Tinker remained uncooperative. "If our reporting looks the same, maybe it's because we have the same government sources."

"Or maybe you have the same master back in DC. Tell me about Fourth Branch."

Tinker stared at Mutton. Blank. There was an emptiness to the stare that told Mutton he'd got it wrong. But part of being a good security man was maintaining an air of omniscience and threat. So he gave Tinker a good hard glare and said, "This is my last warning to you, Tinker. Come clean now or I'm citing you with a violation."

Tinker's eyes dropped. He looked at his hands. He mumbled something about joining covert ops.

"Come again?"

"Joining covert ops. It's just … it's just … My Rolodex," Tinker said. "I've spent hours re-organizing these business cards, looking for a way in."

"Tell me about it," Mutton said. "Your Rolodex."

Tinker's Rolodex contained hundreds of business cards, mostly people Tinker didn't know. They were contacts passed down by generations of political officers to serve at the consulate. The trouble for Tinker with having so many contacts, aside from not knowing any of them, was that the cards were difficult to organize: some of the contacts transcribed as "Al K_" what others made into "El K_"; some made "G_" into "Kh_"; "Ei_" became "Ai_" and "Ay". Some included "al" or "el" and "bin" or "ben" and still others used nothing to that effect at all.

"I thought I'd solved the problem by organizing the cards according to first name. But I realized that I don't know hundreds of contacts named Mohamad and Mohammad and Mohammed, not to mention the scores of Mahmouds, Mamdous, and Hamdus I don't know."

Mutton said, "Why not call in an expert. Try Clements. He's the best Arabist at post."

Tinker, sweating and uncomfortable at the surprise visit from the security officer, said, "Maybe I will. Maybe I will."

~ ~ ~

As soon as Mutton left Tinker dialed Clements: the last thing he needed was to be caught lying to the security officer. Not that he expected any cooperation from Clements, who hadn't said a civilized word to him since Tinker'd caused a decrease in Clements' salary. Tinker picked up the phone and in his low, gruff, covert ops voice said, "Clements? This is Tinker."

"Excuse me, sir. Who?"

"Martin Tinker? In the front office."

"Oh. *That* Martin Tinker."

"Have you got a minute? Can you come to my office?"

"Your office?"

Tinker sighed. "My cubby."

Tinker's office was little more than an old storage nook, narrow and windowless. The back of his chair scratched the wall and his stomach squeezed up against the desk. Tinker's cubby had been a book closet until No Lips took over two large offices in the front office suite for his operatives, who were never there to use them.

"Tell me over the phone," Clements said.

Tinker lowered his voice. "Can't say it over the phone."

Clements hit speakerphone and waved to Pudge. He leaned back in his swivel chair and put his feet on the desk. "Why can't you say it over the phone?" Clements said.

"DON'T SAY IT!" Tinker said.

"Is it –"

"– DON'T SAY IT!"

"Classified? –"

"– YOU SAID IT!"

"Is it –"

"– DON'T SAY IT!"

"Top Secret?"

"How many times … how many times," Tinker panted, "how many times do I hafta tell you to watch what you say over the phone!? Do you know what Mutton would do to our clearances if he heard us talking like that over the phone!?"

"Is that question classified?"

Tinker was breathing heavily. He asked, "What was that?"

"That was Pudge."

"Are we on speaker phone?"

"Would that be in violation of a Top Secret?"

"Look, Clements-"

"-No, *you* look. I want nothing to do with your Top Secret and SDDTS classifications. Don't call over here to talk about something that can't be talked about. Don't call over here at all. I've got a job to do, and I'd like to be paid for doing it."

"You're still angry about losing Language Incentive

Pay?"

"Damn straight I'm still angry," Clements said. Six months earlier, when he learned that his Language Incentive Pay had been cut, Clements stormed into the human resources office to demand an explanation from the administrative clerk.

"I cannot tell you that, sir," the Indian said.

"Why not?"

"It is classified, sir."

"Has my skill rating changed?"

"No, sir."

"Did they raise the minimum for receiving LIP?"

"It is the same, sir."

"Then why? How am I suddenly worth $3,000 less than I was two weeks ago?"

"I cannot tell you that, sir."

"Why not?"

"Because the information is classified, sir." The clerk squinted at his computer screen and nodded. "SDDTS, sir. The highest," he said with pride.

"But you know about it?"

"Oh, yes sir. It is about salaries."

"But I don't know about it?"

"It is classified, sir."

"But it's my salary."

"Please, sir. If you have any question, ask Mr. Storp."

By consulting his stack of paper and cross-checking that against the files in his computer and verifying his conclusion with a call to the Indian clerk, the management officer traced the SDDTS classification of Clements' Arabic skills rating code to a cable drafted by Martin Tinker.

"The TIP report," Storp said. The cable cited Clements as the source used to debunk a *National Geographic* article about human trafficking in the Kingdom. "Something about camel jockeys."

Clements remembered. Months earlier Tinker had called him up and asked him to take a look at something.

"What 'something'?"

"I can't tell you."

"Can't tell me?"

"Not over the phone."

"*You* called *me*."

"I called to ask you to take a look at something."

"Is it classified?"

"Don't *say* that!"

"Don't say *what*?"

"You know what. You can't say that over the phone. It's a security violation. Mutton"

"I can't ask if a subject is classified over the phone?"

"You did it again!"

"Did what?"

"Said cl– Let me remind you we're on the phone here."

"*You* called *me*."

"I called to ask you to take a look at something."

"How can I look at it over the phone?"

Tinker exhaled heavily. "Can you come to my office?"

"Your office?"

"My cubby."

"I'm busy. I have visas to print."

This wasn't true, exactly. The local staff had visas to print. Clements had visas to come up with reasons for not printing. He practiced his default reason each afternoon with Belvedere, the Consular Chief who inevitably received a call from Pervis who received a call from Vanna demanding an explanation for the refusal of certain visas.

"Why don't you just issue to these Muckety-Mucks?" Belvedere asked. Belvedere disliked being made to support the officers under his supervision against the wishes of the officer who supervised him. "Why didn't you issue to Sheikh al Bafarti?"

"Because he's a terrorist."

"I didn't hear that," Belvedere said.

"I said he's a terrorist."

"I can't tell that to Vanna."

"What *can* you tell Vanna?"

"I can tell her the visa's been issued."

"But the visa hasn't been issued."

"Then issue it. Or give me something I can tell Vanna."

"The fact that he's a terrorist isn't reason enough? I think Mutton would support me on it."

"Can I tell her *why* al Bafarti's a terrorist?"

"Al Bafarti won't tell me why he's a terrorist. That's the problem. If he would tell me why he's a terrorist, we wouldn't have this problem."

"What can I tell Vanna?"

"Tell her there's information to suggest that al Bafarti might be a terrorist."

"She'll want to know what information."

"Tell her we're querying Washington."

"Are you?"

"No."

"Why not?"

"Because Washington probably has nothing to prove he's a terrorist. They'll just tell me I can issue the visa."

"Then why don't you issue the visa?"

"Because al Bafarti's a terrorist."

"You said Washington has nothing on him."

"They don't. But they have enough to put him into ACHOO. Do you think I want to issue to somebody who Washington thinks *might* be a terrorist?"

"No."

"Can you tell that to Vanna?"

"No."

"Then tell her Washington needs more information."

"What information?"

"They sent a list of questions to ask him."

"Out of the question. Vanna doesn't want us calling him up and harassing him unless it's to issue the visa."

"Good. We can't ask the questions, we can't issue the visa."

"I can't tell that to Vanna."

When Clements recounted the conversation to his office mate, Pudge said, "You're better off talking to Vanna yourself."

"I was going over to the front office to see Tinker, anyway."

Clements pushed through the one, two, three ballistic doors between the consular section and the front office. Tucked away at the back of the suite he found Martin Tinker crowded behind his desk, chin in hands, staring at a magazine. "I'm meeting with the CG in three minutes," Clements said.

Tinker looked up, startled to have a visitor. "Thanks for coming," he said. "Uhh. Thanks for coming." When Tinker was grateful he became nervous, and when he was nervous he repeated nearly everything he said. "Have a seat. Have a seat."

Clements remained on his feet. "You wanted to show me something?"

"Yeah. Here it is. Here it is." Tinker pushed the *National Geographic* toward him. "The idea for this cable occurred to me last weekend. At the camel races. Look at these photos."

Tinker squeezed out of his chair and came around the desk to stand beside Clements. He turned the magazine for Clements' benefit and peered over his shoulder. "What do you see?"

"What do I see? I see camels. And camel jockeys."

"Ah ha! Right. But what kind of camel jockeys?"

"They're kids. All camel jockeys are kids."

"But what nationality?"

"How should I know?"

"Do these kids look Sudanese to you?"

"How can I say? Sure. They look ..."

"Because I don't think they're Sudanese."

"So they're not Sudanese. What's the article say?"

"That's just it. The article says they're Sudanese."

"So they're Sudanese."

"Do those kids look Sudanese to you?"

Clements looked at the photos. He was unable to determine the nationality of the children. "What's the point, Martin?"

"The point is the Trafficking in Persons report. Last year's TIP report mentions children from Bangladesh being used as camel jockeys in the Kingdom. The Royals weren't happy with what we said about them last year. Vanna says we have to get it right this year."

"I don't think she means 'check their nationality' when she says get it right. Besides, this article is from 1987."

"What do you think she means?"

"You'd better ask her that."

"Ok. Ok. Thanks. But hey, we were at the races last week. What did you see?"

"What did I see? I saw miles and miles of sand. I saw a giant friggin' Ferris wheel in the middle of the desert. I saw baboons and graffiti and the shitty, beat-up asphalt of the non-Muslim highway."

"I mean at the races. What did you see at the races?"

"I saw Arabs. And camels. And camel jockeys."

"And where did the camel jockeys come from?"

"How should I know?"

"You were talking to them. I saw you talking to them. What did they say to you?"

"Talking to them? I congratulated one of the riders. I don't even think he spoke Arabic."

"What did it sound like to you? I mean, you're an expert in languages and Islam and shit, right?"

"Islam and shit?"

"Islam. The religion."

"I'm no expert."

"Well, you have a what? A 4/4 in Arabic. Right?"

"Yes, Martin, I have a 4/4 in Arabic on the Foreign Service scale, and I congratulated some camel jockeys at the camel races last weekend, and some of them were probably from Bangladesh, and others were probably from Sudan, and others from God-only-knows where." Clements turned to leave the cramped and airless space.

"But I have no idea, Martin, because I'm a consular officer and the Non-Immigrant Visa chief responsible for keeping terrorists out of the United States. I'm not here to report on whatever it is you think you're reporting on. I'm not here to develop your 'raw Intel'." Clements looked at Tinker's Rolodex. "Here. Why don't you look up one of your contacts? Somebody who knows something about camel racing? You must have hundreds of cards here."

"Good idea. Good idea." Tinker nodded eagerly and fingered the cards. "Here's one I know. Sheikh al Bafarti."

"The terrorist?"

"No. He's in construction."

"Sure. That's how he moves his money."

"What do you mean, 'moves his money'?"

"To finance terror."

"Finance terror? The sheikh's in construction."

"The watch list has him as a terrorist financier."

"But he's a good friend of the CG's!"

"Talk to No Lips."

"No Lips?"

"From the office that isn't there."

Tinker tugged on his chin. "I think I'll do that." He nodded, warming to the prospect of talking to covert ops.

~ ~ ~

Three months later Tinker's camel jockey cable had come out and Clements was earning five percent less because his language score had been classified SDDTS. And six months after that, with truck bombs exploding in the capital, terrorist safe houses being raided in Hajrayn, and Mutton installing razor wire, guard towers, and Jersey barriers all over the consulate, the only good news was that al Bafarti still hadn't received a visa.

Chapter 15

Tinker's call with Clements had ended badly. What if Clements told Mutton he was plagiarizing cables? Or taking shortcuts in the clearance process, going around Vanna, who anyway read nothing he wrote? He called Clements again, his urgent voice low and harried.

"What is it now, Tinker?" Clements asked.

"Look, I just wanted to apologize. I wanted to make sure everything's ok."

"Is that all?"

"Well, no. Actually, I have a question for you."

"Fine."

"Actually, I have two."

"Don't push it."

"The first is about a visa for Sheikh Mohamed al Bafarti."

"And the second?"

"Well, the second is about. Uh, the second is about No Lips."

"Never heard of him."

After a silence on Tinker's end of the line he asked, "What was that?"

"What was what?"

"That noise."

"Did you hear it, too?"

"Is there somebody there with you? I thought I heard ..."

"Just a minute, Mart– ... –ink we have a prob– ... –is line ... You still there, Mart– ... I think ... Not quite ... -ing you ... –it better now? –be –should come over here ...."

Clements hung up and shook his head.

"Do you think he'll come over here?" Pudge asked.

117

"No way he calls again." Clements turned to his computer. "Look busy. If we work this right we can fix it so he never comes to this office again."

They heard him before they saw him. Tinker moved awkwardly, with lots of knocking of heels and swinging of arms and swishing of clothes, dark expensive suits, some with pinstripes, and ties Tinker thought made him a Club Man. Tinker punched a code on the consular door, turned the knob, then bounced past Belvedere's office and turned quickly into the office where Clements and Pudge stared intently at their screens in an effort to ignore him.

Tinker began in a wild harangue: "All right, this place is ..." He had a hand in the air as he built himself up to a shout, but Clements and Pudge continued to type. Tinker, flustered, started to shout. "First of all we've got these problems with our telephones, which is why I'm over here to begin with. I mean I, I, I ..."

Clements and Pudge continued typing. Tinker cleared his throat. He quieted slightly and said, "What's up, you guys?" After a pause filled with the sound of rapid typing Tinker tried, humbler still, "Uh, Clements ..."

Clements continued typing.

"Clements, uh-"

"-Just a minute, Martin. Here, have a seat." Clements motioned toward a stool.

"Sure. Sure," said Tinker. He continued standing by the door, looking important but uncertain in his navy pinstriped suit. Thin navy stripes crossed his red tie, a diamond crest embroidered at the center. Tinker closed the door and sat daintily on the uneven stool next to the corkboard.

"Leave that open," Pudge said without turning around.

"I don't want any of the local staff to hear what I have to say," Tinker whispered. He crossed a leg tightly over his knee and clasped his fingers around his top leg. He scanned the office, repulsed by the disorder. *Doonesbury* comic strips taped to the walls mocked the invasion of Iraq. Papers hung crooked on the tilted corkboard. Sliding piles of applications, cables, travel orders, and dozens of other documents covered both desks. The top drawer of the Mosler safe stood open. A bottle of Johnnie Walker, half empty, stood in plain sight on a bookshelf stuffed with leaning, leaking binders, pamphlets, portfolios, and dictionaries. Tinker considered the mess beneath the dignity of the office, beneath the dignity of the U.S. Government, beneath the dignity of a diplomat serving on the front line of the war on terror.

Clements felt differently. Among the acts of dignity he performed as a diplomat on the front line of the WOT was to answer e-mails from applicants wanting to know when their visas would be issued. He copied and pasted the following message into his response: *Dear ___, The U.S. Government is engaged in a great war on terror. While we fight to spread freedom and democracy to lands governed by fear and tyranny, our efforts to adjudicate visas and safeguard the Homeland have slowed. We regret that the unfortunate actions of a few terrorists may cause you to miss your ___.* In conclusion Clements inserted a variety of reasons for travel, most frequently adding *Business trip, semester of college, grandchild's birth, visit to Disney Land,* or, when he felt especially surly, *efforts to immigrate.*

Clements finished sending one such message before turning to Tinker. He leaned over and opened the door. "Stuffy in here."

"If you don't mind," Tinker said, using his covert ops voice, "let's keep it shut for now."

"Suit yourself," Clements said. His voice grew softer until it became a whisper. "But keep in mind. This office isn't secure. Everything that goes on here is ...

unclassified."

"Careful what you say," Pudge said.

"Well, that's why I wanted to shut the door ..."

"Speak softly," said Clements.

Pudge pointed at the florescent lights in the ceiling.

Tinker leaned forward and whispered hoarsely. "This is the reason I'm here in the first place. I don't think we can have this conversation over the phone. We shouldn't be having it here ..." Worry gripped his face. He looked at Pudge and Clements with wide eyes.

"You think Interior is listening to our phones?" asked Pudge.

"I'm not sure we should talk about that in this office," said Clements.

"Why don't the two of you come over to my office?"

"You have an office?" asked Pudge, eyebrows raised. "They finally got you an office?"

"My cubby."

"And you think it's safe to talk in your ... your cubby?"

"Well, it's certainly safer than talking here."

"What makes you think our phones are tapped?" asked Clements.

"I didn't say that," Tinker said quickly. "But it seems they are listening."

"Who?"

"I can't say."

"Then how do you know they're listening?"

"I can't tell you that."

"Tell me what?"

"Tell you why I can't say how I know they're listening."

"Who?"

"The government."

"The Saudi Government?" Clements asked.

"*Our* Government?" asked Pudge. "Fourth Branch?"

"Don't say that," Tinker said. He stood suddenly,

backpedaled, kicked the stool with his heel and nearly fell over. "I never said that. Look, why don't you guys come over to my off- my cubby, and we'll talk about it there?"

"Sure, Tinker. Why not?" After all, Clements decided, Tinker wasn't the enemy. And while Clements had never really trusted the political officer, it was entirely possible that Tinker could be useful in digging up intel on al Bafarti that would make a refusal stick for good.

~ ~ ~

A visit to Tinker's cubby was the lesser of two evils for Clements. In exchange for a frustrating, albeit harmless, conversation with the aggravating political officer, Clements stood to eliminate the even more frustrating – and frankly dangerous – questions from the CG about a visa for Sheikh al Bafarti. When Clements arrived Tinker rose from his chair, came around his desk, and rested his buttocks on the edge, arms folded across his chest. Clements refused to sit, hoping to make it quick. He got right to it.

"There was something you wanted to tell us," Clements said.

With none of the usual stammering Tinker said, "I'm going under cover."

"I guess that means we won't be seeing you around?"

"This is serious."

"It certainly is," Clements said. Tinker's delusions were worse than ever. "Have you talked to Dr. Meddler?"

"This op is highly classified. Can't be discussed outside this secure environment. Strictly Need to Know."

"Then why are you telling me?"

"I need you as an alibi."

"What about your boss. Does DB know?"

"He's nowhere to be seen."

"What about Vanna?"

"She commissioned the op. And I need an alibi

121

independent of her."

"So what's the op?"

"Vanna asked me to investigate links between No Lips and Fourth Branch."

Clements waited. Nothing. "That's it?"

"That's it. You'll keep it quiet?"

"Absolutely." No way Clements wanted to be associated with what Tinker had said. "Of course."

"And you'll serve as my alibi. While I'm incommunicado? And help pull me back in if I go off-reservation?"

"Of course," said Clements, though he had no idea what Tinker meant by 'off-reservation'. But he knew he'd have to act fast if Tinker was going to be useful to him. The man was slipping quickly. "Meanwhile, maybe there's something you can do for me."

"Name it."

"We have some information of our own to send back. But we can't do it through normal consular channels. We need to use your classified channels."

Tinker rocked nervously. "I don't know. I already circumvent the clearance process enough."

"What clearance process? Vanna doesn't read your cables, anyway. Just have this sent through the Embassy's political section. They won't ask Vanna, especially if it contains a really good scoop."

"What scoop?"

Clements looked around and leaned toward Tinker. He lowered his voice. "Well, for example, we've got strong indications that Sheikh al Bafarti's a terrorist financier."

"The Sheikh?"

"He sympathized with the Taliban when they fought the Russians."

"Vanna's Sheikh al Bafarti?"

Clements nodded. "He provided the cash to purchase

their weapons – or, I should say, our weapons. Like another Charlie Wilson."

Skeptical, Tinker stood up straight. He circled back behind his desk, as if to protect himself from Clements' influence. "How do you know this?"

Clements shrugged. "Just have to get out and talk to people." Clements didn't mention that the people he talked to were the other Pierce Pierce and Thorner.

Tinker said, "It isn't much. It isn't financing terror against the U.S."

"It isn't terrorism at all. At least, it wasn't. But now that the Taliban are fighting the U.S. and supporting al Qaeda, they're our enemy. That makes al Bafarti an enemy sympathizer. For all you know, those weapons purchased in Afghanistan were used against Amco over the weekend. They could turn their weapons on us, next."

"I don't know."

"Do you need a second source?"

"Of course," Tinker said, although he hadn't thought of that. In fact he was thinking of the praise such a bombshell was going to get him when he cabled it to Washington.

"Pudge will tell you the same thing."

"Any local sources?"

"Pudge is local. He's right across the lobby."

"I mean, can I get someone from the Kingdom to tell me?"

"I think you should cable it now and look for corroborating intel during your covert op. No Lips is sure to have something on this."

"And you'll have my back while I'm undercover?"

"Absolutely. Here. Take dictation."

Tinker sat down and pulled up the cable template. He typed quickly as Clements spoke. When he finished he printed a draft and handed it to Clements:

TOP SECRET/TS
PROG DATE: Z1300091103
POL: MTINKER
005122347

SARB
PRIORITY: RUSH INTEL
AMEMBSARB; GCCDL; BME; NEACOLLECTIVE

REDACTED PER SECSTATE 9, 991, 1011 AND ABOVE

SUBJECT:

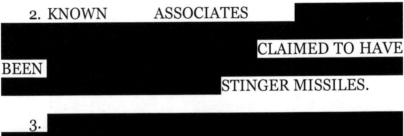

1. SUMMARY: THIS IS AN ACTION CABLE, SEE PARA SIX. LOCAL SOURCES CONFIRM ACCUSATIONS OF TERROR FINANCE ACTIVITIES BY ███████████████ AND OFFER AS EVIDENCE THE FOLLOWING POINTS.

2. KNOWN ASSOCIATES ███████████ CLAIMED TO HAVE BEEN ███████ STINGER MISSILES.

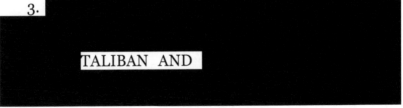

3. ███████████ TALIBAN AND ███████████

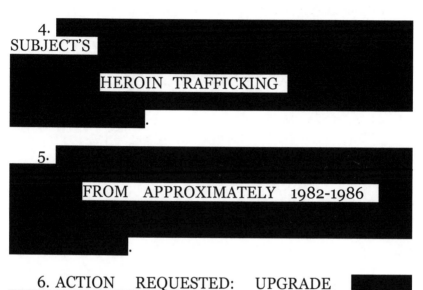

████████████████████EXACT LOCATION OF THE
SUBJECT.

4. ███████████████████████████████████████
SUBJECT'S ██████████████████████████████████

██████████HEROIN TRAFFICKING██████████████

██████.

5. ███

████████FROM APPROXIMATELY 1982-1986████████

████.

6. ACTION REQUESTED: UPGRADE ██████████
██████████████████, DOB █████████ ON
AMERICA'S CONSOLIDATED HOMELAND
OBSERVATION OUTLET (ACHOO) AS 666 AND 911
HITS, PERMANENTLY INELIGIBLE FOR TRAVEL, AS
OF DATESTAMP RELEASE OF THIS MESSAGE.

"This is very good," Clements said. "Very convincing."
"You think so?"
"I think so. You might also want to add '██████
██
████████████████████████.' That might get
you a Meritorious Honor Award."
"What? Say that again."
"███████████████████████████████████
██
██████."

"I don't think you substantiated that."

"I don't have to." Clements drew closer to Tinker and lowered his voice. "Take a closer look under cover. No Lips has this information. I'm certain we can hang him up on

██████████████████████████████████████

."

Chapter 16

Martin Tinker enjoyed drafting cables. Drafting cables in his tiny cubby kept him safe from the terrorists Mutton said were right outside the gate. Drafting cables kept him clear of Vanna, the evil seductress who held his pathetic career like a tiny specimen between her thumb and forefinger. Drafting cables cut his time with the other JOs, who ridiculed him for reasons he didn't understand. Drafting cables, above all, added value to Tinker's status as a Nobody.

As a Nobody, Anybody talked within his earshot unaware that Everybody would read about the conversation later in his cables. Vanna had conversations like that all the time. Tinker's best-read cable – ZIONIST INFILTRATORS DESTABILIZE MONARCHY – came about that way, when an urgent call from Washington interrupted Vanna's instructions to Tinker about who should sit where when she hosted diplomatic lunches. Vanna forgot all about Tinker, the Nobody, and went on at such length about matters of national security that Tinker later pieced together the prize cable:

SUMMARY: ATTENDEES OF THE MAJLIS HOSTED BY SHEIKH AL BAFARTI (SARB00692) OFFERED OVERWHELMING EVIDENCE THAT ENEMIES OF THE MONARCHY ARE BEING ARMED BY INFIDEL NATIONS AS PART OF A ZIONIST AGENDA. THE VIEW THAT THE USG WILL STOP AT NOTHING, INCLUDING ARMING THE TERRORISTS, TO RECRUIT ALLIES IN THE WAR ON TERROR, IS PREVALENT AMONG INFLUENTIAL SAUDIS. END SUMMARY.

Washington responded immediately with kudos, and a request. They wanted details on the evidence discussed at the Majlis. Terrified by the recognition, Tinker responded that the evidence in question was classified SDDTS, and that since SDDTS access was limited to officers in Saudi Arabia, Tinker was obliged to withhold details. He did, however, provide a biography of Sheikh al Bafarti culled from the moldering notes in the bottom drawer of his Mosler safe:

AL BAFARTI, FORMER VICE MINISTER OF AVIATION, MAJORITY OWNER OF LARGEST MEDIA HOUSE IN SAUDI ARABIA, AND SOLE DISTRIBUTOR OF TOYOTA, PANASONIC, PHILIPS, AND THE AL GHARBIYA CHOCOLATE FORTUNE NAMED FOR THE FATHER OF HIS WIFE.

The file said nothing about al Bafarti's construction firm, the Kingdom Exploding Group, and Tinker lacked the courage to add the fact, though he knew it to be relevant and true. He then returned to drafting cables inspired by presidential speeches and old magazines, drafts that he sent for clearance where they piled up higher and higher on Vanna's antique desk.

Martin Tinker was a man of little confidence. He was feeble, with hardly the strength to cinch the knot in his striped silk tie. He was a slender man who'd grown up a slender boy, a Nobody who wanted desperately to be Somebody, Anybody, but Everybody he tried to be caused him consternation, humiliation, and pain. In Saudi Arabia Tinker lived in fear of one thing: the reality check. Reality checked in on him each morning when the foggy shroud of his dreams dissipated before his unbelieving eyes. The role he dreamed of playing, that of a Diplomat bestride the global stage, evaporated to reveal a hollow-eyed, pale-cheeked ghostly white Nobody whose days consisted of taking notes for the beautiful, worldly Vanna Lavinia and whose nights were crowded with the sweats and fears of life on the front line of the war on terror. As his fingers fluttered around the knot he made in his silk tie each morning he watched in the mirror the same slender digits that would betray him throughout the day while turning the pages of old *Newsweek* magazines or hunting and pecking like chickens across his keyboard to fabricate reports from the Kingdom.

Tinker's life had been a miserable cycle of great anticipation dashed upon the rocks of despair going back as far as he could remember. He bought imitation Wayfarers and practiced to be Bobby Kennedy, transporting himself into black and white photographs of the sixties and seventies, sharing power with presidents and diplomats, senators and statesmen, Kennedys and Kissingers. In joining the State Department he saw the solution to all that made him weak. The nervous, shaky, unlucky klutz would become a dignified, poised, debonair Statesman. The images of diplomats striding the halls of power that sustained him through his youth would be the history of his own career. He believed it would grant him grandeur, honor, respect, notability, pomp, circumstance, righteousness, justice for all, trust in God and God's trust in him, all summed up in the strip of fabric tightened like a noose around his neck each morning.

Between his first and fourth attempts at the Foreign Service Exam Tinker graduated from George Washington University, worked at a branch of the Wachovia bank, finished a Masters in Political Science, taught high school history, and began a dissertation on the assassination of Bobby Kennedy. He resigned himself to a life of unrecognized greatness until early 2001, when the secretary of state announced that the Department of State planned to hire over 500 new employees each year for the next four years.

Tinker was ecstatic. The Foreign Service would *have to* lower its standards to recruit so many people. Tinker passed the written exam, soon thereafter the orals, and found himself dressed in a celebratory Brooks Brothers suit he could barely afford and jammed like a sardine with 100 other trainees in an overcrowded room. There Dickie Doubleman, the training coordinator, strafed them with cruel reminders of their exact rank within the steaming bowels of the giant morass known as Foggy Bottom. "Only by clawing, scratching and conniving against each other will any of you crawl out of this dungeon to be considered for an Ambassadorship to even the dustiest of nations, such as Chad.

"If you really want to become Ambassador," said the balding but charismatic bureaucrat, "I suggest you quit the Foreign Service, make a killing in the private sector, and donate money to a successful presidential campaign. For $500,000 you can buy a fairly decent job in Santiago."

Tinker felt his enthusiasm leak out of him in a lonely hiss. They were given a list of 99 jobs in 70 cities that even as a graduate of the School of Foreign Service Tinker didn't recognize. The jobs were an alphabet soup of mysterious acronyms. The class was told to rank their top 25 choices and were warned by the charming assignments officer with the gleam in his eye: "Some of you will be given your first choice. Some of you will be given your 25th choice. Some of you will be given a choice you didn't know you made, mainly because you didn't make it." He looked at the list and made a snappy comment about Njamena, and when Tinker returned to his South Capital apartment that evening he saw again the giant desert country in the north of Africa. Chad. He had seven weeks to worry that he would be assigned to an African desert country named for the middle school bully he'd never forgotten: Chad.

Tinker viewed the assignment process as a competition to avoid being sent to Njamena. He looked for more livable places nobody else wanted to go to, like Saudi Arabia. The jobs there were so unpopular that mid-level officers refused to take them, leaving them open to JOs like Tinker, who lobbied hard for all of them. When training ended the assignments officer told Tinker, "You've got your top choice. Welcome to the very post that issued a dozen visas to the 9/11 hijackers. Welcome to The Kingdom. Welcome to the war on terror."

Tinker swallowed hard, suddenly aware he'd gotten in over his head.

The Near East Affairs Bureau worked quick to get him out of Washington. The white-haired civil servant responsible for travel bitterly told Tinker, "I've seen your kind before, Buster. Too big for your britches. Taking jobs above your pay grade in order to get promoted."

The sentiment was expressed throughout the Bureau. Most officers were promoted to a job like Tinker's after a dozen years or more. Here Tinker had succeeded in obtaining a political reporting job after just seven weeks! The Foreign Service couldn't have that. To accept a JO and invite him to cocktails at the Dacor-Bacon House was unthinkable; but to belittle him was to belittle all other officers in political reporting jobs at the 03 level. Who was this upstart, risking life and limb, to shame his superiors who'd spent their careers sipping cappuccinos in Europe?

What needed to be done was get the problem out of Washington. Ms. Dixon expedited a visa, secured a business class ticket through Frankfurt, and bid him Sala'am. And Tinker, shocked to be accused of anything other than general ineptitude, couldn't find the words to defend himself before boarding his flight for the Middle East, mainly because he'd been given no training whatsoever in the language of the region.

In their haste to be rid of him the civil servants at Main State channeled Tinker through the most obvious recipient of a rush job: The office that wasn't there. No Lips had just crawled into bed after a night of scotch and skirt chasing when the duty clerk alerted him to a cable announcing the arrival. Though he was unaware of any plans by HQ to send in a new officer, No Lips ordered the expeditor to the airport just in case: HQ had been known to leave him out of important decisions.

But when Tinker came through customs wearing a pinstriped suit No Lips said, "There's been a mistake."

"The airline lost my luggage," Tinker replied, amazed that the officer on the ground already knew. It reaffirmed his belief in the magic of the Foreign Service and the all – knowing world of intelligence collection.

"There's been a mistake," the man with no lips repeated.

"I'm Martin Tinker. Political Officer." Tinker held up his orders as evidence.

"Bring him to his residence and have the shuttle pick him up in the morning," No Lips told the expeditor. "Storp will straighten him out."

"Nice to meet you," Tinker said.

No Lips said, "There's been a mistake."

"There's been a mistake," Vanna told Tinker. "The Political Counselor is away. You'll be Acting Political Counselor." Vanna spoke from behind tall piles of paper on her desk. "Too bad DB isn't here to show you the ropes. But if you hit the ground running I'm sure you can make up for your lack of training."

On paper Tinker reported to the Political Counselor. But because DB was away most of the time, in practice Tinker reported directly to Vanna. Vanna was an extremely busy person. Vanna had hair appointments on Tuesdays and Thursdays, and nails on Mondays and Wednesdays; the Country Team met in the capital every Saturday, which left insufficient time to shop for shoes, purses, dresses and lipstick. Wonderful, influential people sent her chocolates and flowers and she owed it to them to have lunch and dinner at their beck and call so they could continue to be wonderful, influential people. She had regular meetings to discuss image and budget with Potts, Storp, and Belvedere, and meetings to discuss security and intelligence with Mutton, No Lips, and Colonel Windsock. If there was anything at all Tinker could have done to help Vanna make Ambassador, she would have gladly cleared time for him on her schedule. But there was nothing the lowly JO could do to advance her career, and her schedule was already so full that she kept standing appointments for massage therapy on Sundays and Wednesdays just to help her unwind. Vanna barely knew Tinker except as a name on the roster, and sometimes not even then. When she did remember his name, Vanna put it to good use if the caller demanded to know: "Where in the hell are those reports from your Mission?!"

"Tinker has them," Vanna told Testes, the Ambassador's deputy. "We've no Political Counselor and a JO doing the work of five men." Vanna cursed Tinker's presence then. Before his arrival Vanna could tell Testes she had *nobody* to do the work of five men. She ordered Pervis to squeeze Tinker onto her schedule, right between her facial and her lunch with Sheikh Saad Ali Reza.

"Who's Tinker?"

"The Acting Political Counselor. And prepare the paperwork for a formal reprimand."

She would teach the JO to mess with her reputation. She found Tinker an infuriating person. The ease with which she took advantage of him made her feel she wasn't doing all she could to fully exploit him. She wanted to squeeze every last drop of blood, sweat, and tears from his frail, overworked frame.

Tinker also sensed resentment from the other JOs. They were polite enough at first, inviting him along to hit balls on the driving range. But he couldn't match their enthusiasm or their spirited accounts about the worst of the visa applicants. Pudge told the stories as if recounting college pranks, and Clements supported the telling by adding deadpan, sardonic details. Their storytelling had become a game of one-upmanship, each one vying to add the strangest piece.

"Prince Qutub wanted to know why I couldn't issue his visa," Pudge said.

"Isn't he still a freshman after four years of school?"

"He's failed every course except Art Appreciation."

"And Power-Walking.

"He's averaged 2½ credits a semester since 1999."

"Half of them D's."

"Including power-walking."

"Which he took twice!"

It was difficult for Tinker to create humor or drama out of his own work taking notes for Vanna while she sipped tea with government officials who didn't trust her enough to tell her anything most journalists didn't already know, or thumbing old magazines in search of material for his cables. He was unable to hide his awkwardness as they drove golf balls in the early evening, whacking them across the sandy lot, the breeze kicking up dust and the crows circling noisily in the trees just outside Vanna's residence. The rest of them didn't care much about the golf. But Tinker couldn't take part in any activity without assuming his performance was a reflection of his character. He was embarrassed by the way his hands fumbled with the club. He was uncomfortable to hear the JOs mock Vanna. They hooted drunkenly and called out "Vannity!" as she drove past in her golf cart. Thorner had the nerve to tee up a shot and swat it across her bow, bouncing the ball off the fender. Vanna smiled and waved, but Tinker cringed knowing that in the morning she'd call him on the carpet for a complete review of what the JOs were saying about her.

Tinker had lived for so long in a state of complete and total misery, ignored by his parents, abused by his bosses, and belittled by his peers, that his shoulders rolled forward in a perpetual hunch and his face had grown long. He hid behind his Wayfarers and took solace in seeing himself as the image of Bobby Kennedy: young and smart, but unpopular and mistrusted for his proximity to power.

Tinker's solitude was reinforced by his assignment to the cramped cubby carved out for him by GSO and the office that wasn't there. When intelligence suggested the war on terror would heat up in Saudi Arabia, No Lips threatened Vanna with executive privilege. "We're authorized to expand our domain at this mission. We need a presence outside the doors behind doors behind doors."

"Authorized by whom?" Vanna challenged.

"Fourth Branch."

Vanna grew compliant. "Just tell me what you need."

"We need more space in the front office suite."

"The new political officer is just a JO. You're welcome to that office. Just make sure he has a place to sit where I can find him. And Chief, make it so I never see your people."

"They'll be like ghosts."

"You want my men to put a desk in there?" Cautwauler asked in disbelief.

"CG wants it." No Lips had intelligence enough to know that the secret to getting the GSO's help was to use Vanna's name in vain.

"We've got to measure the space."

"What's to measure? The desk fits."

"It's pretty small. There are federal regulations about decent labor practices. Why not designate it for one of your guys? It's not as if they'll actually use it."

"Nobody would believe a space that small is an office. We need to establish credible cover."

"So we're putting an officer in there?"

"If there's an officer in there, people will have to believe it's an office."

So operatives from the office that wasn't there took over plum space they never used, and Tinker holed up in the former book storage room crammed with moldy back issues of *National Geographic* and *Newsweek*. There he drafted cables by copying magazine articles word for word, reversing the order of the paragraphs, then reversing the order of the sentences. In some cases he reversed the order of the words in each sentence. He invented dialogue. He added comments overheard on the driving range or in the CG's office. He blended gossip and history and churned out creative cables and annual reports on Human Rights, Religious Freedom, and Trafficking in Persons. These cables, filled with wild fancy and false conclusions, drawn from eavesdropping and unfounded assumptions, should have been corrected and cleared by Tinker's boss before going to Vanna. But since DB was rarely around, Tinker's facts went unchecked straight to Vanna's desk where they piled up higher and higher.

Until Mutton started sniffing around in search of something – anything – that would make them all safe. His interrogation with the skittish Martin Tinker pointed to a frightening intelligence gap. Afterwards he returned to his office, took the nub of pencil from his ear, and jotted a list of intelligence vulnerabilities on the back of his list of security vulnerabilities:

1. Martin Tinker's Cables
2. No Lips
3. Fourth Branch ...?

He dropped the list in the shredder and went to see the more concrete of his potential vulnerabilities.

Chapter 17

The man with no lips was Mutton's main rival for Vanna's affection. At least, that's what Mutton liked to think. He couldn't bear the thought of Sheikh al Bafarti as his main rival for Vanna's affections.

No Lips ran an office hidden by doors behind doors behind doors that were magnetic locked, cipher locked, watched through cameras, and concealed by shipping crates stacked up high in the corridor. Mutton had long mistaken the entrance for a broom closet. Each time he walked down that corridor at the rear of the consulate an unseen speaker emitted lonely, familiar country tunes by Dwight Yoakam, Merle Haggard, and other forgotten greats.

How Mutton longed to know what went on back there! Tucked away behind heavy, secretive doors, No Lips was sure to be guilty of every kind of violation, from common deceit to the purposeful corruption of agents through pornography and prostitution, controlled substances and cash. Mutton needed look no further than the Ten Commandments to create a list of top ten violations, and he wouldn't stop there. For one thing, Mutton felt certain Vanna had allowed No Lips to taste the same pleasures he'd enjoyed in her shoe closet.

But there was an even greater incentive than jealousy in putting the screws to No Lips. No Lips worked in the safest office on the compound, tucked away behind heavy, secretive doors. Mutton figured the best way to improve his chances of survival on the front line in the war on terror would be to spend as much time as he possibly could inside the office that wasn't there.

A few days after the Amco attack, Mutton invited

himself to attend the chief spook's daily intelligence briefing.

"Men," No Lips told Thorner, GLASSCOCK, and the other Pierce Pierce, "this is War. Don't let the acronym fool you. This is not a WOT. We are engaged in an epic battle with an enemy we can't always see. The raid on the Amco refinery, the trouble in Hajrayn last week, the hostages up in the capital, these are warnings to us all. We had no intel hinting at any of it." No Lips looked at Mutton through bulging, hooded eyes before delivering his sharpest rebuke. "And we still have no post-mortem from Interior. Which means that some of us simply aren't doing our jobs."

The tall, grim spook burped into his fist with indigestion. He eyeballed each of his men and let his eyes linger on Mutton. No Lips wasn't well. He had Fourth Branch breathing down his neck to get them intel that would justify the war on terror. His case officers weren't handling their agents and their agents weren't producing. No Lips hoped the security officer's presence would serve as a hint at violation and spur them to action. He dropped two lemon-lime Alka-Seltzer tablets into three fingers of Maker's Mark, quaffed it at a gulp, and crunched down the undissolved tablets. He wiped his non-lips on the back of his hand and continued the harangue.

"Just beyond those doors are more doors, and more doors, but once you get outside the chancery and beyond the main gate secured by the local military, and up the street a little, out of range of the .30 ml cannons, you are for all intents and purposes behind enemy lines. In this particular war there is no distinct line in the sand we can point to and say 'that is the front line.' And we are standing directly on top of that line that cannot be pointed to. Am I not clear?"

"Crystal," Mutton said, pretending to understand in

defiance of his confusion.

Pierce, Thorner, and GLASSCOCK were glad to have Mutton chime in. All three masked their confusion behind silence: the last thing they wanted was for the chief to prolong the briefing with explanations or more stories from his days fighting the Cold War.

"Good. Because I'm going to get to the request from Fourth Branch in just a minute."

"Fourth Branch?" Mutton asked.

"Need to know," No Lips said, staring Mutton down with an icy glare. He considered his men one-by-one. Thorner, all hatred and bitterness, hating Muslims because they weren't Jews, Jews because they weren't Christians, and Christians because they weren't Muslims. His religion was Misery, and he sought assignments that would make him as miserable as possible. When he didn't get assigned to Afghanistan, he complained that the system had fucked him again, until he learned that his assignment to Saudi Arabia was even worse than an assignment to Afghanistan.

"Hallelujah," he said, and cursed himself for his pious response. God had answered prayers that Thorner hadn't even said, which proved how useful God and prayers were in this miserable, crummy, stinking world.

Thorner may have hated the Kingdom as much as he hated everything, but GLASSCOCK, the violent, cold-blooded killer hated the Kingdom with a special passion. He'd wanted a job in Iraq with its unlimited opportunities suited to his specialization with explosives. "The problem is," he was fond of saying, as he curled and shook the hand he hadn't blown off accidentally as a child, "the Administration has no hand." His job as bomb-maker was to help build global support for the war on terror by increasing public disgust at the terrorists' tactics. He did this by training the terrorists to make bombs and blow up civilians. He channeled explosives into their unholy hands. He was a short, disfigured, unsightly little operative and he was excellent at his job. No Lips couldn't stand the look of him: he had no proof of authorization for GLASSCOCK's op, other than the killer's proficiency at it.

No Lips looked last to the other Pierce Pierce, the handsome, devilish Vice Consul who looked so much like the Pierce Pierce who worked the visa line by day. Both sought treatment with Dr. Meddler for Schizophrenia. To some, Pierce Pierce was a Vice Consul denying visas in window number five; to others Pierce Pierce was the man who wasn't there, providing cases of Johnnie Walker in return for gossip about the Royal Family.

The Kingdom's elite knew both Pierce Pierces and wanted to be friends with each of them. The Pierce Pierces had charmed their way to celebrity by attending weddings, birthdays, and falcon hunts in the desert. They were invited to everything and introduced to everyone and their presence could be overshadowed only by their absence. Impeccable Arabic, fluent Russian, and an intimate familiarity with the oil industry endeared them among Arabs and Russians alike. It helped that they could expedite visa requests.

"This isn't the Cold War, gentlemen," No Lips said, picking up his favorite refrain. "It's not Berlin in the eighties, where a goddamn wall stood for all the world to see the front line." Just above the place where the chief had no lip was a thin mustache that twitched and trembled. Perspiration beaded on his forehead and his migraine pounded his temples. The chief got down to the thrust of his monologue: BLONDIE, DOPEY, and the WOT.

"How much money have we poured into BLONDIE?" he asked. "And what has she done but tell us things we already knew, and expose our ignorance about a number of things we didn't know?"

"I wasn't aware there was anything we knew," Pierce said, meaning to speak up for his agent. He'd planted the golden-haired beauty to teach English at the Ministry of Interior where her wanton sensuality weakened the knees and loosened the lips of even the most loyal Royal Family insiders. He'd been inspired to install such a wench at the Ministry after just one short lesson with Maimouna, the girl with the jiggling twins and the pouty lips who gave Arabic lessons in a private room at the back of the consulate.

"One thing we know is that BLONDIE's a money-grubbing floozy. What I don't know is who else she works for."

"You think she's a double agent?"

"I think she's as dangerous as that tart in our language classroom."

"You think Maimouna works for Interior?"

"If you have to ask, you have a problem. Fix it."

"I can put DOPEY on her tail," Thorner said. "I've got him right where I want him. His consumption's on the rise. He needs us more than ever."

"Correction. He needs more than ever from us."

DOPEY was the son of an influential advisor to the Royal Family. Studying in the U.S. had turned the young man from the true path of Islam, and Thorner had been taking advantage of his drug addiction, gambling debt, and general moral depravity to dig around in the royal dirt. Thorner was using unvouchered funds and crops off the Afghan front in return for DOPEY's services, but the material he provided was becoming less and less reliable.

"What will Congress say when they learn we're pushing dope on America's kids and giving away the proceeds to a foreigner named DOPEY? He threatens to expose assets more valuable than himself. It's like those crazy fucks in Baghdad listening to CURVEBALL."

"I've got him on a leash like the animal he is."

"He's this close to destroying whole networks," No Lips said, shuddering at what would happen if he didn't take DOPEY out by his favorite means: poisoning. "He's going to undo all of our sacrifices in the war on terror. Which brings me to my third point, gentlemen. The war on terror. Fourth Branch has tasked us with locating the front line of the war on terror. You men have traded crate after crate of Johnnie Walker Black for this kind of information, and what have you got to show for it?"

"A lot of requests for more booze," said Thorner.

No Lips puckered his face and sucked in. "If we can't solve this riddle we'll all be out of a job. Our intel suggests that we won't find the front line of the war on terror. Pierce, why not?"

"Because it's behind us?" he guessed.

"Because we're behind it?" guessed Thorner.

"Because it doesn't exist?" suggested GLASSCOCK.

Mutton cleared his throat and stepped forward. "Chief. It's because it's a line in the sand and keeps shifting. Now, will you please just tell me what the hell is Fourth Branch?"

No Lips tasted Maker's Mark on his burp and felt inspired. "Very close, Mr. Mutton, but no cigar. It's because we're standing on *top* of it. The line is not a line at all. It's a grid. It's a web, latitude and longitude, cradling the globe."

Fourth Branch would be pleased, No Lips thought. They'd be so tickled pink by the intel that they'd cut off all communication with him for good, which was all he ever wanted in the first place. He felt an enormous relief about the information he'd revealed to himself until he swallowed his bourbon and Alka-Seltzer and realized: his conclusion placed him squarely on top of the front line of the war on terror. He trembled and his nerves fell apart. He comforted himself with the things he'd learned by heart. "We serve our nation here on the front line of the war on terror. You may not see the line. It's an invisible line not marked by concrete and stone and barbed wire and guns. It's not Berlin in the eighties. But the front line is there. The terrorists are there. Fourth Branch is there. Trust no one."

Mutton trembled. Thorner yawned. Pierce checked his watch. GLASSCOCK tightened his fist in frustration to be reminded that there was a war going on and that he played but a bit part in it.

They all pondered the premise that they stood on top of the front line of the war on terror. Months ago the U.S. Army had swept across the desert and rolled into the heart of Baghdad. American Forces had been hunkered down in the city fighting urban warfare ever since, with more insurgents springing up every day. For Pierce this meant the front line of the war on terror had been drawn in the sand a thousand miles to the north. The Defense Department, not themselves, were standing on top of it. But he didn't want to prolong the meeting by pointing this out, which would have inspired a long-winded explanation in which No Lips defended his own intelligence. Pierce had agents to run and a deal with Decker for a duck and cover drill during his language lesson. Pierce surmised that for him the location of the invisible line that could not be drawn actually lay beneath the table in the language classroom where he hoped to enjoy an intimate moment with Maimouna, the twin-chested language instructor.

But for Thorner, whose only date was with a bottle of Johnnie Walker, torturing the chief was a pleasure second only to the pleasure of torturing Tinker. "What about the *Abraham Lincoln?*" he asked.

"What about it?"

"It's in the Gulf somewhere; just off the peninsula. The president himself landed an F-16 on it and announced the end of major combat operations. 'Mission Accomplished'."

No Lips said, "He was referring to the end of the invasion of Iraq, not the end of the war."

"But with Iraq finished, isn't the line that cannot be drawn back in the mountains somewhere between Pakistan and Afghanistan?" said Thorner.

Only GLASSCOCK took comfort in the conversation. He'd derived another premise from No Lips' sense of military geography: if they were standing on a front line that couldn't be drawn, then so were every Tom, Dick and Harry in the U.S. of A. and all around the world. Civilians everywhere were involved in a very grave way in the war on terror. They might even be called enemy non-combatants. They therefore could be destroyed without being counted as collateral damage, which would keep GLASSCOCK from looking like a murderer when it came time to write his Employee Evaluation Report.

"Does the CG know this?" Thorner asked. "I mean, as the most senior State Department person here. Shouldn't she, at the very least, know the location of the front line of the war on terror?"

"I don't trust the CG," No Lips said. His indigestion, fluttery bowels, and the almighty hammer of migraines came on thick and fast at the thought of the lusty Vanna in boots. He gripped his forehead with one hand and rubbed his stomach with the other. "We need to focus on the front line. If we are standing on top of it, no way we should be open, let alone hosting parties. This is the intel required to shut it down once and for all. All we need are the facts to prove it." No Lips knew he'd need something real to cancel it right. He'd invented intel before, resulting in catastrophe. If he was going to invent facts to get out of an inconvenient situation, he was going to make sure they were true.

"Bombing," said GLASSCOCK. "Smithereens."

Yet another source of migraines and indigestion – GLASSCOCK! He was out of control, running about the wilderness handing out bombs to the enemy, training them to destroy cars, buildings, and unsuspecting humans asleep in their beds. The nut took target practice right there on the compound!

No Lips didn't trust GLASSCOCK's agents. He felt they must be at least partially responsible for the hostages bound and gagged at Amco. Training. Material. Always the unseen hand. Always. The chief had already asked GLASSCOCK for proof of authorization, hopeful of a single document, signature, or shred of evidence that some higher authority had approved his operation.

"Naval Observatory?" GLASSCOCK had said. His mission was authorized by the head of Fourth Branch, a secretive, creepy old man with a mechanical heart and a constant sneer. This posed a problem for No Lips: questioning the mission put him on the wrong side of the highest authority in the land; yet allowing it to continue put him on the wrong side of an even higher authority whose existence he preferred not to admit. No Lips might have lived with the civilian deaths if he could show that someone other than himself had signed off on them. He couldn't even trust the chief at the embassy. When he'd asked Trumpeter to flag headquarters about GLASSCOCK's work, Trumpeter shrugged.

"No can do, old buddy. If this leaks we'll be in the shit."

"If we don't get it in writing, we'll be in the shit."

"Tell you what. I'm headed Stateside next week. I'll personally brief the Director. I'll have him scribble his seal of approval on a cocktail napkin."

"Don't yank my chain, Trumpeter."

"Look, you want the operation or not? My opinion, it's a good one. Exactly what we're here to do. But believe you me, nobody back home wants this in the public eye. Operation GLASSCOCK has a spymaster somewhere at Fourth Branch."

"Let me have a copy of the order."

"Just keep sending your reports."

"The order-"

"They receive attention at the highest levels."

"Trumpeter, dammit. The order!"

"It's a slam dunk. And if that's not enough for you, if your nerves are too jangled for that, you can always back out."

If No Lips had had any lips, they would have peeled back against his teeth at Trumpeter's accusation of cowardice. But since he had no lips the chief dropped the issue and pretended at bravery.

Now he couldn't escape the woozy sensation that his ass was way out over the ledge, swinging in the breeze. He had orders from Vanna to gin up intel clearing Sheikh al Bafarti of having a hand in financing terror, to pump his friends at Interior for news related to Hajrayn, which would distract them from providing the information Fourth Branch was hounding him over: locating Weapons of Mass Destruction in the Northern Desert. Now he had an intel gap on Amco. And he had GLASSCOCK blowing things up throughout the Province, a mangy little Catholic with one hand and a sack full of explosives. Meanwhile Embassy station was receiving credit – and funding! – for predicting the attacks. Trumpeter was up to his eyeballs in praise for warning American Citizens that an attack was imminent. What a prediction!

No Lips had seen this before, during the Cold War. Counter intelligence. Someone had slipped a mole inside his shop. Vanna, Trumpeter, Mutton, *someone* was sabotaging him from within. No Lips took another swig of Alka-Seltzer and told his staff, "Gentlemen, intelligence is the weapon, and intelligence is the enemy. Fourth Branch wants us to capture a little of both. And Pierce, get your consular colleague in here. The one in charge of American Citizens Services and the one in charge of visas. Something's come up and I'll need their contacts at the morgue. And I have a report from the Watchlist people that I need to discuss with them."

No Lips couldn't help wondering, watching him there now, if Mutton didn't have the upper hand where Vanna was concerned. The chief knew a thing or two, things Vanna had hinted at as he himself took certain depraved pleasures with her footwear.

For his part, Mutton could only continue wondering about the existence of Fourth Branch. Maybe Clements or Pudge could help him out.

Chapter 18

Pudge's errand for No Lips required armed escort. Mutton loaded his Sig and rode shotgun to the medical examiner's office. The place reeked of death and chemicals. An orderly in a pale green coat, Red Crescent on the lapel, led them to the vault. There the victims of traffic accidents – Chevies and GMCs colliding with camels in the desert boonies – lay on aluminum tables.

Mutton held back. He'd done his share of morgue duty as a cop. No need to gawk.

The orderly opened a drawer. Pudge's gut dropped at the sight of the scarred, burnt-looking heads. He fought nausea looking at the melted rubber faces, the frostbit skin. They told a tale of violent abuse: a stove skull; cloudy eyes; gouges; bite marks.

"Dogs," the orderly said.

"Pardon?" asked Pudge, checking his nausea.

"The bites. They are from the teeth of dogs."

Pudge told the orderly, "Close it." He'd had his share of morgue duty lately, to verify the bloated remains of Buddy Cringle. The stench had taken up permanent residence inside his head. "They're ours," Pudge said, as instructed by No Lips. "Send the certificates over to the consulate."

He and Mutton raced straight to the wild comfort of Sunday happy hour at the Marine house. Pudge needed a drink before describing for No Lips the desiccated heads of three former intelligence officers killed in Iraq. He needed a drink even if it meant tolerating the company of Red Kippinger, the communications specialist who bumbled through life with only partial vision and hearing. Kippinger, who worked for Larry Porcas in IT, was drinking with Larry's wife, a pretty Filipina on the prowl for any chance to embarrass her troll of a husband.

Williamina tormented her husband in a variety of ways. She encouraged him to buy the Harley-Davidson he'd always wanted, then mocked his orange suspenders and leather vests. Williamina strapped on leather chaps and straddled the big machine behind Larry and let everybody know the motorcycle was the only useful thing between his legs. Williamina made a point of telling everyone the circumstances under which she and Larry had met.

"We meet in bar," she told Pudge. She leaned on the bar clutching a green bottle of Heineken with one hand and gripping Pudge's sleeve with the other. Larry sidled closer and pretended not to listen.

"A lot of fine couples meet in bars," Pudge said.

"No. I work in that bar."

"A lot of fine girls work in bars."

"No. You no unnerstan. I not serving drinks."

"A lot of fine girls don't serve drinks in bars."

She tipped her head back and opened her mouth to laugh, stroking Pudge's forearm. "You are funny. But you no unnerstan."

"No. I unnerstan."

"No. You too young to unnerstan."

"Oh, I unnerstan."

"No. I bar girl."

"I bar boy."

Williamina threw back her head and laughed.

"I meet many fine girls in bars," Pudge said, thinking of the Georgetown bars and the drunken college girls with the rich fathers and the expensive cars. He thought of Sarah. He thought deeply and heatedly of Sarah Stricker who had gotten him into this mess on the front line of the war on terror in the first place.

Williamina giggled. "Larry come in wearing sailor suit. He in Navy. I give him – "

Larry spun suddenly and cut her off with a nasal laugh. "I woke up with this tattoo and that 18 year old covering my body." He shook his head. "Mm-hm. Twenty years younger. You weren't lying about your age, were you sweetheart? Hee hee hee."

Williamina rolled her eyes and licked the rim of her bottle before pouring the beer down her throat. Larry giggled, stuck a cigarette between his lips, and called for more beer as Pudge downed his martini and slipped away to face the man with no lips.

Young, fair, blue-eyed handsome, Pudge came from a background of wealth and privilege and easy laughter. He walked with supreme dignity, his head high, his shoulders back. His empty hands swung easily by his sides. Born with a silver spoon and a witty tongue in his mouth, he joined the State Department after graduating Georgetown's School of Foreign Service, groomed from childhood as a Foreign Service brat for the diplomatic life. He looked forward to tours in London, Paris, Madrid, perhaps an excursion tour in Buenos Aires or Santiago when he felt adventurous, but the career he had planned for himself meant shaping policy in Rome, Berlin, and Geneva, just like his father and his father's father before that. His link to men like No Lips was sealed at birth.

Saudi Arabia was an adversity Pudge bore with a kingly philosophy: even the great John F. Kennedy, like his own grandfather, had soldiered through the Second World War. He was doing his time as all plebs did time, and he took comfort in the fact that, though loathsome and undignified and well beneath his station, he was serving his nation in a time of war. He was appalled at the personal qualities of his colleagues, and only in Clements did he find an equal. To ease his frustration Miss

Wellstone prescribed double martinis any time of the day, and the alcohol softened the hardship into which he'd been cast.

The numbing effects of booze made it easier for Pudge to tolerate fools like Martin Tinker, who he was surprised to find in the office with No Lips when he showed up to report on what he'd found at the morgue.

"What's going on?" Pudge asked.

"I was just telling the chief about my visit with Conklin," Tinker said.

"You visited Conklin? Who told you to visit Conklin?" As American Citizens Services Officer it was Pudge's responsibility to visit the American Economic Officer being held by the Kingdom as an enemy non-combatant and an extra-terrestrial detainee. "Why didn't you call me?"

Using his covert ops voice and looking nervously at No Lips Tinker said, "Uhhh, I can't tell you that."

"Can't tell me what?"

"Can't tell you why I had to have classified conversations with the prisoner."

"What classified conversations? The guards never leave his side! Last time I was out there the guards said they want to arrest you."

"What's stopping them?" No Lips asked.

"They don't want Tinker around."

No Lips said, "Martin was telling me they've got Conklin dressed in orange coveralls."

Tinker trembled at the memory of his visit with the emaciated prisoner, shivering in his jumpsuit. The guards had let Tinker into a tiny cell with a damp floor, a room that stunk of wet dog. Dim light filtered in from a tiny window high up on the wall. Conklin shivered in his chair on the far side of a plain grey table. The shrunken mouth behind the tangled beard had begged for information.

"They keep asking about Guantanamo," Conklin said, his voice hopeless and far away.

"I brought you a deck of cards," said Tinker.

"They think I'm some kind of spy."

"The guards confiscated it."

"What's going on at Guantanamo?"

Tinker considered the possibility that Conklin was a plant, part of a greater scheme by No Lips to test his mettle for covert assignments. "They did allow a toothbrush," he said, pushing it across the table.

"Tell me about Gitmo."

"Soft bristles. Dentists recommend soft bristles."

"Tell me about Fourth Branch."

"Fourth Branch?" Tinker was eager to get out of the cell. The nauseating odor and aching damp were bad enough. Now he was being asked questions about the most secretive entity in the U.S. Government. "Is there anything else I can bring you?"

"Newspapers."

"They're prohibited."

Conklin pulled down the corner of an eyelid. "It's not like I'm asking you to slip a knife inside a cake," he said.

"I can bring letters."

Again, the eye. "I want a cake."

"I can bring episodes of Archie Bunker. They won't allow Seinfeld. For obvious reasons."

Conklin's face went from forlorn detachment to sudden rage. "What's going on at Guantanamo?!" He strained against his shackles, trying to leap across the table at Tinker. "What is Fourth Branch!?"

Tinker nearly fell out of his chair. He found his balance and retreated to the door where he shouted for help. "I can't tell you!" Tinker stood with his back to the door, as far from the prisoner as he could get. "For your own good. They'd prohibit future visits."

"If you can just – "

"I can tell you nothing – It's classified – It's something I saw on CNN – I've got to go – " Tinker slipped out, more afraid of the fury in Conklin's eyes than of the stink and metallic echoes that clanged against the walls of the stifling prison.

"If Conklin's lucky, the Kingdom will follow their own due process. Eventually they'll deport him," Pudge said.

"And if he's not lucky?" asked No Lips.

Pudge shook his head slowly. "He'll be released and sent here to work for Vanna."

"Do they still have him shackled to the floor in painful positions? No contact with the outside world? No newspapers?"

"Nothing but censored letters. He hasn't slept in weeks. They pipe in the call to prayer every half an hour at high decibel."

"Food? Drink?"

"They're pouring water down his throat and asking him all kinds of questions he can't answer."

"Like what?"

"Like why would a Zionist pig want to infiltrate the Kingdom? They asked him if he thought the detention of the Muslims at Guantanamo Bay was making him safer."

"How did he answer?"

"He asked them what was going on at Gitmo."

"What else?"

"Did he think the invasion of Afghanistan made him safer? The invasion of Iraq?"

"What's he saying to it all?"

"He has no answers."

"Maybe he *does* work for the Administration. How are his spirits?"

"He hasn't had a drink in months. But I try to make him feel better. I tell him about what we face here at the consulate. I think he prefers detention to working for Vanna. Speaking of ..." Tinker stood. "That'll be all for me. I have that cable to send."

"Remember," No Lips said. "Addressee is strictly Fourth Branch. And mask that fresh intel as Super Duper Double Top Secret. SDDTS. They'll have their intel to support the war on terror but you need to source it with a few lines from *Newsweek*."

"Yes, chief."

"And don't tell Mutton. That hinky sonofabitch will share it with Vanna and shove it down my throat as a reason to close us down. Piss Vanna off and sayonara to her closet full of good times. Clear?"

"Clear," Tinker said, though he had no idea about any closet full of good times.

When Tinker had gone No Lips turned to Pudge. "Tell me what you found at the morgue."

"Three heads. Just like you said. M.E.'s sending over the certificates."

No Lips took a drink. "You deserve to know. The heads. They belonged to bodies. Once. They crossed the desert as treasure, born by caravan. *Mujahideen*, drumming up support for the insurgency in Iraq. Need a drink?"

Pudge nodded.

"Last week's raid in Hajrayn was a big success," said No Lips. "The Kingdom's forces neutralized six of their 50 Most Wanted. Unfortunately for you, they also turned up this mess."

"How do we know they're Americans?"

No Lips reminded Pudge of his SDDTS non-disclosure agreement and let silence hang while he conveyed a threatening look. "Last month three contractors went missing in Iraq."

"That's no secret."

"Three headless corpses turned up in the Euphrates."

"Still no secret. FOX and CNN both covered it."

"It comes down to rudimentary math," No Lips said. "Three headless corpses, three heads on ice."

"That's your intel?"

"Let's just say that infidel heads on ice are much more effective at recruiting villagers to the cause than *jihadist* websites in a landscape devoid of Internet. It's the 7th Century out there in the boonies." No Lips savored his drink. "You know, they owe their success to us. If it weren't for the abuse at Gitmo, they couldn't raise half the army they've got.

"As far as anyone's concerned, these were ordinary Americans doing an ordinary job. Unfortunately for them, they were doing it in Iraq." No Lips pulled back the curtain behind his desk. "Take your pick."

Pudge selected Johnnie Walker from amid the crates. "What happens next?"

"These three receive the highest honor."

"But they're dead."

"Of course they are. You don't get a black star on the wall without the requisite death."

"And their families?"

"They'll never know that these men provided valuable information. Compromised Saddam's top generals. Veep himself will bestow the honors. This was a Fourth Branch op."

Chapter 19

Mutton drove alone to the Ministry of Interior. He didn't trust the drivers. He trusted Hassan, but Hassan was Yemeni, and Yemenis fell outside the binational intelligence-sharing agreement. The fully armored, blacked out Suburban rode heavy and sluggish under the bleached sky.

Jersey barriers, sandbags, humvees and troops surrounded the sprawling white marble palace that housed the Ministry. Mutton twitched his stub of pencil between thumb and forefinger as he approached the drop arm. The guards weren't rough about it but they took everything: Sig, holster, knife, even his stub of pencil. Mutton didn't fuss. He did the same to Ghani each time he visited the consulate.

"I was surprised to get your call," Mutton said as they walked the cool, echoing halls.

"My friend. You have no faith."

Ghani held open his office door and waved Mutton to a chair. He sat behind a big, empty desk. At his back, a glaring window opened onto the sea. The light at his back cast Ghani's face in darkness, forcing Mutton to squint. A trick of the trade – gives one man mastery over the other. The no-frills office felt like a sergeant's office back home. State-sponsored functionality, nothing more. Soldiers weren't meant for desks. They were meant to be out leading men, or killing them. Ghani offered tea. Mutton asked for water.

"The prisoners aren't talking."

"Why not?"

"They die before we get anything. Certainly before we can verify what they tell us."

"Must be your technique," Mutton said.

Mutton saw past the glare to the twinkle in Ghani's eyes, the turned up corners of his mouth, that damned fine dimple on his chin so deep Mutton saw it even through the thick foliage of his stubble. Face buried in shadow, still Ghani charmed. "Our techniques? My friend, where do you think we learned our techniques?"

Mutton shook his head.

"Oh, yes. I assure you we are very much on board with the American model. Your colleague, Mr. Grant – "

"Please." Mutton stopped him before Ghani could say anything more about No Lips. "I don't want to know what name the man goes by." No Lips carried a name in every pocket and three backstories in his shoes. "But fine. Let's just say your men have had some training."

"Hardly just my men. The entire Ministry."

"Point is, if you want to call it an American model, you have to understand. For us, it's applied only to foreigners. In covert settings. We don't interrogate our own citizens, and certainly never at home. Our citizens have rights."

This interested Ghani. Ghani liked working with the Americans, but he found them difficult to read. He found that even the ones he liked – Mutton, Grant, the beautiful Vanna Lavinia with her fancy shoes and gifted ankles – were hard to trust. Even harder to understand. The rules were strict, but the exceptions stricter. He didn't understand how anything got done.

"Is an interesting point, Mr. Mutton. But you know that in Saudi Arabia we follow the Prophet, Peace Be Upon Him. His unchanging laws apply equally to all."

"Not here to argue law or theology, Ghani, but you have a whole road out there dedicated to non-Muslims. I tell you from experience it is a shitty piece of beat-up asphalt for the non-Muslims. You cannot have infidels in your two Holy cities, and so you've got a road to go around. So much for equality in Islam."

"I speak of equality for Muslims. The rest are infidels." He turned up the corners of his mouth, unapologetic on the point, and Mutton could not feel offended.

"Ghani, to your Hajrayn prisoners."

More of the American model, direct and to the point. Ghani took comfort in being able to read Mutton so easily. But only so much comfort. He could not trust Mutton, not fully. Mutton had proven his lack of faith: Ghani knew why he'd been given the tour of consulate security features. A test. And in testing Ghani, Mutton had revealed his lack of faith.

Even so, as a man of faith Ghani had no interest in seeing the terrorists win. He had no interest in seeing the Kingdom's guests come to harm. His debt to Allah, Peace be upon him, required that he protect even the Infidels. It required he tell Mutton what he had learned.

"There is one thing we have extracted that you may find useful," Ghani said, drawing Mutton to the edge of his chair with his smooth, low voice. "The first point, it is obvious. All of the prisoners were employed at some point on the construction sites in Hajrayn."

Mutton's neck tingled. "They lived there," he said. "It's an easy coincidence."

"True. But, some had also worked for the Kingdom Exploding Group on other sites. Outside the city."

The tingling increased.

"Handling explosives."

Mutton said, "This is all background. Circumstantial. What about the interrogations? Anything more concrete?"

Ghani sat forward, his face coming out of the shadow. With the glare no longer blinding him Mutton saw the man for who he was: a straight shooter, another dick, a cop, busting the bad guys. "You and I know these guys are just dumb animals. Bottom feeders. No connection to the top."

"No magic Mercedes?" Mutton said, helping him along. "No loose-lipped landlords or nosy neighbors?"

"No. None would know anything of substance. But – One of the suspects was picked up in error."

"Error?"

"I mean, he wasn't in any of the safe houses. He wasn't supposed to be there at all. He just got caught up. In the sweep."

"And?"

"By Allah's grace, we got to him before his patrons did."

Mutton sat back. He could only grin. He hadn't grinned like that in a long time. He hated the brown, hawk-nosed Arab fuckers but at the moment he could lean across and rub his cheek against the sandpaper scruff of Ghani's.

"We have a saying back home," Mutton said. "You'll like this. You get the first link and establish the chain. Link by link you build the chain. Then you yank the chain until the guy at the top falls right in your lap."

Ghani smiled too. Colorful American cop. "I like that very much, Mr. Mutton. And I have a name for you. You can use it however you will."

"Is it raw intel, or analysis?"

"This intel is so raw it could only have been spoiled by the analysts. The man who drops in our lap is none other than the great patron of this city, a Yemeni by tribe, the builder of our roads and hospitals. He is currently rebuilding Hajrayn. It is the sheikh." Ghani disappeared back into his shadow. He would say no more, but it was enough."

"Were you in the room?"

"I will save us both your inevitable questions. My counterparts, myself and the others who witnessed the interrogation, do not consider this actionable intelligence. And the prisoner will be held in isolation indefinitely. So as to protect the Sheikh. The intel belongs only to you."

Mutton stood, his head swimming in clarity and gratitude. Ghani emerged once more from his hiding place. Seeing him in renewed light Mutton felt moved to a confession of his own.

"You knew," he said. "The tour at the consulate. You knew it was a test. You knew I was challenging you, revealing the traps. My friend, I am deeply sorry." He put his hand on Ghani's shoulder and lowered his head in real and ritual shame.

Ghani took Mutton's hand. "Now we have both passed. *Alf mabrook*, Jeff Mutton. A thousand congratulations."

"*Alf mabrook.*"

"Now do what you can with the intel."

Mutton tapped the wheel with nervous energy. He wouldn't be able to use Ghani's intel in the traditional way. He couldn't run it up the flagpole, call it highly credible material from a vetted source with first-hand access. No letting the analysts in DC stare at it through their crystal balls, studying it, holding it up to the light, discussing it a thousand ways before telling him what he could do with it. No, unless he could find a creative way to deal with it the info would remain little more than a conversation between two lawmen fighting asymmetrical warfare against an invisible enemy.

He would get zero backing from Vanna. Forget about her accepting it without punching holes in every inch of the meal ticket.

Sending it back – to who? It would only get back to Vanna, who held that shameful episode over his head.

His passion for her shoes! It had driven him too far. In the wrong place, at the wrong time. It was the only such instance! The great moral failure buzzed his ears because he'd forgiven the man who'd done it to him first so many years ago. He'd turned the other cheek! And was it a big red kiss from rose-petal lips that greeted his final cheek? No! It was a cosmic raspberry. Forgiving those who'd trespassed against him had gotten him nothing.

Angelic Jeffrey Mutton, third-grader in red cassock and white surplice, measuring out Church wine in the sacristy at St. Barts. A dark winter's morning. The dreaded weekday Mass.

"Mass is cancelled, my son," Father Towler said. "The organist is ill."

"The organist? But-"

" – Relax. You can stay here until the school opens." He meant the adjacent parochial school Mutton attended.

"What about the Sisters?"

"I will bring the body of Christ to them after school."

Young Jeffrey thought of the day ahead. He dreaded the thought of facing Sister Henry without her having taken the Host. She was cruel as it was, even with the Jesus coursing through her veins. How would she be without it?

"Can we go to them now?"

"You fear the Sisters. But you need not." Father Towler knew well from confession how Mutton felt about the nuns. "I will protect you. Come to the Rectory and I'll teach you a game. It will make you strong." Father Towler took Mutton's coat off the peg and gave it to him, removing any choice but to follow the priest. "It is a game we can play any time you like. Any time you wish to avoid the horrors of your math tables and your cursive writing exercises."

Towler never touched him, not really. He was sincere about the promise of sanctuary. But Mutton still felt soiled and sinful after dressing up in ladies shoes – heels, strappies, peek-toes, boots. Mutton loved the boots, it was true, and Father Towler had many: red cowgirl boots; black pirate boots. Sometimes the priest lay between Mutton's legs, gripping his ankles and writhing on the floor. The old man would lick the heels of the boots he made Mutton wear, crawling toward him on hands and knees like a starved dog. He'd rub Mutton's ankles before disappearing into the bathroom only to re-emerge and do it all over again. Mutton thought the game crazy but it beat facing Sister Henry. So he played.

Mutton asked Father Towler how the game would make him stronger.

"The Lord works in mysterious ways," Towler said, applying cherry red polish to Mutton's toenails before putting him in sparkling silver peek-toes.

Mutton continued to visit the rectory throughout the remainder of third grade, often two and three times a week, patient and hopeful for the day his promised power would rise up in him, flowing forth from its divine source above. But before the school year ended Father Towler was removed from office, silently transferred away from the Parish, and Mutton faced the horrors of the remaining weeks with little help from the Holy Spirit beyond happy memories of the crusty shag rug on which the priest had lain, writhing in holy ecstasy while the young Mutton stomped him with the heels of an assortment of fine ladies footwear.

~ ~ ~

The day his career began to crumble, the day Vanna would hold over his head like the sword of Damocles, Mutton had arrived at the consulate in the breezy hour before the evening call to prayer. He liked the consulate that time of day: the crows livened it up with their flapping and wheeling; the wind cleansed the air, and the construction sites in Hajrayn lay dormant, no explosions rumbling the earth. The '84 Coup de Ville, a grey, wide-bodied, fully armored vehicle with blackened windows, idled in front of Vanna's residence. Mutton waved to the Yemeni driver having a smoke and leaning against the Caddy. The driver wished Peace upon Mutton, who returned the greeting.

Mutton rang the bell and waited. He was reaching to ring a second time just as Vanna opened the door. "Look at youuu ..." she cooed. "Don't you look nice." Her head bobbed up and down on Mutton, appraising him openly. Did he smell wine on her? Yes.

"That's a nice ... dress ...." Mutton said, wary.

She wore a tight black dress, much too short for strict Muslim company. And it was tight, revealing her trim, athletic figure. A gold Crusader Cross dangled from the chain around her throat and settled above her bosom. "The color flatters you," Mutton said, knowing he couldn't go too far. "I like the cross."

She covered it with her fingertips in false modesty. "You noticed, my dear."

"The gold brings out the right shade of your ..."

"Why thank youuuu," she said, again covering the cross and cooing. "I have so many of these from my time in Tel Aviv." She beckoned him in, turning on bare feet and sashaying into the house. "But come in, come in."

Mutton stepped into the bright foyer. The house was dark: darkness behind the kitchen straight ahead; darkness to the right from the wing reserved for public entertaining; a television flickering in the darkness of the sitting room to the left. Mutton felt an emptiness to the house. Vanna turned and walked toward the home's living space.

"I need to freshen up," she said.

Mutton followed Vanna, stopping in the sitting room

where the television played black and white footage of battalions invading Normandy. "Back here," Vanna called. Was something caught in her throat? There was a pitch to her voice Mutton hadn't heard before.

Mutton approached the bedroom and stood on the threshold.

"Here I am," Vanna said. She stood before a mirror, head tilted, toes wiggling in the plush carpet. "These earrings."

As DSO Mutton had escorted the maintenance crew to inspect Vanna's closets and to test the safe haven door. He was familiar with the bedroom as government property. Now he felt like an intruder, watching Vanna inspect herself in the full-length mirror, until she caught his eye. She tugged the gold chain that held the Crusader Cross.

"– earrings?" She smiled. "Jeff?"

"Yes?"

"The earrings?"

He cleared his throat, aware of a surge in his groin. "The gold flatters you," he said, the first thing that came to mind.

Her smile reflected in the mirror over her bare shoulder. She turned on him and reached for the bulge she knew was there. She had her mouth over his before he could speak and then her tongue was sliding around with his, a command performance, her tongue demanding his to dance. He ran his fingers through her hair and she pulled him back inside the closet, all the way to the wall where she knelt and drew him to the carpet, the straps already off her shoulders. He heard a click, ignored it, caught up in her heat.

Then he smelled it, a familiar odor. He thought of his ex. Then, from further back, the distant past, a silhouette in black. He couldn't make it out but the vision maddened him, filled him with ecstasy, a holy surge of carnal joy. All around him, shoes. There were so many, rows and rows of them on shelves the GSO had built. Mutton tasted wine on Vanna's breath but all he smelled was the musky odor of her shoes.

"Step on me!" he cried, remembering Father Towler and pulling away from her.

"What?"

"Put on those boots! Step on my throat!" He demanded abuse.

"But – "

"Do it!" He was desperate for her, and he wanted her to crush him. He wanted to look up her dress from below, trapped there red-faced and breathless, straining against the high arch of her pointed boot, a full glimpse up her long, muscular calves and thighs and into the place where the white linen would be, and beyond. He wanted it close enough to see but not reach. She should destroy him.

"No Lips," she said, destroying him more than he wanted.

"What?"

"That's what No Lips likes. That's his brand of torture." She had her lips to his, her teeth grinding his. Then she looked away and cried, "My God!"

Mutton couldn't open the door. He barely tried, knowing how the mags worked. Defeated, he hit the alarm, a feed alerting Post One.

"Mr. Mutton, you tell one little person what happened in here and all will know that you begged me to piss on you. Pervert. Next time, fuck me like a real man."

When Decker and Hunker let them out the two Marines didn't seem all that surprised. And Mutton never got a next time.

Mutton tapped the wheel and hit on a way he might use Ghani's intel. He'd drop it on Tinker, right in his lap. Tinker could use some raw intel for his reporting, even if he wound up masking it with glossy news articles from 1982.

Chapter 20

Eager as Tinker was to write up Mutton's intel on Sheikh al Bafarti, he couldn't get to it until he finished his report for Fourth Branch. Tinker feared Fourth Branch because he had no idea what it was. All he knew was they wanted intel supporting the war on terror, and Tinker wanted to get it for them. But he also knew that such a report could only be written in coordination with operatives from the office that wasn't there, and since they were never to be found in their big, empty offices next to his cramped quarters in the front office suite, Tinker's consultations produced imaginative results.

In order to provide intelligence that conveyed a reality justifying desired policy positions, Tinker reviewed hundreds of Administration memos, presidential speeches, and commentary on FOX Sunday morning talk shows. From this repository of chatter Tinker deduced that the Administration had been vindicated on the question of Iraq, would soon be free to draw down from Afghanistan, and had every right to use taxpayer money to fight a war on terror. He learned that terror was the result of tyranny and a lack of economic opportunity around the world. He pasted such snippets into a cable template. He reworked the sentences until they sounded bland and bureaucratic. And when he re-read the summary paragraph Tinker learned that Saudi Royalty approved of taking out Sadam Hussein, predicted quick success against the Taliban, and supported a war on terror as a means of ending tyranny and lack of opportunity for people across the Middle East.

Impressed by his text Tinker next consulted a stack of magazines, added color by describing photographs, plagiarizing captions, and copying whole paragraphs in reverse order.

Tinker's plagiarized cable, written in consultation with people who weren't there, fluffed up with colorful facts from 1982, and uncleared by Vanna, was routed to the political office at the Embassy in Riyadh, where a handful of officers read it with envy. How had a JO at a satellite post crafted intel so clearly reflecting the beliefs of their masters in Washington? Seeking recognition as co-authors they changed "this" to "that", "those" to "these", "them" to "their", "will" to "won't", "can" to "should", "have" to "have not", and so many other points that the new copy threatened to alter policy direction. The revised document was handed to the Ambassador's Special Staffer, the goateed young Robert Furgle, who brought it to Ambassador Glyder bearing the red-bordered cover sheet marking it Top Secret. Furgle read it aloud to the Ambassador when Glyder's attention could be diverted from the oil market ticker.

"The president will never go for that," Ambassador Glyder said. "Fourth Branch wants intel that vindicates us in Iraq, minimizes our concerns in Afghanistan, and gets Congress to fund our allies in the war on terror."

"How do we do that, sir?" asked Furgle. "What is Fourth Branch?"

"We must marginalize the extremists in the Kingdom. How was this cable ever cleared at the consulate?"

"It wasn't, sir," Furgle said, still wondering what the Ambassador meant by Fourth Branch. "Not by the CG."

"What's her name again?"

"Vanna Lavinia, sir."

"That Miss America-looking woman?"

"She's a former Miss Texas, sir."

"That language wasn't cleared?"

"No, sir."

"Where'd it come from?"

"A JO down there. With a few improvements from our political shop here at the embassy."

"Let me see the original."

After Furgle read Tinker's original, the Ambassador requested a copy of the President's speech at the Naval Academy. Furgle returned with the speech, distracted the Ambassador once again from the ticker, and read the speech aloud.

"CG didn't clear on the original cable?"

"No, sir."

"Dad-gummit, that wasn't cleared!? What on God's Green Earth is the president doing reading uncleared text!?"

"But he's the president, sir."

"Exactly. He's only the president. Whatever must Fourth Branch think of this?"

"What's Fourth Branch?"

"Get down to the consulate right away and investigate the situation."

"Yes, sir."

"It appears that policy is being formed in D.C. based on uncleared reports from the field."

"I'll look into it, sir."

"I mean the most significant policy decisions: the invasion of Iraq; the war in Afghanistan; maybe the entire war on terror!"

"I'll track it down, sir."

"Fourth Branch is responsible for policy direction!"

"Yes, sir. You can count on me. But sir, what is Fourth Branch?"

"And ask them about security down there. How safe are they, anyway? I haven't received any security reports from them in weeks."

"Yes, sir."

"Before you go, would you put the ticker back on? You

know how it relaxes me."

Set at ease by the numbers rolling across the bottom of his screen Ambassador Glyder gained perspective on the problem. Policy appeared to be getting its direction from the field rather than Washington. And yet the decisions mirrored the Administration's views. It could mean only one thing: Fourth Branch had dispatched a mole to generate the intel required for the war on terror. The Ambassador watched the numbers on oil futures rallying past. He and his patrons were realizing triple figure increases! The WOT was proving profitable, and all was well with the world.

Meanwhile Furgle sent a blistering message warning the consulate to cease all reporting. He ordered the Ambassador's residence be made ready, and scheduled the Ambassador's car for a 5 pm pickup. Vanna forwarded the message to Pervis who forwarded it to Storp who forwarded it to Tinker, who'd already seen it. "Make sure Mutton's aware of this. And clear my shoes and magazines from the Ambo's Caddy," Vanna ordered, then waved the JO off.

Tinker went home for a shave and to upgrade his suit so he would look intelligent and useful when he greeted the Ambassador. He waited inside the terminal, an overused place with yellow fluorescent lights and dingy tile floors. The airport was crowded at all hours with Muslims from East and South Asia, Mesopotamia and the Levant, Central and Eastern Europe, and dark Africans from the Sahel and North of the Sahara, many of them dressed in white Hajj towels, except the women who were shrouded from head to toe in black.

When he saw Furgle's bulbous forehead and his bushy goatee approaching through the crowd, Tinker stood on his toes hoping to spot the taller figure of Ambassador Glyder, most likely in a square-shouldered powder-blue suit and a tall, cream-colored Stetson. Furgle emerged from the crowd and Tinker saw that in addition to his wheeled luggage, Furgle carried a black attaché case manacled to his wrist. The JOs circled each other like sniffing dogs.

"Where's the Ambassador?" Tinker asked.

"In Riyadh. Where else?" Furgle checked his watch. "To be precise, he's at the residence watching the ticker with a drink before dinner."

"The Ambassador's residence here was made ready."

"Suits me fine."

The Caddy pulled out of the airport and into busy evening traffic rushing ahead of the sunset call to prayer. Tinker asked, "How long are you staying?"

"However long it takes."

"However long what takes?"

"Clearing up this mess."

"What mess?"

Furgle put on a conspiratorial face and leaned toward Tinker. He patted the attaché case on his lap. "Let's just say it's got a red-bordered cover sheet and a Top Secret designation." Furgle nodded once and settled back into the leather seat, looking at Tinker sideways. "This stuff trickles down all the way from the top."

"The White House?" Tinker asked. Furgle answered by bringing his pointer finger to his lips and nodding subtly at the driver.

"Fourth Branch," he whispered, adding to Tinker's confusion. "I'll need to see the CG first thing tomorrow."

"She has a standing appointment until noon."

"After lunch, then."

"Two o'clock?"

"Fine. I'll also need meetings with Mutton, the Chief, Cons, Admin, the Communicators, and DB."

"DB's at the Embassy."

"Then I'll meet with the Acting."

"That's me."

"Oh. Right."

"So?"

"I'll meet with the CG first. This stuff trickles down."

Furgle's attaché case was still cuffed to his wrist the next day as he sat before Vanna in her luxurious office. Vanna sat in her straight-backed chair, her legs crossed, with Furgle before her on the low, uncomfortable couch. Tinker sat off to the side with a steno pad on his lap.

"Ma'am, I think you know why I'm here."

Vanna stared blankly at the goateed staff assistant. "Why don't you explain it to me, Mr. Furgle?"

"Very well, ma'am. The Ambassador is concerned that the President has been delivering speeches that include uncleared text."

"Uncleared? As in, confused?"

"No, ma'am. As in, not cleared for broader dissemination."

"That *is* a concern."

"Yes. And, well, these uncleared texts originated here. In the Kingdom."

Vanna held a finger to her lips, pumping one calf, knees showing at the hem of her skirt. Furgle cleared his throat and squirmed. Vanna leaned forward and reached for the crystal bowl on the coffee table.

"Would you like a sucker, Mr. Furgle?" She held the bowl toward him with both hands, her burgundy nails long and curved around the decorative crystal. Furgle reached for a candy. Vanna took one, unwrapped it, and held it between her lips.

"I can also offer you chocolates, my dear Furgle. Our contacts send us very good chocolates. Made right here in this city. I shall have to send some back with you for the

Ambassador. When are you leaving?"

"Ma'am. About the remarks. The cables."

"It is a worry, isn't it? We can't have the president going off and reading language that isn't cleared. The implications for national security are enormous."

"Yes, ma'am."

"You're talking about intelligence failures; protocol failures; policy based on falsehoods; a disrupted chain of command and communication." Vanna paused. Furgle waited for her to continue, grateful that she understood the problem without his having to suggest her role in it. Such a suggestion would have a negative effect on his career. "How can I help?"

"Well ..." Furgle searched for a way to proceed. "The *Ambassador* is concerned that the cables may have originated in this Province."

"Here? But there are only Martin and myself. And the men who aren't here. DB, also not here. Conklin, our Econ man, never made it past immigration at the airport. As you can see, we're extremely understaffed here. Believe me, we are quite vacant."

"The Ambassador is aware of that, ma'am."

"Is he? Mr. Furgle, I'm sure that I personally haven't sent any uncleared cables to Washington. And Tinker isn't authorized to do so." She held up her hands, palms out, again with the look of innocence. "So where does that leave us?"

Furgle coughed. "Ma'am? I'm sorry. I don't follow."

"Well, clearly. Let me put it this way. The problem, you say, is that the president has used uncleared text that may have originated here."

"Correct."

"And I've accounted for my political staff."

"That's right."

"And you're aware that we're short staffed."

"Yes."

"Then you have two options. There are the men who aren't here, and there is the staff that we are missing. I would suggest you focus your investigation on those two sources."

Furgle fumbled with the handcuffs linking him to his attaché case. The CG's point confused him. But since confusion was bad for his career, Furgle played along. "I guess it would, 'clear' you," he said, making quotations with his fingers. The handcuffs tumbled clumsily down his wrist with an awkward rattle.

"I thought so, Mr. Furgle." Vanna loosened up. "Robert, right? So, tell me, Robert, how long will you be with us?"

"I'm not sure. Until I finish the investigation."

"Of course. Take your time. You shall have our fullest cooperation. I only hope you'll be here through the weekend. We'll be having a party, as long as the present threatcon doesn't change, or our dearly skittish security man doesn't pull the rug from under us. And I do hope to see you around. Understaffed as we are, I am swamped with paperwork." She looked over her shoulder at her desk. Furgle's eyes followed her gaze and landed on the stacks of cables there. "I'm sure you're anxious to get started, Mr. Furgle. You have a lot to investigate with the men who aren't here."

Chapter 21

Clements and Pudge followed the other Pierce Pierce along the back corridor to the office that wasn't there behind doors behind doors behind doors. Pierce reached between the stacked crates marked "DIPLOMATIC" and pressed a buzzer that made no sound. He told them to stand in full view of a camera staring down from a nest of wires high up in the ceiling. They waited, like Dorothy, the cowardly lion, and the tin man outside Oz, for a clicking that released the lock on a door that Clements saw only after Pierce had pushed him through it.

Beyond the door Clements breathed the fresh, cool air from giant Trane air conditioners blowing hard over brand new leather furniture. No Lips led them silently past looking glass wonders and first world amenities to a private office where he motioned them to sit and took up his own seat behind a large, empty desk. A thick black curtain hung behind him.

"Sign these," No Lips said, pushing several pages across his desk.

"What are they?" asked Pudge.

"Declarations."

"Of what?" asked Clements.

"Loyalty."

"And this one?"

"Discretion."

"And this one?"

"That's an SDDTS Clearance Waiver Non-Disclosure Form."

"What are they for?"

"Reminders. Of the sensitivity of this briefing."

"Why not just remind us?"

"I like the psychological bind of a signature."

After they signed, No Lips held each form up to the light and scrutinized them, squinting his eyes. The black curtain stirred behind him. Clements shivered in the chilly air. "Problem?" asked No Lips.

Clements shook his head.

"HQ says you have Need to Know clearance."

"Need to Know what?"

"About the Royal visit, Stateside."

"We already know about it."

"Do you know that some of the travelers are on the other side?"

"Other side of what?"

"Some in the Family support our cause. Some are working against it."

"Can we get a list?" Clements asked. "Might help us keep the wrong ones out."

"Can't give you that."

"But you have one?"

No Lips blinked once. "We have lists of every bureaucrat, functionary, lackey, footman, butcher, baker, candle-stick maker, cook, cleaner, barber, expediter, and Royal S.O.B. in the Kingdom."

Clements' ears rang. "Did you say cook, cleaner, and barber?"

"If that's what you heard."

"Butcher, baker, candle-stick maker?"

"It does sound a little like Mother Goose, yes."

"And you know which are working which side? Can we see the list?"

No Lips shook his head.

"Can I match your list against our reports?"

No Lips shook his head.

Clements furrowed his bulging brow. "I may have issued to three terrorists matching your description."

"I haven't described anything."

"The cook, the cleaner, and the barber. The butcher, the baker, the candle-stick maker."

"Figures of speech. Fairy Tales. Fantasies from Grimm."

"They might be entering the States as we speak."

"Not if Homeland Security is doing its job."

"So you're sharing intel with DHS?"

No Lips paused, shook his head. "Go ahead," he said. "Ask me the names."

Clements made up names that hadn't been listed in the ACHOO cable. No Lips stared ahead. But when Clements spoke the names of the cook, the cleaner, and the barber whose bearded visages and blazing eyes continued to haunt him day and night, No Lips' eyelids came down like big heavy vaults.

Clements froze. He grew dizzy. He plainly saw the pale faces masked by wild beards and lit by dark, piercing eyes; the short thobes and worn sandals; the righteousness, determination, and divinity of purpose. He'd sent the revocation letters to the Royal Palace but had received no response. Through the fog of a growing dizziness Clements heard No Lips.

"Can't confirm any of that."

"Where are you getting this from? Why have these names been added to ACHOO?"

"Detainees from Hajrayn are starting to talk. Interior has taken our suggestions to heart. There is no information that a little shortness of breath can't reveal."

No Lips voice reached Clements like an echo on an empty canyon vault. "Well, if we're all through now," No Lips said, pressing his hands on the empty desk and pushing himself out of his chair. "You fellows signed the SDDTS Clearance Waiver Non-Disclosure Forms? I do appreciate it. I'll just escort you out. Oh, where are my manners?"

No Lips turned and reached into the black curtain. He held a bottle of Johnnie Walker toward them. Only Pudge had the strength to reach for it.

Clements followed with heavy feet. His legs felt watery and his bowels loose. He went numb below the waist, then tingling and hot as the blood rushed through him. He felt the deep terror of an irrevocable mistake, like discovering he'd left his passport on the train just as the train was leaving the station. Surely the butcher, the baker, the candlestick maker had traveled. The enemy had taken up residence in the Homeland.

No Lips opened the door onto the musty corridor with the towering stacks of crates marked DIPLOMATIC.

~ ~ ~

Back at their office Pudge tried to soothe his friend. "Is it really a problem?" he asked. "DHS will stop them at the border."

"You saw the way he handled it. No way he's sharing intel. No way he lets another agency chalk credit for stopping them."

When they reached their office Pudge poured Clements a drink. "We don't even know they're guilty."

"Just names on a list?"

"Innocent until proven guilty."

Chapter 22

Mutton had men on every street, cameras on every wall, and guards at every gate. He had magnetic locks and cipher locks and razor wire and Delta barricades but none of it was enough. He wanted land mines, trenches, a fast-closing gate and a squad of guards with shoot to kill orders.

"Do we really need all this?" Storp asked, pulling the procurement request from the bottom of his stack.

"We need this stuff *now*," Mutton said. "I tell you we are going to be attacked."

Storp rubbed his plump, pasty face, exhausted at playing the middleman between Mutton and Vanna. Choosing sides was a losing proposition: back Mutton and live, but get an onward assignment to Njamena; choose Vanna and be promoted to Management Counselor, but good luck working for Vanna the rest of his life. No, Storp's only hope was to find a way that pleased Vanna and Mutton both. His plan was to divert some of Mutton's security funds to Vanna's pet projects while also approving the security upgrades without actually getting them started.

"You've seen the results of that razor wire installation," Storp said. "Vanna's pissed about all the plastic bags stuck up there."

"Is she happy we haven't been attacked?"

"Look, I'm on your side. But your requests have to go through standard procurement procedures."

"Meaning?"

"Meaning GSO will contact three vendors for each new item. Each vendor conducts a work assessment before we close the bids, which will be judged on a variety of factors

– not on time and cost alone, but a variety of factors."

"Our priority is to get these upgrades done as quickly as possible."

"And our priority is to spend taxpayer money in a responsible fashion."

"I think the taxpayer would consider it responsible to protect the officers serving on the front line of the war on terror."

"Speaking of which," said Storp, "this compound does have internal security matters to take care of."

"Such as?"

"Well." Storp shuffled through his stack. "I'm glad you asked. As long as DS has all this funding to offer, we could use some of it to repair the road."

"How's the road a security matter?"

"Let's say somebody trips."

"That's hypothetical."

"Not really. Vanna herself has damaged many shoes on the potholes."

Mutton's face flushed at the mention of Vanna's shoes. "That's safety," he said. "Not security."

"There's also the rec center."

"What's the rec center got to do with security?"

"With a rec center on the compound, our officers won't have to go home to get their exercise. They won't have to go home for anything at all. They can just enjoy themselves here."

"The last thing I need is more officers on this compound."

"You're responsible for their security whether they're on *this* compound, or any other."

"Only if they're following my Security Directives."

"That reminds me. Do the directives apply to TDYers? Guys like Furgle?"

"Who's Furgle?"

"I would think you knew. The Ambassador's Special Staffer? Conducting an investigation."

Mutton's face reddened. "What investigation?"

Storp shrugged. "SDDTS," he said.

"Not without my approval," Mutton said. He took the stubby pencil from behind his ear and nearly snapped it between his thumbs and forefingers. He got out of his chair and marched down the corridor, across the lobby, and into the office reserved for the Ambassador. There he found the goateed A.S.S. typing notes from his interviews.

"You have to stop this investigation," Mutton ordered.

"Why?"

"Because I wasn't informed. If you're not careful, I'll open an investigation into you."

Furgle nodded. He might be the Ambassador's Special Staffer, but he was still just a JO. Diplomatic Security investigations had a way of ruining promotion potential. "I don't know a thing," Furgle said. "Let's just forget about it."

Nobody told Mutton to what to do. He launched an immediate investigation into Robert Furgle, and asked the Special Staffer what he'd come to investigate.

"This investigation goes all the way to the top."

"The White House?" Mutton asked.

Furgle shook his head. "The *top*."

Mutton's nose tingled and his skin crawled. Furgle could only be talking about one place, a place he was frightened to hear named and unwilling to mention; a place above the bureaucracy that nobody had clearly defined and nobody could point to. He stepped closer to Furgle in an effort to intimidate. "Who authorized your investigation?"

Furgle gulped. "Fourth Branch?" he asked, uncertain of his awareness of any such entity. He hoped Mutton would explain.

"What are you investigating?" Mutton asked.

"Cables."

"What cables?"

"Cables containing uncleared language."

"What's 'uncleared language'?"

"Language used by the president that shouldn't be used?"

"What have you found?"

"Only that there's an organization more powerful than the White House."

"And the cables?"

"It's true: I found cables containing language not cleared for use by the president."

"Where'd they come from?"

"From right here. At this Mission."

"Have you reported any of this?"

Furgle lifted the attaché case manacled to his wrist. "It's all in here."

"I'll take that," Mutton said, and Furgle didn't protest.

Mutton's insecurity flared. He was accountable for things he knew and could be accused of dereliction for the existence of things he didn't know. So he established a defense with Security Directive Sixty-Nine. SD-69 required that all action, gossip, cables, meetings, interviews, spending, communications, operations, contracts, visits, delegations, memoranda, mistakes, errors, bad ideas, failures, and other miscellany be channeled to him for security review through his secretary, effective immediately. And because Williamina Porcas had been employed to make coffee rather than to channel any action, gossip, cables, meetings, interviews, spending, communications, operations, contracts, visits, delegations, memoranda, mistakes, errors, bad ideas, failures and miscellany for his review, Mutton could plausibly deny receiving any such news.

Armed thus with the powers of a Priest, privy to the secrets and sins of the Mission, but protected from acting on them by the immutable laws of Porcas's refusal to do anything other than make coffee, Mutton dashed off to the beach house where he found himself grumbling to Miss Wellstone about the drunkards who came to work in a place where alcohol was prohibited.

"It's been good for us," said the association manager. "FARSA makes a tidy profit thanks to prohibition. Anyway, enough to pay for the beach house and the boat. Another Heineken?"

Mutton accepted the freezing green bottle and loosened up in the cool breeze blowing under the thatch-roofed bar. Out in the glare of the afternoon sun the Red Sea undulated gently, the sun glinting off the ripples and peaks.

"Unless," Miss Wellstone said, "the CG gets her way and ropes our profits into her recreational center fund."

"You mean this rec center idea is real? I thought Clements said FARSA was going to use the profits to replace the *Sheikh Djibouti.*"

"The only way we're getting a new boat in here is if we put Vanna's name on it."

"That's extortion."

"It's certainly worth investigating. Another Heineken?"

Mutton sobered. Slightly. He thought an investigation into the CG was just the sort of project that might save them all. And in order to collect the kind of information he needed, he temporarily lifted SD-69.

Mutton's interview with Potts revealed the consequences of hosting a Fourth of July event, which would provide an excellent opportunity for a truck bomb, commando-style raid, or attack by RPG from the Kingdom

Hospital.

"I've been practicing the Sousaphone for months," said Potts. "Fine instrument. Unfortunately, the CG doesn't want to celebrate with the Sousaphone. She'd rather celebrate with a Pledge of Allegiance to the war on terror."

"Who would pledge allegiance to the war on terror?"

"Nobody. That's why we're trying to get it cancelled. Any way you can help?"

"I'm trying. What I need are leads."

"Have you talked to our friends in back? No Lips is always ready to supply evidence that supports the favored opinion."

But when Mutton disappeared behind No Lips' broom closet door, the chief asked Mutton to sign an SDDTS Clearance Waiver Non-Disclosure Form. "I feel more comfortable," No Lips said, "knowing you know that I know that what I say will stay between the two of us."

"What you say might not stay between us."

"Then I'm not telling you anything."

"What if I told you we had a common enemy."

"Terrorists are everyone's common enemy."

"What if the common enemy was the CG?"

"If this is a threat about shoes in the back of her closet ..."

"Look, it's ok. She does the same to me." Mutton nodded his assurance.

"Then ... We're ..."

"We're on the same side."

No Lips froze with surprise and momentary pleasure. Pleasure was a feeling he rarely experienced and it loosened the place where he should have had lips. "Here's what I know: I personally would like to send back intel that gets the Fourth of July canceled. But I'm under strict orders. I'm only permitted intel that supports certain views."

"Whose orders?"

"Fourth Branch."

Mutton shivered. "I don't know what that is. Whose views?"

"Fourth Branch."

Mutton shook his head in disbelief. "What else?"

"CG's running moles inside my shop. Strictly amateur."

"Who?"

"Storp. Tinker."

"Want me to spook them?"

"Their presence *does* jeopardize several important ops. Including one that might just get the Fourth of July cancelled."

"I'll put a stop to this."

Mutton's interrogation of Storp confirmed the chief's revelations. "Why would you do it?" Mutton asked.

"My career is tied to hers."

"You can be charged with conspiracy. Espionage. Treason."

"Maybe in prison I'll find real freedom."

"What are you talking about?"

"This document." Storp pointed to the stack of printer paper in the center of his desk. "It's giving me paper cuts. I won't need it in prison." Storp shook his head pitifully, and Mutton felt a sudden sympathy for the management officer.

"Have you talked to Dr. Meddler?" he asked.

Storp nodded.

"What's he say?"

"He confirmed what I already knew: I do what she says and I get promoted. I refuse, I get Chad."

"Did Meddler point out that even with promotion, you'll still be working for her?"

Storp nodded. "You see the situation I'm in? Already a prisoner. Maybe I'm better off serving time for treason."

Mutton snuck out of Storp's office. He couldn't stand to see a grown man cry. He left him blubbering behind his desk, resolved to put an end to Vanna's reign of terror.

Mutton had the same results with Tinker after flashing his badge and threatening jail time. He stopped his harangue to hand a tissue to the terrified JO, sputtering on about falsified cables and reports and memos and emails.

"Slow down. What are you talking about?"

"Uncleared language."

"What's uncleared language?"

"The CG hasn't cleared a single one of my cables. I don't think she even reads them. Talk to Furgle. He was investigating the uncleared cables."

"I already talked to Furgle."

"Then what about the CG? What about the stack of cables on her desk?"

So that was it. Having run the gauntlet of possibilities and circled back to the place he'd started, Mutton went to face his enemy. He swore he would be strong. No more cowering. No more blackmail. But Vanna remained as glib and cool as ever.

"Mr. Mutton," Vanna said. "I hope this isn't about the security upgrade again?"

"No, ma'am."

"Then you must be satisfied with the way your barbed wire is collecting every piece of rubbish that floats up on the dreadful sea air in this salty city."

"No, ma'am. This is an investigation."

"And what are we investigating?"

Mutton mentioned what he'd heard from No Lips regarding Storp and Tinker. He mentioned words like conspiracy and counter-intelligence and treason.

Vanna waved him off. "But Mr. Mutton. It's so simple a ruse it fooled even you. I'm fully aware of their ineptitude. If I really wanted to spy on them, wouldn't I have sent in someone with skill?"

"But why look into their operation at all?"

"Before you ask that question, you should know that this office has been cleared of whatever it is Furgle was looking for."

"It's still not clear to me what he was looking for."

"Then you aren't much of an investigator, are you?"

Mutton felt stung by Vanna's ability to turn the blade back on him. In an effort to get the upper hand he pulled out his badge.

"Ma'am, I'm a federal investigator. Lying to me or withholding evidence from me during an investigation is a jailable offense."

"And what are we investigating? Shoes?"

Mutton stayed strong. "Treason."

"You're looking in the wrong place."

"Where should I be looking?"

"You should start by asking Mr. Furgle. He's working for some very powerful people. For your own sake, I hope that you provided him with your fullest support."

Mutton felt the sting again. "I don't really understand what he's after."

"His investigation hinges on important communications with a very important office. The highest in the land."

"The White House?"

"I remind you we are at war. No branch of our government can afford dissent. The war on terror. The war in Afghanistan. The invasion of Iraq. What is it all about?"

Mutton guessed, "Nine eleven?"

Vanna shook her head. "It's much bigger than that."

Mutton hadn't a clue.

"Oil," Vanna said. "Our allies in the Kingdom say it's worth more than we pay for it. Our masters happen to agree – they, too, would profit from higher oil prices."

"You can't eat oil."

"Don't be naïve, Mr. Mutton. We can't afford to alienate the Kingdom. So who's the real criminal?"

"The terrorists?"

"That's the obvious answer. And it's wrong. Who's been ripping off the Gulf's oil producers since the beginning?"

Mutton had no answer. He had the low, fluttery feeling that he wouldn't like the answer, like warm liquid running down his legs. But he didn't dare let his lips utter his guess.

"Don't be afraid to say it, Mr. Mutton. The real enemy is the consumer. They pay so little at the pump. And now Fourth Branch is making up for lost time. It's only fair, don't you see? Considering their investments."

"I'm afraid I don't – "

"You don't know Fourth Branch?"

"No."

Vanna sat up straight in her armchair. "An elected official not limited by checks on Executive authority because he has one foot in the Legislative Branch, and not limited by checks on Legislative authority because he's got one foot in the Executive. Sound familiar?"

Rather than a light bulb Mutton suffered a black out trying to recall Junior High Civics.

"Throughout the history of the Republic, the incumbent of this office has interpreted the Constitution conservatively and succumbed to the checks on both branches. Not so, this Vice President."

"The Fourth Branch?"

Vanna nodded. "The Vice President. He will establish global military dominance. He will implement his wishes by frightening the populace. He will make them accept terror, or charge them with treason for ignoring it. He's raised a specter that cannot be disproved. We have a patriotic duty to give him everything he asks for. This is one genie that won't fit back in the bottle."

"What is he asking for?"

"Simple. Our job is to ensure strong ties between the Kingdom and the United States."

The specter of 9/11 emerged from the fog. The bald head. The cynical grin. The mechanical heart. The master of the war on terror. Who was winning the war on terror?

"Mr. Mutton?"

Terror was winning. Victory would be for Terror. Terror begat Hatred begat Terror. A Biblical 69. Mutton looked away from the CG. It was as he had memorized:

"Those who hate me without reason
Outnumber the hairs of my head;
Many are my enemies without cause,
Those who seek to destroy me."

"Mr. Mutton?"

Mutton considered the consequences; there were consequences for Mission staff and consequences for America; consequences for the allies and consequences for the adversaries in the war on terror; consequences for the Kingdom and consequences for the world. It discouraged Mutton to see that the CG, Fourth Branch, veiled officials accountable to none, could cause misery on such a large scale.

Mutton retreated to his office. He closed the door and hunched over his desk to read his illegible notes. New culprits sprung up everywhere: Mutton's notes even pointed to his own culpability. He could be found guilty of scribbling. At the very least it appeared as if Mutton were interfering with an investigation. He was as guilty as

Vanna. By failing to see it happen, he'd as much as let it happen. As DSO, as an American Citizen, he'd let it happen. He, like the American people, continued to let it happen.

Only one course of action remained: Mutton reinstated SD-69. The more he learned, the less he wanted to know.

PART III

Chapter 23

The public address came alive with the high-low alarm, followed by the usual announcement: *This is a drill. All personnel must assume the duck and cover position ...* The alarm continued to wail across the flat sandy lot in the humid afternoon under the watchful eye of the Kingdom Hospital.

The general services door snapped shut, catching Tom Cautwauler on the ass. He told himself yet again to have the clerk get the carpenter to fix the door, then tipped forward his fedora and lowered a cigar toward the match he struck behind cupped hands. A breeze kicked up in the pre-dusk air. With the breeze would come the crows. This would be the last night for so many of those black bastards, thought Cautwauler.

He stood on the little patch of lawn where the sprinkler sputtered and rocked, barely tossing water onto the grass. He squinted across the dusty grounds. The door opened and the senior procurement clerk came out, holding the door carefully before letting it snap shut.

"You learn," said the Indian. "After 35 years. You are not the first to be hit on the ass by that door." He pointed with the cigarette he held between his fingers. "No GSO ever has time to fix his own door."

Cautwauler tilted back his head and laughed. "Haaa-ha." He continued the rest of the laugh in silence, and the Indian stood by, arms behind his back, head bowed innocently as if he'd intended nothing funny at all.

The crows were beginning to settle in the trees. Just beyond the trees the tattered American flag was picking up in the breeze over the chancery.

"Will they set the plague tonight?"

"Maintenance will task the gardeners in the morning. This time tomorrow, no more crows."

"And no more whining from you-know-who about slip-sliding away on guano."

The clerk said nothing. It was not his place to mock another officer, and certainly not the Consul General. He finished his cigarette and flicked the butt into the ash bucket. "Workday over," he said. "I'll see the warehouse received everything we paid for on my way out."

Cautwauler watched him go, and soon the procurement agent's receding figure was replaced by the approaching outline of Martin Tinker. Cautwauler had no time to stab out his cigar and escape Tinker's inevitable request. The breeze had picked up and the clamoring of the crows in the Fichus trees reached frenzy. This was the only pleasant part of the day for Cautwauler. Once the orange sun sank into the sea, the humidity returned to blanket the night. Now Tinker was going to ruin the breeze. Tinker's random complaint, request, demand, suggestion, what-have-you, would ruin Cautwauler's satisfaction at knowing that the crows were about to eat their last supper. Tinker's random complaint was exactly why Cautwauler barely came out anymore while he awaited his orders for Iraq.

Tinker stepped toward Cautwauler on lively toes, until he noticed the sprinkler dribbling on the grass. He looked down at his shiny black shoes, at the sprinkler, at Cautwauler, then again at his shoes. Cautwauler sucked on the cigar and slowly let out smoke.

"Hi," called Tinker from the edge of the grass. He lifted his hand in a wave.

"Out for the fresh air?" asked Cautwauler. He sucked his cigar.

"Actually," said Tinker, "to tell you the truth, I had a question for you."

"A question?" Cautwauler looked at the crows. "You want to know how to kill a couple hundred crows?"

"I hate those birds. They ... crap, all over the sidewalk. These birds have ruined many good receptions at Vanna's residence. I hate those birds."

Cautwauler didn't look at Tinker. He kept his eyes on the birds, cigar poking out of his mouth, hat tilted back, forehead lifted to the steady breeze. He did his best to ignore Tinker.

"Actually," said Tinker, exposing his shoes to the wet grass and daring to step closer to the GSO. "Actually, I had another question for you."

"Uh huh."

"You've seen the latest warning? The threat to all residential compounds? Well, I was wondering. I've got this ... concern."

Cautwauler lowered his head and took the cigar from his mouth. He looked behind him for the ash can. The evening had been ruined.

"You see, I've got a lot of documents ..."

"Documents?"

"I've got a lot of important documents. Very valuable. Irreplaceable."

"Documents."

"*New York Times. National Geographic.* Old publications. I have every *New York Times* from – "

Cautwauler stabbed out the cigar and started toward the office. "So you've got newspapers."

Tinker followed quick. "Well, if you've seen this latest warning, it indicates there might be an attack at a residential compound. Commando-style. Hostages. Beheadings. Car bombs ... What I'm worried about is, you see, these documents. If there are any car bombs outside my home, I don't want the papers getting burnt up. They're irreplaceable."

Cautwauler had reached the door. But this was a first, and he was amused. He kept his hand on the doorknob and said, "I see your point. So what are you asking for?"

Tinker brightened, surprised by Cautwauler's interest in his problem. "I've got this large closet. What I'd like to do is, I'd like to line the interior with steel. Something fireproof. Bombproof. I think I can fit all my documents in the closet, and close it off. Of course, I understand there would be some expense to this that I might need to – "

"No, no," said Cautwauler. "Stop right there. I think I see what you're saying. You're asking the GSO to bombproof your closet to keep some old papers safe. Why not write up a work order? Shoot it over to Ed. As Acting GSO, he'll see where this job fits in between tonight's slaughter of a few hundred crows, requests for mouse traps – *with cheese* – and the procurement and installation of a couple million dollars worth of security upgrades." Cautwauler lowered the front brim of his hat and glared at Tinker.

Tinker gave an uncomfortable smile.

"Don't worry," Cautwauler said. "It's just an advisory. A reaction. You're perfectly safe now that the USG has predicted a slaughter."

But Cautwauler didn't believe what he said. Security was deteriorating. Where were his damn orders for Iraq? Even that war zone would be safer than the Kingdom. With one last email to send before he called it quits, Cautwauler pulled open the door of the general services building. He entered the office, and the door snapped shut on his ass.

Chapter 24

Clements, Pudge, Ed, and one of the Pierces carried their beers through the cloying humidity. Mutton watched from the newly erected guard tower, the sawdust fresh in his nose. The termites and humidity would soon get it. Ok, and so he'd build another. And another. He needed quick, cheap fixes to keep the place safe *now*.

The Sri Lankan next to him spoke no English. No matter: the guard knew which way to point a shotgun, and he could be trusted not to turn it on Mutton. Mutton felt in his thin, quick blood they would be over-run any day now despite the razor wire and new guard towers on both sides of the wall. Even Hassan Ali had gone from cool to cagey.

Pudge hit from the 9th tee to the 8th hole. "Easier," he said. "Closer."

"What happens when we get to the first tee?" Ed asked.

"I break out another beer."

"Is Mutton ok with it? He doesn't want any drinking in view of the hospital."

"That's only because he thinks it'll provoke anger toward us," said Pudge.

"And there already is anger toward us, so ..." Clements finished his beer and fished around in his bag for another. "The faster you drink, the colder it is."

Ed hit toward the eighth hole. None of the foursome had reached the flat circle of Astroturf. Pudge lay his Astroturf mat on the dirt and lined up his shot to the pin.

They shuffled through the heat squinting behind sunglasses. Pudge stopped, dropped his mat, and nudged the ball onto it with his toe.

"You're not lined up with the pin," Pierce said. "You'll

never get to the pin."

"No hurry. What else is there to do?" Pudge swung. His ball landed further from the pin than it had been. He picked up his mat. "This would be more fun with caddies. Maybe in Paris." Pudge's onward assignment had come in: he would be one political officer among a dozen, a portfolio focused on the rise of Muslim ghettos and the French response to it. "Let me guess," Pudge said. "Racist. Xenophobic. Paranoid. Who can blame them?"

"You'll only be working on it when not arranging shopping trips for Congressional Delegations and their spouses," Clements said.

"Spouses and *daughters*, my friend. Don't forget the daughters."

"Why are all the available assignments related to Islam?" Clements asked. "Even small African missions in countries with almost no Muslims are opening positions tied to Islam."

"I just hope the martinis are good in Paree. How am I going to give up all this?"

Pierce stopped by his ball and lifted his glasses. He squinted into the low orange sunlight reflecting off the dust. "The hell is that?" he asked.

"Crow," said Pudge.

"What's wrong with it?"

The black object inched forward through the dust, its beak jacked open.

"Poison," said Clements. The crow gasped and scratched through the dust toward the pool. "Don't you read your email?"

"It came from Cautwauler," said Pudge. "He probably deleted it unread."

"Cautwauler? I thought he was in Baghdad."

Ed said, "He leaves next week. He's having trouble with his travel orders. Boy, was he pissed when he found out he had to fill out a work order to get his travel orders."

"What about the crows?" Pierce asked.

"Cautwauler poisoned them," Clements said.

"We've been instructed not to touch them," said Clements.

"And for God's sake, don't EAT them."

"You didn't see an email with the subject 'DON'T EAT CROW'?"

"How could you miss that?"

"Don't eat them?!" Pierce demanded. "What kind of sick shit is that?"

"Apparently Patches wasn't on the distribution ..."

The calico cat had left her post by the rear chancery door to watch the dying throes. She sat beside one of the crows, regal, gloating at the birds impending demise. At the approach of the three officers Patches looked up and yawned. She licked her paws and preened.

"Hyah!" shouted Pierce. The calico only blinked. She looked at the crow and returned to her preening.

"It can't be good for a cat to eat poisoned crow."

"I think Patches is smart enough not to eat poisoned crow. But some of these others ..."

They shuffled toward the post office and the eighth tee. Several more black objects stirred in the dust. They seemed to be crawling in the general direction of the pool. A low buzzing rattled the air. From the Fichus trees around the post office a crow dropped out and landed with a thud on the dust.

"Christ!" said Pierce.

"Peace be upon him," said Clements.

As they neared the post office the number of crows, crawling or dead, increased. They were thickest around the lazy twirling sprinkler dribbling water on the patch of grass outside Liston's moldy bungalow. Half a dozen of the mangled things had reached the sprinkler before expiring.

They lay in the wet grass, their beaks open.

"What kind of poison is that?" Pierce asked. "This is – "

– a loud mewling cut him off; a cry filled the early evening. They turned toward the pool and peered through gaps in the cinderblocks. A horde of strays had turned up by the pool to watch the helpless flapping and spinning of the crows. Scores of birds had expired on the concrete. Several floated in the water. In the far corner a pile of cats climbed over each other, backs up, tearing and ripping at the pile of black feathers.

"This is exactly why I'm leaving government service," the other Pierce Pierce said. The story he told was that he would be joining a Russian oil firm doing business in the Gulf. "I'm getting out. Make my millions while I can."

Ed watched the pile of cats tearing at the poisoned crows and the army of Chadians picking plastic bags out of the razor wire. He looked up at the twenty floors of the Kingdom Hospital staring down. What observers up there might be watching the crows die on the American compound? Mutton sweated in the tower next to the Sri Lankan guard, both armed with shotguns, eyes trained on the gate and the hospital.

The gate opened and a black Mercedes pulled into the chute. The gate began to close, slowly.

"He's here," Clements said.

"Who?"

"Sheikh al Bafarti. He's come for tea with Vanna." Clements headed toward the front door of the chancery. Mutton climbed down from the guard tower.

~ ~ ~

"Tell the Sheikh what you told me regarding his visa," Vanna ordered Clements. She held her cup daintily, legs crossed at the knees. Al Bafarti sat in an armchair, dressed in an immaculate white thobe and headdress. Clements was sunk into the couch, the cushions forcing his knees together. Mutton looked on from the armchair, examining al Bafarti as if in search of the reason he had been invited to join this particular group for tea.

"Washington hasn't cleared."

"What kind of clearance, exactly? Maybe you can explain the process to the Sheikh."

"Clearance is required when our database links biographical data to known – " Clements was going to say "criminals". Instead he said, "For applicants whose records are of interest to law enforcement agencies, for one reason or another."

Vanna pressed. "So you're saying the visa is held up for 'one reason or another'?"

Mutton watched Al Bafarti. The small brown sheikh followed the exchange like a man watching Ping-Pong, his dark eyes darting back and forth.

"The law requires Washington's input before I can issue."

"But Sheikh al Bafarti is our good contact."

"I will call," Clements said. "I'll ask when we can expect a decision."

"You see, Sheikh? All we have to do is ask," Vanna said.

The small man nodded gently. He was impeccably groomed. His mustache and beard were neatly trimmed, and his eyebrows, almost joined, were clean and straight. He sipped his tea. "I truly appreciate it," he said softly.

"I know you do. That is why I am eager to help."

"Timing is everything, madame. You know how I wish to accompany the Crown Prince later this month."

"And you know how eager I am to see that happen. I would enjoy the opportunity to go, myself. Either as a member of your entourage or at the request of, others ...." Vanna paused and let her self-invitation float out there.

"Of course, it will require that my visa be issued." The

sheikh gave Clements a good-natured smile. "My visit carries important implications for our two countries."

"You've got that troublesome glimmer in your eye, my dear sheikh. Won't you enlighten us?"

"Of course. Quite simply, my enterprise, the Kingdom Exploding Group, would like to open operations in the U.S. We would like to accompany the Crown Prince when he meets with your president. It will mean everything to us and our investors. A sign of good faith." He leaned forward a little slyly and said, "We have a gift for him. We would like to make a surprise announcement."

Vanna leaned forward. "Can you give us a hint?"

The sheikh put his tea on the saucer and set the saucer on the table. "We want to announce our first project in the U.S."

"Which is?"

The Sheikh gave his charming smile once again. "Madame, with respect. A secret this big must be kept to oneself. My dear, surely you understand the need for secrecy. Let me just say that the project will be regarded as true philanthropy from the people of Saudi Arabia to the people of the United States. To make amends between our countries."

"But Sheikh, you are a true philanthropist already."

Al Bafarti ducked his head.

"I assure you our young Vice Consul here will do everything he can to see your visa issued on time. Isn't that right, Mr. Clements?"

Vanna looked at Clements, who had only one thought: If the Kingdom Exploding Group opened its operations in the U.S., there would be no end to the visa requests. "That's right," he said. Al Bafarti thanked his host softly, then rose to go.

"One other thing before you go, Sheikh. I wanted to introduce you to Jeff Mutton. Our security officer."

"Very nice to meet you."

Mutton shook his hand.

"Mr. Mutton has long needed assurance about the construction across the street. Sheikh, I am confident that meeting the chairman of the Kingdom Exploding Group will ease his mind about the regular explosions that rattle our cages."

"Madame, you are very funny."

"Mr. Mutton will show you out," Vanna said, after the Sheikh had kissed her hand.

As they walked toward the lobby al Bafarti said, "You have a very large compound. What do you do with so much land?"

"We have a lot of buildings." Mutton held each door for the sheikh as they exited the secure area, the first set of lobby doors, and the final door opening to the outside. Mutton saw the sheikh's driver get in and start the black Mercedes.

"These doors all look so heavy."

Mutton shrugged.

The sheikh offered Mutton a soft, feeble hand. Mutton felt he was crushing a marshmallow. "Are all the buildings as secure as this one?"

Mutton pretended not to hear. He said, as if continuing his original answer, "Of course we also have a golf course ..."

"Ah yes, the golf course. I have seen it. You know, there is a wonderful view of the compound from my hospital, just across the street."

Mutton looked up at the hospital and shivered, as with the flu.

"I love you Americans," the sheikh said. He let go of Mutton's hand. "Imagine, a golf course at your place of work. There is nothing you take too seriously." The sheikh's black Mercedes pulled up at the end of the walk.

"I thank you, Mr. Mutton. I can expect to hear from you about my visa?"

"I'm sure Mr. Clements will call Washington. Visa security is one thing we Americans take very seriously. All security. That is why we have so many protections in place."

Al Bafarti smiled. "Ah, Mr. Mutton. But you know what we Arabs believe? We believe that best for security is to know your friends and neighbors."

Chapter 25

Shards of sunlight glanced off the polished white sedan. Inside, five bearded men listened for the command from above. The street shimmered with heat. Few cars moved before the mid-day prayer.

The radio crackled. The voice from Crow's Nest, barely audible, advised them of the sedan's approach. The men tensed, then relaxed. God was great.

Twenty stories up inside the Kingdom Hospital, the commander watched. The battleground lay plain before him. None had seen him. None knew the commander. It mattered only that through them all ran the Will of God. The men strained toward the windows, eager to spot the vehicle carrying the occupier and the enemy.

A black Crown Victoria, green diplomatic tags, turned off the street.

"Al Hamdu Lila," the driver said. "That is the target."

The walls surrounding the consulate provided no shade. The soldiers guarding the enemy stronghold sweated and drowsed in their helmets and armor, dreaming of paradise.

The sedan stopped before the enemy gate. The indolent machine-gunner, propped under a shade atop the military pickup, leaned over and banged the driver's window. The truck rumbled to a start and lurched from its blockade of the gate.

Now! called Crow's Nest. The white Caprice jerked heavily into the street. The four passenger's gripped their AK-47s below the windshield.

Close in! ordered the voice on the crackling radio.

"Al Hamdu Lila, it is not a drill."

"Al Hamdu Lila."

Allah's blessings surged through them as the Caprice raced toward the gate rolling open. The driver shouted: "Alahu Akbar!" and gunned the engine.

His companions shouted: "Alahu Akbar!"

Before the Caprice reached the consulate a sturdy barrier rose from the asphalt. The Caprice stopped short. The soldiers dropped their weapons and ran from the gate.

The four doors opened at once, a bearded attacker jumping from each, the day charged with gunfire and the confused shouts of the soldiers running away from the battle. The attackers dropped two black duffels as they breached the gate creeping slowly closed.

They fired at the sky. The blue shirt guards inside the guardhouse watched through explosion resistant glass. The attackers fired wildly as they ran past the black Crown Victoria, windshield and front end crumpled against the drop arm, the engine smoking, the bloodied driver and the passenger pressing themselves against the floor of the dead, smoking car.

Chapter 26

The hi-lo siren drowned Clements' voice. He shouted to the applicant through the glass: "Just a drill! Should only be a minute!"

"PLEASE. IT IS LOUD." The bearded man covered his ears. "WHAT DO I DO?"

"DUCK. BENEATH THE COUNTER." Clements pointed.

The Afghani was the last applicant of the morning. Behind him the waiting room was empty. A local guard, an Indian in a blue uniform shirt, strolled in. He squatted beneath the table used by applicants to fill out forms. Clements dropped the blinds and squatted beneath the counter. Pierce and Pudge were already there. Ed had gone to the GSO bungalow.

"Why couldn't they have done this fifteen minutes later?" Pudge asked.

"Language lesson?" asked Pierce.

Pudge nodded, regretting a missed chance to crouch beneath the table with Maimouna.

The alarm continued. "Where's the announcement?" Pierce asked.

Loud popping erupted.

"Quite a drill," Clements said.

"No drill," Pierce said. "That's live fire. AK-47s."

Moments later – a dull muffled thud – more popping – another thud. The intercom came to life with static, then the Marine: *GAS! GAS! GAS!*

Clements asked, "Anyone have a Quickmask?" Nobody had one. Clements' mask was in his office.

More rounds fired. The popping closed in. The local staff chattered giddily in Arabic.

"Definitely not a drill," Pierce said.

Clements counted the doors between himself and the outside. There were four ballistic doors between the consular section and the chancery entrance.

~ ~ ~

The blue-shirted Sri Lankan guard in the tower unslung his shotgun. He never fired a shot. The lead attacker took aim from one knee, fired a killshot to the head.

Two attackers sprinted from the gate straight toward the rear of the chancery. Three ran left toward the front. Each carried an AK-47 and a heavy, black duffel.

~ ~ ~

Storp instructed his staff to crouch on the floor. His secretary, the procurement agent, the budget clerk, Nurse, and the protocol assistant crouched in front of his desk. Storp remained in his chair behind the desk until a bullet pierced the window and struck the soft cinder-block wall. Storp dove from his chair and crawled along the carpet to join the staff. "NOT A DRILL!" he shouted. Another bullet hit the wall, followed by a trickle of pulverized concrete.

A few meters from Storp's office the rear hatch of the chancery slammed shut. A fierce metallic clanging rang off the door. Round after round struck lead. The marines mustered noisily at the weapons room. Their hustled voices exploded down the hall. Storp heard them punch the code on the weapons room Hirsche pad.

~ ~ ~

Two attackers ran toward the low bungalow: the Marine house. Several young Americans in shorts and tee shirts ran from the house. The attackers fired on them. The Americans reached the chancery and slipped inside. Bullets bounced away from the lead door as it shut behind them. The attackers tossed homemade bombs through the bungalow windows; explosions flared; the

Yemeni cook, trapped by fire and smoke, roasted before he could suffocate.

Outside the house thick black smoke boiled up over the motionless green fronds of the palm trees and into the hot bright day.

~ ~ ~

The Pakistani and Sudanese clerks crouched in the rear offices of the flimsy general services building. Toward the front the Indian clerk crouched beside Ed. Hearing the gunfire, the explosions, the shouts, the booming from the Marine house, Ed thought about the others in the motor pool office, the maintenance shed, the carpenters, plumbers, and mechanics, all working in unsecured locations. Ed remembered the contractors, the gardeners, the char force, the South Asians working in the heat and humidity. None of the outbuildings was built like the chancery. Ed crouched under the desk close enough to smell Thomas' sweat. They said nothing amid the explosions and gunfire. Thomas had brought from its hiding place in his desk a plastic Jesus figurine.

~ ~ ~

At the front of the compound one attacker kicked open the motor pool door. Another lunged in. The crouching dispatcher shook beneath his desk. A dozen drivers hunkered on the tile floor. Valentine was on his feet, servicing the telephone. The lead attacker shot him one shot in the head. Valentine dropped and blood spilled from the hole in his head, making a quick pool across the white tile floor.

"Americans!" shouted one attacker.

The dispatcher, hands around his head, moved awkwardly on his knees from behind his desk.

"Americans!"

The dispatcher called: "No Americans! Ma fee Amreekeeyeen! Ma fee! Ma fee!"

The bearded men in dirty white pajamas, with crazed eyes and wild hair, rounded up the drivers and the dispatcher and marched them, hands raised, outside into the blazing heat.

~ ~ ~

Mutton burst into Vanna's office, Decker behind. Both in Kevlar, carrying stubby rifles. The rectangular window above Vanna's desk, bullet-shattered. Debris littered the Persian carpets.

"VANNA!" Mutton called. "IS IT CLEAR?"

"UNDER HERE!" she called, hysterical. "Under here! They're shooting at me! THEY'RE SHOOTING AT ME!"

The stacks of paper piled on her desk had cascaded to the floor, covering the carpets in a slippery mess. Crouched, moving like a crab in his heavy vest, black Colt M4 automatic in both hands, barrel down, Mutton came around the side of her desk. Vanna was on her knees, hunched over, hands over her ears. Mutton reached down. Vanna took his hand. Her other hand gripped the straps of her shoes. She rose until Mutton ordered, "Stay low!"

They crouched along toward the door. Mutton kept his body between Vanna and the high, narrow windows.

"CLEAR!" Mutton shouted.

"ALL CLEAR!" Decker replied.

Tinker and Pervis were crouched just outside her office. Decker, in helmet and goggles, stood with his rifle pointed toward the windows. Vanna saw debris across the floor along the corridor, lights broken, glass ground into the carpet.

The small band of Americans moved together toward the rear of the chancery. Mutton pressed a bell beside the big, heavy vault, twice short, once long, once short. After an excruciating pause the door cracked. The square black barrel of a pistol appeared, then an eye, eyelids wide, straining to see through the gap.

"CLEAR!" Mutton shouted. The door opened wider. No Lips peered into the corridor before lowering his pistol. They entered and sealed the vault.

The sound of smashing and grinding filled the vault. Liston's men and No Lips' men smashed equipment in a deeper vault. They smashed machines with hammers and picks and fed massive amounts of paper into the mouths of shredders growling like beasts.

"Are we preparing to be over-run?" Vanna asked No Lips.

"We've *been* over-run."

"How many?"

"Don't know," Mutton said. "Ghani reports half dozen. Maybe more."

"What do we do?" Vanna asked.

"Head count. I'm rounding up the others."

"Who's accounted for?"

"This is it."

"Can we turn off that alarm? I can't hear myself think."

"Not until we have everybody. Kippinger and Porcas have the command center. Around the corner. I have to pull the others back."

"Has there been a breach?"

"The compound. Not the chancery. I control this wing. That's all. Ghani's got our gates, but that's where it all began." Mutton held back reminding her of his constant hectoring about the gate.

"So ...?"

"Not good. I'm clearing the other wing. The Marines have the front and rear hatches. We've fired the gas canisters."

"So what's first?"

"Head count. Call the embassy."

Vanna dropped her shoes to the unfinished concrete floor and took in her surroundings: a close, unventilated room, rough cinderblock walls lined with unopened packing crates, pallets of water and MREs, boxes of old documents, castaway computers, printers, fax machines, shredders. Around the corner Vanna found the communications set-up: computer, printer, a black and a red telephone. Larry handed the black phone to Vanna.

"Non-secure line, ma'am. We have the Embassy."

"Get me the residence," she ordered.

"Ma'am?"

"My residence. I want to talk to my staff."

Kippinger dialed, handed over the phone.

"Mustapha? Listen. What? Listen to me. What?" Vanna pressed the phone tight against her ear but couldn't hear over the grinding and shredding and smashing. "CAN'T THEY STOP THAT FOR JUST A MOMENT?!" she shouted at Larry.

Kippinger went around and stopped the destruction. In the silence Vanna cupped the mouthpiece and quietly told her butler to put the jewelry on her dresser into the vault.

~ ~ ~

Near the flagpole at the entrance an attacker shot dead a guard climbing down from his tower. He approached the flagpole, unwrapped the lanyard, jerked. The flag stuck. He tugged. Several canisters bounced on the asphalt around him. White clouds of smoke billowed up. He tugged the lanyard. The flag didn't budge. Smoke enveloped him and his eyes swelled and his throat burned. He fought back tears and jerked the lanyard. Finally the American flag, a frayed and dull old flag, descended the pole. The smoke dissipated.

~ ~ ~

Mutton and Decker, crouching low, came to Storp's office first. "STORP?" Mutton shouted over the alarm.

"WE'RE IN HERE!"

Mutton entered quickly, pointing his weapon reflexively at the bearded Indian budget clerk. The crouching clerk shot his hands toward the ceiling. Mutton saw his badge. "STAY LOW!" he shouted to the cowering group. "We're evacuating to the safe haven."

"All of us?" Storp asked.

"All together." Mutton didn't have time to separate the non-Americans.

~ ~ ~

The general services door banged open. Two bearded men pointed their weapons at Thomas and Ed.

"Americans!"

"No Americans," Thomas called, trembling, hands by his ears, crouched on the floor. He trembled badly. He looked quickly at Ed then lowered his head. He trembled. One attacker jerked him to his feet. Another beat Thomas' cheek with his rifle butt and Thomas dropped the Jesus figurine. The attacker shot Thomas in the face and his body crumpled to the floor. "Americans!" he shouted.

One kicked down the door to Cautwauler's private office. The office was empty. One attacker pointed his rifle at Ed while the other marched swiftly to the back offices and found two clerks crouching behind desks.

"Americans!"

"Ma fee!"

The attacker yanked both men to their feet and shoved them toward the exit. The first shoved Ed into the blinding day, his shoes tracking blood out the door. Thomas' blood.

They marched the hostages to the front of the compound, dozens of men: Lebanese, Yemeni, Pakistani, Sudanese, Christian, Muslim, Hindu, all marching, hands to the sky. They marched past the smoldering Marine house, partially collapsed, the inner gypsum walls bubbling and boiling and black with smoke. They gathered the hostages on the patch of lawn by the chancery. They were joined by hostages from maintenance, motor pool, the warehouse.

"We want Americans!" The hostages had their hands in the air. "Where are the Americans!? Wayn al Amreekeeyeen!?"

An attacker lowered the muzzle of his rifle against a clerk's ear. "Americans!" he shouted. "Infidels!"

The clerk looked toward the chancery. The attacker pulled the trigger.

~ ~ ~

Clements crawled from the counter to his office in search of a Quickmask. The firing outside continued. No announcement from Post One. Clements tucked in beneath his desk, next to the ballistic window. Shadows moved across the blinds. Shadows of attackers, shadows of high, puffy clouds, Clements didn't know. His cell phone perked up.

A colleague from the Embassy. "What's going on down there?"

Clements muffled his voice. "I don't really know."

"CNN has footage of black smoke coming out the compound. What's going on?"

"I don't really know."

"Are you okay?"

"I don't really know. We're hiding"

"Turn off your cell phone."

Clements thanked his friend and clicked off. Frightened for the first time, Clements switched off the phone.

Thuds beat the big secure door opening onto the hallway – THUD THUD THUD. Fists or boots pounded the door. Clements crawled forward to peer out, head low. Mutton's face in the narrow window. Mutton shouted and pounded the door. Clements crawled across the carpet, reached for the knob, pulled. Mutton and Decker crouched in and shut the door.

"Is it clear?"

"I think so."

"Everybody ok?"

"I think so."

"How many are you?"

"We're all here."

"How many?"

"I don't know." Clements thought. "Ed's not here."

"Where is he?"

"He's outside. GSO."

"Shit," Mutton said, lips tight. "Shit. How many here? SHIT. FUCK. OUTSIDE?"

Clements thought. "Fifteen, including myself." His knees felt limp.

Mutton moved low around the corner and directed everyone toward the exit. Belvedere came out from behind his desk rubbing his eyes like a man waking from a nap. Mutton separated the local staff and opened the safe haven along the public affairs corridor. Decker followed Mutton down the corridor and brought Potts and his staff from public affairs. They locked the local staff inside the safe haven.

"Stay low," Mutton ordered. "Follow close." Mutton led them down the admin corridor toward the secure vault. The hi-lo alarm squawled.

~ ~ ~

The lead attacker watched the Hospital for a sign. No sign from Crow's Nest.

The invasion had taken minutes. The standoff was endless. The gunmen held a few dozen prisoners – locals; Muslims – on the lawn. The coward Americans remained locked inside. From the black duffels they had taken their largest explosives and set them to the doors. The explosions only blackened the glass and steel. Bullets ricocheted back at them. They had shattered glass in places but nowhere wide enough to crawl through.

The marines would not fight. They had run inside. No American had been captured. The flex-cuffs and razors and video recorders in their black duffels were useless. No Americans pleading for their lives. They needed to cut open the throat of one American: something to show the world Allah's might.

STILL no sign from Crow's Nest. Smoke billowed up toward a circling helicopter. If Allah willed it, the Royal Family's traitorous forces outside would be defeated. Crow's Nest would send reinforcements over the walls. Then they would destroy the doors and enter the building. The real killing would begin.

"Americans!" he shouted. The hostages, hands in the air, trembled at his feet.

~ ~ ~

"HEAD COUNT!" Vanna shouted. "HEAD COUNT!" She rushed to and fro, shoes off, hair wild. Mutton had disabled the alarm by pulling the wires.

"Count off by section," Storp said.

"The Ambassador wants to know who's accounted for!"

"I've accounted for all sections but the front office," Storp said.

Vanna said, "Who's here from the front office!"

"You are, ma'am."

"That makes one. Who else?"

"Pervis. Tinker. That makes three," said Storp.

"What's the final count?" Vanna asked.

"We can't account for 35 local staff," Storp said. "The rest are with us or accounted for on the other side. Two Americans off-compound; one American outside, on compound."

The smashing and grinding continued in the small, disorganized space. Still Clements felt safe. There weren't enough chairs, but Clements felt comfortable standing among his colleagues. Even the smashing and grinding felt reassuring. Clements didn't know how long they'd have to wait, but he didn't feel exposed. Closer than ever to the front line of the war on terror, he felt calm. For once, he knew the precise location of the enemy.

A new, piercing sound rose above the drone of grinding and smashing. The protocol assistant yelped into her phone in a high-pitched, panicked Arabic. She wailed loud, insistent, inconsolable. Clements' stomach clenched. The knot twisted. He felt light-headed, nauseous. The frantic mood of collegial nerves fell away to despondent sobriety.

Meddler tried to console the woman. She wouldn't be consoled. To No Lips Meddler said, "Let me out."

"What?"

"Out."

"Can't. You'll endanger the rest of us."

"I can put a stop to this."

"How?"

"By walking among them. Naked. An act of peace, with no clothes on."

No Lips signaled Thorner and the other Pierce. They grabbed Meddler from behind. "Secure this man. For his own good and ours."

"He doesn't understand," Meddler protested, struggling against their chicken hold. "It's an old Jesuit non-violence trick. Works every time."

Thorner and Pierce worked him down into a sitting position.

The grinding and smashing continued.

Vanna shouted frantically through the phone to the Deputy Chief of Mission. "I can't confirm the dead."

She listened.

"I can't confirm the number of local staff outside. One American. Outside. Yes, I said outside."

She listened.

"Ed. Mohammed Khan. Yes, an American. Yes, I'm sure."

She listened.

"I can't confirm the number unaccounted for."

She listened.

"Mutton was in communication with the Commander."

She listened. The vault had grown hot and close, the noise overwhelming.

"He's sweeping the chancery."

She listened.

"He hasn't confirmed the number of attackers."

She listened. The protocol assistant, broken and sobbing, folded over on the floor. Storp's assistant tried to comfort her. Whispers spread: staff were dead. The assistant's grief was too great to interrupt. Vanna looked at her. "At least two local staff. Confirmed. Yes." She whispered a single syllable. "Yes, confirmed. Maybe more."

She listened.

"He can't confirm the location of the attackers."

She listened.

"They can't confirm where they have taken the hostages."

She listened. The smashing and grinding continued.

"Human shields? Fine. I'll tell Potts. Not hostages; human shields. Media calls?" She looked at Potts. "No. No calls. Yes, we'll refer them to the embassy."

Vanna, barefoot and shiny with sweat, paced the vault.

~ ~ ~

On the fifteenth floor scores of onlookers surrounded Crow's Nest. *The crowd pushed for a view of the battleground.* Crow's Nest *was unable to communicate with* Lions Den. *The National Guard had mustered outside the gate.*

The gate opened. An armored vehicle drove on. The Kingdom's soldiers marched behind the armored vehicle advancing slowly toward the front. A second vehicle drove on, then the pick-up mounted with the .30 millimeter FAL. Fifty national guardsmen advanced against the Lions.

The Lions circled the hostages and stood inside the circle. The armored vehicle came around the chancery, troops marching behind. The attackers opened fire.

The troops returned fire. Hostages fell. All the hostages dropped to the ground, some wounded, some dead, some paralyzed with fear. The attackers returned fire until one by one they fell to the ground.

~ ~ ~

Two short rings, one long, one short. No Lips cracked the hatch and put his pistol to the opening. He peered out behind the barrel, then opened the hatch. Mutton and Decker entered.

"We can keep it open. Chancery's secure."

"And outside?"

"Ghani's men are sweeping."

No Lips waited for more.

"Nine dead. Nine of ours, confirmed. Four of theirs. One attacker still alive."

"Who?" Vanna asked.

"Ours?"

"Yes, ours," Vanna said. "Our dead."

"I don't have all the names," Mutton said. He knew at least some of the names. "I don't have confirmation. I'm going to sweep." He ordered them to remain on the secure side. "The entire building is cleared. The local staff on the other side are safe. We're sweeping the compound. Nobody is to open the chancery door without my say-so."

Clements turned on his phone and saw that he had several missed calls and a text from al Bafarti's expediter expressing concern for his safety.

Chapter 27

Fluorescent tubes flickered in the half-lit corridors. Neat piles of debris, pyramids of dust and glass, dotted the carpet. Soot blackened the glass on the ballistic doors. Bullet holes pocked exterior cinderblocks. Wires dangled from the disabled sirens high up on the walls.

Outside, blackened earth and moldering embers marked the ruined Marine house. A single concrete wall stood amid the smoking debris. A black Crown Vic, riddled with bullet holes and yawning with a stove windshield, crouched in the dust on flattened tires. Dark crimson puddles stained the sand and walkways and grass.

A new American flag drooped in the hot, still air toward the earth.

The pyramids of dust and glass slowly disappeared into the large plastic receptacles brought in for the cleanup. Giant sealed containers were hauled out of the vault on the shoulders of anonymous Americans and loaded onto trucks under escort before being loaded onto cargo planes and flown out of the Kingdom. The fluorescent strobe effect continued along the corridors. Local employees not lying on hospital beds or morgue drawers departed the Kingdom on emergency leave.

A detachment of 50 Fleet Anti-Terrorism Security Marines established concertina wire perimeters around the compound. Their helmets and goggles peaked above sand bags. Large-bore weapons were hitched to black tripods standing like alien spiders on the dust. The Marine Security Guard house continued to smolder and smoke.

Each dusk and dawn the new flag was lowered and raised accompanied by the city's *Muezzin* and the raucous cawing of giant, wheeling crows. The crows filled the dusk in a busy, wheeling stir. Cautwauler's poison had destroyed the flocks only to make room for more. Where once there had been hundreds, they now numbered thousands.

The consulate remained closed to the public. The place was dead still. The Ambassador arrived from the capital to inspect the damage.

Mutton led a small group out the rear hatch where Decker sweated in his full body armor, seated and leaning forward on his rifle. In daylight's glare outside the hatch Mutton showed the Ambassador where the lead and cinderblock were scarred and pocked. "The attackers fired on the Marines as they ran to the chancery. Unarmed, across open ground, under fire." The Ambassador took a close look at the pocked cement. "Act of complete heroism," Mutton said.

The Ambassador nodded.

Mutton took the wheel of the golf cart; the Ambassador rode in the passenger seat; Vanna rode backwards with the Ambassador's armed guard. Clements and Storp followed in the GSO cart to Bravo gate.

Mutton said: "What we know from Commander Ghani is this. The attackers waited in the hospital lot across the street. When they saw our vehicle – " Mutton indicated the black Ford squatting on the dirt, doors bent, windshield smashed, windows spider-webbed, body ventilated with bullet holes " – they tailed it to the gate. The Delta barrier kept them from driving on. The attackers jumped out and ran through the gate on foot. Fortunately, they dropped two duffels in the process."

The Ambassador nodded grimly, pulling at the soft, loose flesh beneath his chin. "Who was in our car?" he asked.

"One passenger, one driver."

"What happened to them?"

"The attackers fired on the vehicle and ran past. The Ford was trapped here by the drop arm." Mutton pointed to the mangled iron bar. "Driver rammed it. Both exited the vehicle. The passenger made his way to the work shed and hid in a closet. The driver wasn't so lucky. Shot in the back, the neck. He's in critical condition."

Critical condition meant lying with his entire upper body in a cast, both arms broken and encased in plaster, hugging the air before him. The Ambassador looked sidelong at Vanna, who wiped the sweat from her brow with a handkerchief.

"What were the Kingdom's forces doing?"

"Not pretty. The gunner on the technical ducked behind his lead plate; a second guardsman ran to the truck and smashed the headlights with his rifle; the others dropped their weapons and ran from the fight. Ghani hasn't told me all this. But our cameras picked it up. Our local force did better: one ran unarmed out to the street, grabbed an abandoned rifle, and tried to get back on compound. But the gate had closed before he could enter."

"What was in the duffels?"

"Heavy explosives. Flex-cuffs and rope. Razors. Video cameras."

"Publicized hostage situation." The Ambassador sucked his teeth. He looked more closely at Vanna. "So that's how they got in. Then what?"

"The attackers split up. Two this way, around the back; three toward the front; all the time firing on our guards. Local guard force discharged 20 rounds. The attackers made their first kill right here, firing on that guard tower. Killed the guard instantly."

They climbed back onto the cart and drove toward motor pool, stopping outside the dispatch office. Mutton said, "They haven't finished cleaning. Sure you want to go in?"

"The drivers are inside?"

"We're setting up a dispatch inside the chancery," Vanna interjected.

"But the drivers are still in there?"

They entered the building. The floor was stained pink in wide outlines, the white tiles sticky. Half a dozen drivers sprawled on low sofas, exhausted, leaning back into the deep, soft cushions. The Ambassador greeted each of them individually, shaking their hands, looking into their eyes. The thick stink of blood drove the group outside, their shoes tacking against the floor as they lifted their feet.

"Get them out of there," the Ambassador ordered Vanna.

Vanna waved to Storp who radioed Porcas about the temporary dispatch.

"Get them out of there *now*," the Ambassador ordered.

Mutton drove to the flagpole outside the chancery. "One attacker spent seven minutes lowering the flag. Once it was down he set it on fire, ran it back up. We think it was a signal to additional attackers, perhaps watching from the hospital. Meanwhile the others rounded up local staff from our outside offices and led them at gunpoint to the lawn over there."

The Ambassador looked up at the flag drooping atop the pole. A gardener in green coveralls was hosing down the path leading from the flagpole. The Ambassador waved grimly at the gardener, who lifted his hand and continued to spray water on the path. Clements passed, nearly stepping on some pale, greyish debris. He looked closer and nearly vomited.

"Another of our local guards climbed down from his tower and engaged the attackers here," Mutton said. "He was shot in the head."

They continued toward the chancery entrance. The façade and doors were pocked and scarred, black corrosion where the IEDs exploded against the doors. "The doors held," Mutton said. "Post One fired tear gas from the vents up there, but it was ineffective."

"Why?"

"Old. It's a weak version to begin with. But the canisters had expired."

The Ambassador rubbed his shiny forehead. "Will the doors hold?"

Vanna said, "They're chained shut from the inside."

"Are they secure?"

Sensing that she was about to lose control of her compound Vanna said, "The glass isn't damaged. The doors held."

"I am asking if they are secure." The Ambassador spoke in measured irritation.

"Yes," Vanna said.

The Ambassador held his hands at his hips, flaring out the ends of his dark wool suit coat. He pursed his lips and nodded slowly as he took in the scene. He looked at Vanna, taking her in as if she were a part of the scene. "Well," he said.

"Sir," Mutton continued. "One of the attackers came around the western side of the compound, firing into the chancery. Several bullets pierced our windows; shot up lights, a television, furniture; our return fire drove them back."

The tour continued north of the chancery. "Marine house," Mutton said. "Went up like a tinderbox. Attackers tossed grenades and IEDs through the windows. They went directly to it. They knew exactly what they wanted to hit. The cook, trapped in the kitchen, burned alive."

Mutton pointed toward the heights of the Kingdom Hospital. "I suspect they surveilled us from there. Have been. Ghani agrees. They knew who was entering what building at what time of day. I can't figure why they attacked when they did." Mutton drove his toe against the earth. "If they had attacked an hour later, most of us would have been at the snack bar. They could've entered that building in seconds, or destroyed it as simply as they destroyed this one."

The Ambassador shook his head. He continued pulling on the loose flesh beneath his jaw. Vanna refused to meet his eyes.

"Where was the National Guard at this point?"

"Ghani was waiting for clearance from Interior to enter the compound." Mutton drove to the patch of lawn under the fichus where the final showdown took place. "That's what he's telling us. When MOI finally cleared them, Ghani's men and reinforcements engaged the attackers here. They killed three, wounded two. One of them died at the hospital. They still have one in custody. This is where we took the majority of our casualties."

"Ed Kahn. He was killed here?"

"Yes, sir. And eight others. Two dozen wounded."

Between mandatory psyche-evaluations with Nurse and mandatory crisis management exercises with a team from DC, Mutton made security arrangements for the Ambassador's press conference and helped the local staff prepare a memorial service for fallen colleagues. He was grateful for anything that kept him from writing up reports about the attack. The consulate remained closed to the public, greatly diminishing the daily threat of visa applicants accessing the compound.

"Just when I need threats the most."

"Why is that, dear?" asked Nurse.

"It's a form of therapy."

Nurse laughed until tears rolled down her cheeks and

Mutton realized she was crying.

"Are you ok?" Mutton asked.

Nurse blew her nose and wiped her eyes.

Mutton's sessions with Nurse were very good for her. She wasn't coping well at all with the absence of Dr. Meddler, who'd been flown out on the first chopper as a danger to both himself and the staff.

"Are you recommending anyone else for psyche-evac?"

"You know I can't talk about other patients."

"I just thought you might need to talk."

"Thank you, dear. You'll be glad to know that Belvedere seems to be cracking."

"That's not news."

Nurse wiped her eyes. "It's hard, visiting wounded staff."

Mutton nodded.

"I just need to pour my heart out to someone."

"I understand. You have a lot of hospital visits to make."

"Remember. If you need to talk to anyone about your feelings, I'm here."

"I don't need to talk about my feelings."

"I find these sessions tremendously helpful," Nurse said. "They cleanse my soul."

"Is that why I'm here?"

"No, dear. I'm here for you. Now run along. We have crisis management to attend." The Crisis Management Team had flown in to coach the staff on how to react to a crisis.

"We're here to help you cope with a crisis," the team leader said.

"All of us just did cope with a crisis," said Pudge.

"And we'd like to learn from that. But first, I have a list of scenarios to run through."

"How about a scenario where a U.S. consulate is

attacked?" asked Liston.

"By five heavily armed extremists," said Specs.

"You just had that scenario."

"So let's learn from it," said Pudge. "What happens next time there's such an attack?"

"That's the purpose of this. To prevent the next time."

"I have some ideas on preventing the next one," Mutton said.

The team leader looked at Mutton, puzzled. "But I thought you failed to prevent this one," he said.

Mutton found slightly more closure in the press conference. The event was held in an ornate, gold-gilt room at the luxury hotel reserved for guests of the Royal Family. The place swarmed with security hours before the Ambassador showed up in the Coup deVille Vanna no longer enjoyed the privilege of calling her own, and the room was packed with journalists searching for evidence of the front line of the war on terror. Ambassador Glyder sat beside Vanna at a table on a dais and gave a summation of events in dead monotone.

"What this attack reminds us," the Ambassador concluded, growing lively now that he'd reached his salient talking point, "is the need for international support in the war on terror. A coalition is defeating the terrorists in Iraq so they won't export terror to neighboring countries and the rest of the world. And the United States will hunt down the terrorists, smoke them out, and kill them all. An attack like this can happen at any time, in any place. And with that, I'll take your questions."

The BBC correspondent rose amid the packed house and stepped up to the mic.

"How do you, how does the U.S., react to the death of an American citizen on your own heavily guarded compound? I mean, this comes at a time when you were supposedly on high alert, and had already implemented significant security measures. So what I'd like to know is, where does the U.S. go from here in terms of ensuring the security of its officials – and for that matter private citizens – living overseas while the country pursues a policy that makes them all targets."

"Thank you," said the Ambassador. "Our sympathies today are with the families of all the employees we lost, including Mohamed Amr Khan. What this attack reminds us of is the need for international support to defeat the terrorists in Iraq so they can't export terror to the rest of the world. And we will hunt down, smoke out, and kill all the terrorists in the war on terror."

A reporter from Sky News asked, "Do you blame the government of Saudi Arabia in any way? Are you holding them accountable for the deaths? Are you investigating why it took so long for their forces to engage the attackers?"

"The events of this past week are under investigation and it would be inappropriate for me to comment beyond reminding the media that Saudi Arabia is our ally in the war on terror. This attack points out the need for the international community to support our allies and defeat the terrorists in Iraq. We are hunting down and smoking out and killing all the terrorists in the war on terror."

"Sir, a question on Afghanistan," said the reporter from AP.

"Before you go on, let me just say that this attack reminds us of the need for international support to defeat the terrorists in Iraq so they can't export terror to the rest of the world, especially to Afghanistan."

Only when the CNN reporter asked for a quote specifically from the Consul General did the Ambassador look sideways to Vanna and give way for her to speak. Shiny with sweat in the bright hot press lights, Vanna asked him to repeat the question.

"Can you recount for us what was going through your mind during the attack? You were under attack for five hours. The consulate was upgrading security features. I wonder if this attack could have been avoided if those upgrades had been completed? Does the need for upgrades suggest a lack of confidence in the Kingdom's security?"

Vanna's sweat-shining face answered cool and poised, expressing complete confidence in the protection provided by her government and by the government of Saudi Arabia. "What was I thinking during the attack? Honestly, I don't remember. But I do remember thinking that America needs the international community to come together in Iraq to defeat terrorism there. Only then can the rest of the world be made safe from terrorists."

~ ~ ~

But closure really began for Mutton when the staff held a service for their fallen colleagues. They invited an Imam to invoke the Koran, and a minister to recite the gospel. The surviving staff turned up at an agreed-upon time, paused for a moment of silence, and dedicated nine plaques commemorating the names and birthdates of their fallen colleagues. The plaques were embedded in the earth on the elliptical patch of front lawn. A royal palm was planted beside each plaque to provide perpetual shade. For the first time in his adult life Mutton felt his eyes burn and fill with water until he let the tears roll. When it was over he wiped his eyes with the back of his sleeve.

Chapter 28

An exodus of travelers seeking flights out of the Kingdom immediately descended on the travel office. Washington had authorized an extra R&R and nobody wanted to miss out. The men from the office that wasn't there fled to Monte Carlo and Singapore and Pudge went to Paris to find an apartment. Belvedere, on psyche-evac in Washington, lobbied hard for the extra R&R, but the Office of Retirement and Planning where he'd been employed refused. The Porcases went to the Philippines, DB took notes at a conference in London, and Vanna, fearing the worst for her Fourth of July party, was incommunicado on a Caribbean cruise. Potts, who'd taken a civilian position with the Defense Department and was headed to Iraq, was packing up for good. Mutton went to see him off and found him in high spirits.

"I was tired of working in war zone conditions without war zone pay," Potts said.

"In the war on terror, the whole world's a war zone."

"Precisely. And some war zones pay better than others."

"You aren't in it for the money. You're a patriot."

"You're right," Potts admitted. "But DOD provides better job security. More wars. More work for me. And the military has marching bands. I'm tired of these tin can reception CDs. Military also has good flags."

"Let's hope the flag waves over a democratic Iraq."

"First they'll need a government. We should have decades of good, honest work winning the hearts and minds of Iraq."

Clements alone staffed the consular section, open only

for emergency services to American Citizens. It remained closed to visa applicants and terrorists. GLASSCOCK took charge of the office that wasn't there, propping his feet on No Lips' desk and appropriating his scotch. In Vanna's absence Storp designated himself Acting CG, and to prove his omnipotence carried around a stack of paper three times the size of the old one. Pervis had no reason to report to work, but Storp didn't bother telling her this so she came anyway, inflaming her sciatica on uncomfortable furniture because Cautwauler had gone to Iraq without delivering the ergonomic stuff. Tinker, who continued forging cables, began sending photographs of himself to *Time* in hopes they would publish something about his heroism, which he'd demonstrated by surviving an attack quivering beneath his desk. Mutton stayed on point because there wasn't a security officer in the service willing to relieve him of his duties, not even temporarily. Nobody believed the worst was over.

The most difficult part of the day was getting to and from the consulate. The large white van stopped at each compound to pick up each officer unlucky enough not to be on R&R. Nobody in the van felt much like talking. Kippinger and GLASSCOCK groaned with hangovers while Pervis groaned with sciatica; Storp read from his triple stack of paper while Tinker flipped through ancient magazines; Mutton escorted the van in his own armored '77 Caprice: there was no way he was getting into the death trap of a shuttle. But the shuttle had to run, because there was work to do even with the consulate closed, work like attending to American citizens who continued to die in the Kingdom.

As the officer in charge of American Citizens Services during Pudge's absence, Clements was responsible for handling death and repatriation cases, such as the death of the American airport prisoner, classified a suicide by the

Kingdom's authorities.

The Zionist spy has taken his own life rather than submit to the laws of Saudi Arabia, the Sharia Court announced.

Conklin's remains were dumped in the non-Muslim cemetery outside town, where cats and crows and other beasts stalked the dust. Upon verifying the death Clements noted Conklin's significant weight loss, his sunken eyes, his beard grown full and laced with grey. The corpse brought to mind the fanatics and zealots whose visas Clements had refused in window number seven, and the men in orange jumpsuits squatting in cages at Guantanamo Bay.

Mutton took leave, eventually, because he had to. Nobody would have understood had he chosen to stay behind. But service on the front line in the war on terror had produced in him a craving for misery and pain, an agony not unlike the long, weeping remorse that led to his divorce and his desire to sniff the feet of Vanna Lavinia. He couldn't bear the thought of an ordinary day, of falling asleep without his crackling radio, of an hour at the office without crawling beneath his desk while sirens screamed overhead. He wanted to be there the minute the consulate re-opened. He looked up at the Kingdom Hospital and shook his fist in defiance: face-to-face with his destiny, Mutton shouted aloud for salvation by RPG. But salvation never came; instead Mutton booked a ticket to Vegas.

During his ascent out of the Kingdom he saw how dark the country was: a breathtaking darkness just shy of infinite. The bright cluster of city lights ended abruptly, surrounded by a desert of black into which he had no hope of seeing. For all the wealth it generated, the Kingdom remained a vast, unanswered space. In this empty quarter the perpetrators of 9/11 had been swaddled and raised, trained to believe, trained not to think. Nothing could enlighten this place. The generations of hearts and minds that stewed under the scorching sun of this desert shared no communion with civilization. They belonged to themselves. They belonged to a version of Islam incompatible with today. They belonged to the 7th century.

Twenty-four hours later Mutton sailed above the great American Homeland. He saw a similar blackness: a swath of America that was wasteland, emptiness producing ignorance, excess producing an unchecked will to consume and destroy. A desert. The two worlds, polar opposites, had come to the same end. Religious zealotry. Bigoted xenophobia. Ignorance. Bloodlust. Had Mutton's flight arrived in New York, approaching the cavities on its skyline, he might have felt only rage against the Kingdom. But he connected in Detroit and as he took the final descent through the abundant desert darkness toward the unholy light of Vegas, Mutton was driven toward understanding and recognition of the human frailty of both nations.

Mutton felt no impulse to gamble. He wanted only to feel the energy of the streets, the buzzing neon, the noisy crowds filling the strip. He enjoyed the freedom to wander. He watched the tourists, the dreamers, the cowboys, the conventioneers, the foreigners, the Americans, all of them looking for the same thing: a good time, fulfillment of dreams, a chance at quick and easy wealth. The Promised Land.

Mutton thought of all the hopeful young men standing before Clements and Pudge, citizens of so many places, from all over the world, each of them hoping to see America. This was the America they wanted. The America of excess, of movies, of dreams. The land of the free. The home of the brave. Where all men are created equal. Mutton thought of Clements and the other JOs in consular, deniers of so many dreams.

The war on terror had warped them as it warped everyone. Even the bearded zealots with the wild eyes and hatred of America had wanted a version of the Dream: hadn't the 9/11 hijackers visited Vegas? What had driven them to perversion? It was not Islam. They hadn't even worn beards!

Each night Mutton sat alone among the pimps and Johns, the hookers and pervs, the cops and bouncers and criminals and thugs. The winners and losers. The ordinary, the eccentric, the lucky, the rich, and the broken. He kept his eyes on the television but no explanation came. More depressing for Mutton was to see the bar flies turn their backs to the television. They shrugged and knocked back their beer and filled their plates from the endless buffet. They gloated about gains in the DJI and the NASDAQ. What could they do? Terror would visit them, too. Sooner or later terror would visit them all.

Caught between heaven and hell in the city of earthly delights Mutton eventually came upon the Devil Himself. Amid the hypnotic jangle of winning and losing that filled the Mirage Casino, where Mutton finally caved to temptation and visited the tables to see what fate had in store, he recognized the small, brown figure of his nemesis. Sheikh al Bafarti stood among a dozen other well-dressed, immaculately groomed citizens of the Kingdom, his mustache and beard neatly trimmed, his eyebrows, nearly one, clean and straight over his distinctive, arching nose, his dark eyes small and bright, twinkling merrily and reflecting the million brilliant lights that flashed on hundreds of slot machines around him. Appearing there on the gaming floor, Sheikh al Bafarti was an apparition, a ghost, a remnant of some remote but vital part of Mutton's composition, an Old Testament character, a Nursery Rhyme figure alive and in the flesh.

"My dear Mr. Mutton!" the Sheikh said. He wore an expensive suit, a cream-colored Stetson, and black cowboy boots. He betrayed no surprise or amazement at finding Mutton beside him. Indeed, the sheikh seemed to be expecting him.

"*Massa al H'air.*"

"Good evening? That's all you have for me? After I've traveled so many miles to visit your Homeland?" The sheikh abandoned his formal reserve and wrapped his arms around Mutton. He smelled of cologne – not the woody scent of Arabia Mutton expected, but the soft, fruity aroma of some Western cologne.

"I guess I should congratulate you on receiving a visa. But isn't the consulate closed?"

"I have friends, Mr. Mutton. Our dear Consul General was helpful, of course. But, well- One need not dwell on it here." The clamor of the slots, of money lost and won, of wild fantasies conceived and fulfilled, crashed all around them.

"Aren't you expected in Crawford?"

"Next week."

"So you're tempting fate in the City of Sin."

"Ah, but for a Muslim, this isn't sin. What happens outside the Kingdom, stays outside the Kingdom. We control temptation in the Kingdom. But here in America, temptation is everywhere. I cannot help my impulses. If it is vice that Allah provides, it is vice I will enjoy." Al Bafarti gave a crude smile and pumped Mutton's biceps. "I come here to meet temptation."

"I thought you were coming as a philanthropist."

"In time, Mr. Mutton. Next week. During the Crown Prince's visit to Crawford. But please, join us! Join our entourage as my guest. Vanna, too, will be there."

"Thank you, I cannot."

"You will meet the Crown Prince."

"No," Mutton said, feeling the word in his heart. "I'm returning to the Kingdom."

"But the consulate is closed."

"There is work to do. I still have lives to protect, after all. You know we lost many lives in the attack."

Al Bafarti lay a hand on Mutton's shoulder and looked into his eyes. "Mr. Mutton, please accept my deepest sympathy for what happened to your colleagues. It is a terrible, terrible tragedy."

Mutton shivered. A nod would have been more appropriate.

"You really cannot join us in Crawford?"

"I cannot."

"Then I should tell you now."

"Tell me what?"

"My little secret. What it is I am here to do. Why I must bring the Kingdom Exploding Group to America."

Mutton looked the Devil in the eyes and waited for him to spill his plot, to expose his network of terror finance, a reckless, wild confession on the night before his forces attacked again, when it was far too late to stop them.

"A hospital."

"A hospital?"

"Yes. A hospital. Eventually, many hospitals."

"But the U.S. has many ... Why ...?"

"In honor of my father. He migrated to the Kingdom from Yemen."

"Walked the entire way," Mutton said. "I know his story."

"His generation did a lot of walking. So many came from Yemen. My father built the Kingdom Exploding Group from the ground. His signature building, the Kingdom Hospital."

The slots jangled in Mutton's ears as fully as the duck and cover alarm ever had.

"Do you believe, he never made money? The financial advantage in hospitals lies in upkeep and equipment. Not construction. When I took over I saw right away the profits were in roads and bridges. So I focused on building roads. The Kingdom Exploding Group unified the peninsula even more than the Royal Family."

Mutton let the jangling of winning and losing fill his ears.

"Watch next week. Our visit with your president – we will make a rather large announcement. But now, for fun! To the tables!!" And with that, Bafarti left him. He disappeared among the crowds, as if he'd never conjured himself forth, never squeezed Mutton's biceps at all.

Mutton no longer felt like playing. There would be no merriment in the roll of the dice. Armageddon was on its way. Doomed, Mutton turned from The Mirage and found a place to sit alone, in the bar once more, drinking frosty green Heineken, his eyes glued to FOX.

~ ~ ~

He returned feeling worse than when he'd left. With the consulate closed there was little to do. In the snack bar the staff gathered around the large screen television tuned to FOX. Clements had introduced Heineken to the lunch menu and Mutton drank for its therapeutic nature. Besides, FARSA had been disbanded and had stock to move. Over a round of green bottles Clements, Thorner, Mutton, Liston, Buzz, and Specs sat, shoulders hunched, watching the coverage of the Crown Prince's visit to Crawford.

This will be the first meeting of the two leaders since 9/11, the waxy male anchor told the waxy female anchor, enthusiastically interpreting what the cameras plainly showed.

What makes this visit so special, said the waxy female, *is the chance to ease tensions between the U.S. and the Kingdom.*

Relations have been tense since 2001. But today, we are told, the leaders will announce a renewed agreement of continued cooperation in the war on terror.

FOX cut to live coverage of the Crown Prince's arrival. Dozens of large black Suburbans and Navigators and Escalades drove past the cameras. The president stepped toward the lead vehicle and greeted the Crown Prince with a hug, followed by the awkward bowing and scraping, hugs and pats on the back between the leaders and the coterie.

"Woaahh," said Pudge. "Did the president just kiss his hand?"

"At least he followed up with a bear hug," said Clements. "Rrrrr."

Simon brought a tray of Heineken. On TV the two leaders drove off together in a golf cart. The footage then jumped ahead to a press event following the talks, both leaders driving up to the assembled press. The president, flanked by the Vice President, the secretary of state, and secretary of defense, opened the press conference with an aw-shucks and snappy remarks. Then he got down to business.

"Crownie – you don't mind if I call you Crownie, do ya?"

The Crown Prince was gracious enough to smile.

"As a token of my affection and personal gratitude, I offer you this gift. This Texas-sized memento of my affection. I hope you'll wear it with pride."

"What could that be?" Pudge asked.

"I don't know," said Buzz. "But I want to see what's under that shroud on the table. Are they unveiling a skyscraper?"

"Too small to be a Stetson," said Pudge.

"Not cowboy boots," said Liston.

The president urged the Crown Prince to open the small box. "Is that a belt buckle?!"

Clements asked.

"A Texas-shaped belt buckle!" Pudge confirmed.

"He doesn't even wear pants," said Clements.

The president put his arm around the Crown Prince and pulled him close.

"Crownie, I want to thank you for visiting my ranch here in Crawford. It's not the first time I've welcomed the Kingdom's royalty to my home, and I hope it won't be the last."

The president proceeded to address the cameras directly.

"The Crown Prince and I had fruitful discussions," he told the world. "We reached an important agreement that will provide a blanket of oil security for America. As a leading contributor to OPEC, the Crown Prince's concession to increase production will mean a lot to ordinary Americans."

Through a translator the Crown Prince thanked his host, but while the president smiled and guffawed good-naturedly for the cameras and winked at the Vice President, the Crown Prince reiterated his dismay at American policy toward the Middle East and the long-suffering Muslims of Palestine. "Now the people of the Middle East," said the translator, "will choose what is right for the people of the Middle East."

The winking, nodding, president grinned at the comment, which he heard as praise.

"Something tells me that's not all he said," said Clements.

"That's why I love watching FOX," said Pudge. "I

prefer simplifications."

The president held his finger to his ear, then laughed. "Crownie? Thank you, Crownie. And this is why we are such good friends. We can agree on everything from oil to democracy." He looked back at the Vice President again, nodded and smiled.

"Mr. President," the Crown Prince said, this time eschewing the translator and using English himself, "I too have a gift for you."

The president shucked his head.

"I thank you for our longstanding friendship. As a demonstration of my sincerity, I would like to present a sign of my government's commitment to our mutual security. With us is my dear friend, Sheikh Mohammed ibn Abbas al Bafarti, Chairman of the Kingdom Exploding Group. Next week, he will break ground on his inaugural project in the United States: a 40-story hospital overlooking downtown Houston." The Crown Prince paused to let a footman pull the shroud off a scale architectural model of the building and landscape. When the applause softened, the Crown Prince continued: "Mr. President, it is an honor to name the hospital after our great friendship: the George W. Bush Cardiac Care and Trauma Recovery and Center."

"Crownie," said a tearful president, "from the bottom of my heart and on behalf of the entire United States, I thank you." He looked over his shoulder at the scowling Vice President, winked, smiled, and bobbed his head.

Chapter 29

The Office of the Inspector General determined there was only one fate for the consulate: close it down. Sell the property. Move the staff to onward assignments.

"But not before I'm gone," Vanna said. "I need help packing up."

"I thought your people would do that for you," Storp said.

"You are my people. You are all my people."

The Ambassador-to-Be froze them in place. Even those who'd packed out and checked out and flipped out were made to stay and plan her final farewell. Ambassador-to-Be Vanna Lavinia had decided not to host a Fourth of July celebration, after all.

"I want a Farewell instead," she told Storp. "And make sure the entire Omani mission is invited. My new friends."

Belvedere was brought back from his assignment in the retirement office, and Pervis would have to wait to fill a position doodling in her steno book for the crazed Ambassador in Ouagadougou. Tinker couldn't yet start his dream job as Ambassador's Special Staffer for the bureau of Near East Affairs, where he hoped to impress lots of cute interns with his Brooks Brothers suits and secret Foreign Service ties. The other Pierce had driven up his personal services value in a bidding war between the royal family, the Russian mafia, and certain covert operators from Langley who'd arrived in the Kingdom as talent scouts, but he too was frozen in place behind doors behind doors behind doors. Only Pudge had escaped, starting his job in Paris, where he'd figured out the quickest route to an ambassadorship was in dating the Ambassador's daughter.

Mutton's constant harping about security and his reputation for inciting fear got him assigned to Fourth Branch, where the leadership saw political gold in having somebody on staff with first-hand experience creating terror. Vanna gave Mutton the news herself.

"All your badgering about security has paid off, Mr. Mutton. Your record of fear-mongering here has come to the attention of Fourth Branch. I recommended you for the position myself, when I met the Vice President."

"What will I be doing for Fourth Branch?"

"Same as you did here. Promoting international terrorism."

"You mean *preventing* international terrorism?"

"Mr. Mutton. As far as the Administration is concerned, the prevention of terrorism can best be realized following a significant increase in terrorism. You'll be there for the latter."

The men in Liston's shop were in no hurry to begin their onward assignments. The only constant in their lives was the evolution of their high-tech equipment, which in this case had been destroyed with sledgehammers, grinders, and acid, and flown out still smoking and crackling on C-130s. The team would be dispersed to Afghanistan, Pakistan, and Dubai, where some exciting new technology awaited for their eavesdropping on Tehran and other members of the Axis of Evil.

When he learned he would be sent to Afghanistan, Thorner grumbled about wanting Iraq, which was where GLASSCOCK was headed as a reward for fomenting instability in the Kingdom. And the death of DOPEY had strengthened No Lips' reputation as a vapors man, getting him re-assigned to an undisclosed location administering poisons to the permanently damaged inmates at Gitmo.

"Torture?" asked No Lips. "I thought we didn't do that."

"Advanced interrogation," Trumpeter called it. "For subjects who've outlived their usefulness."

Storp was given the responsibility of closing the consulate according to the FAM and the nine-inch stack of papers he carried. He commanded the consulate as Acting CG, since there was no way Vanna would serve as a lowly consul general now that she was Ambassador-to-Be. Storp started with the backlog of unread cables in the front office Moslers. They contained warnings from Mutton, talking points for the president, derogatory information on Sheikh al Bafarti, and the minutes of dozens and dozens of Vanna's meetings. Under his personal supervision Storp had the cleaning crew load the piles into brown paper bags and haul them to the incinerator, where the angry black smoke drove the swarming crows from the trees.

Storp next supervised the closure of the office that wasn't there, which meant the destruction of crates and crates of booze and porn and shrink-wrapped pallets of twenty-dollar bills. To shut down FARSA Storp consulted with Clements regarding the booze, the boat, the property at the Crown Prince Resort, and a significant amount of liquidity in the bank.

"Put it into real estate," Storp ordered. "Grow it for when State reopens this place. The Royal Family is already complaining about having to travel to the capital for visas, so you know this is only temporary. And speaking of complaints. The CG- I mean the Ambassador-to-Be, is deeply upset that FARSA never built a Rec Center. She really wanted a building named after her. This won't be good for your career."

Clements shrugged. He figured he'd already survived the worst thing that could happen to him in the Foreign Service. Career ambivalence had a salutary effect on his health, integrity, and self-esteem. The only problem was that he'd have to enjoy his health, integrity, and self-esteem at the worst post in the entire Foreign Service, for he was headed to Njamena.

"Vanna does have a permanent legacy here," Clements said.

"What?" asked Storp.

"The nine plaques commemorating our fallen colleagues."

~ ~ ~

It was Larry Porcas, in his orange suspenders, black leather vest, and white beard, who came up with the idea of a Harley-Davidson theme for the farewell party. So far-fetched was the idea that it loosened the knot of hot tension that gripped the conference room, where mold crept thick and fast up the walls. Even before Vanna entered the windowless room and took up her seat at the head of the table, the officers had been bickering about the mold.

"Look at it!" Mutton said. "Do you have any idea what the Bible says about mildew!? Can't the GSO do something to kill it?"

Storp said, "We have no GSO. He's in Iraq, and the Acting GSO – "

Storp stopped himself. Even he knew it was poor taste to blame administrative inadequacies on a dead man.

"Is it not a health risk?" Belvedere suggested, looking to improve his chances of another medical evacuation.

"Leviticus 14:33-42," said Mutton. "I tell you, it's all in the Bible."

Storp said, "To register it as a health risk, we have to get Nurse to write it up."

"Has anybody seen her?"

"She's on leave."

"Right after the passage about cleansing infectious diseases from the skin," Mutton said. "Open sores. Oozing pus and fluids. *The house must be vacated and closed up for seven days."*

"Can't the Regional Psyche folks do it? Crisis management?"

"They work for admin. A work order from them would constitute a service to a service. We need another section to initiate the request."

"The Bible says, *If the mildew has spread, then the priest must tear out the stones and scrape all the walls.*"

"Service to a service? What does that mean?"

"It doesn't mean anything," said Potts. "That's why it can't be done."

Belvedere said, "I'm initiating the request. And while I'm at it, I'm initiating a request for medical evacuation."

"*If the mildew continues to reappear, then it is a destructive mildew, and the house is unclean, and must be torn down. Anyone who goes in that house is also unclean.*"

"In writing."

Belvedere tore a page from his steno book, scratched a few words and slid it down to Storp at the foot of the table.

"E-mail," Storp said.

"We're going to need to purify this house," Mutton said. "You people need to read the Bible. Listen: *To purify the house we must take two birds and some cedar wood, scarlet yarn and hyssop. Kill one of the birds over fresh water in a clay pot. Dip the cedar wood, the hyssop, the scarlet yarn, and the live bird, and dip them into the blood of the dead bird and the fresh water, and sprinkle the house seven times!*"

"I can taste the mildew!"

"Hey," said Potts, "the mold is actually all the greens I get in a week."

The bickering stopped when the door opened and Pervis poked her head in. "Everybody here?" she asked. Without waiting for an answer she entered and shut the door quickly, ensuring nobody escaped.

A moment later Vanna entered through a second door in the gypsum wall. She whisked to her chair at the head of the table and placed her forearms on the dark wood, then sat up straight and surveyed the room from as high as possible. A wide smile slid across her face. "Everybody? *Why* are you so *gloomy*?"

Mutton couldn't take his eyes off her. Neither could anyone else. She'd come back from her cruise with a deep bronze tan. Mutton kept seeing glimpses of the pretty pink toenail polish that had driven him crazy, peeking through the seductive hole in the front of her shoes. How he'd missed the sight and the smell of her shoes! He considered dropping his stub of pencil for an excuse to bend over and steal a whiff along the way. How many more opportunities would he have? But he banished the craven thoughts when Potts spoke up with a challenge in his throat.

"We're gloomy because of the party. With the consulate looking the way it does, frankly, we should not even consider a party – "

Vanna cut him off. "It's too late for that, Mr. Potts. We're having a party." She parted her lips and traced her finger dreamily along the table. "My Farewell. How do we celebrate? I want to hear suggestions about the shared cultural values between the United States and the Kingdom. Mr. Storp?"

Storp tapped his stack and said hopefully, "How about a Texas-themed barbecue?"

"We are *not* doing Texas."

Storp scratched "Texas" from his list. "Volunteerism? To highlight the work of charity organizations."

No Lips shook his head. "Too many of the Kingdom's charities are fronts for terrorist financing."

"All charities can't be bad," said Vanna. "What about the ladies who participated in my fashion show?"

"We can't highlight a fashion show without photographs," Potts said. He remembered the abuse Vanna had heaped upon him when her female guests complained about being photographed.

"Point taken," Vanna said. "Aren't there volunteers at the hospital?"

"All women. Same problem with photos and publicity."

The mood grew tense. Every passing second was another second stuck in the airless, mold-infested room, an opportunity for Vanna to snap, to blame, to accuse.

"Pee-pulllll ..." Vanna pleaded, a rare posture for her. "Helloooo? I would think that with a dozen or so of us here we could come up with a theme to show our shared values."

Potts said, "What about the Chevy Suburbans hauling around the Kingdom's families? American cars, Kingdom families?"

"Inefficient American cars gobbling up the Kingdom's petrol?" Windsock asked.

"The U.S. as a vacation destination," said Storp.

"For terrorists," said Clements.

Vanna reproached him with a glare. "How about Disneyland? We could set up the pool area to look like the Magic Kingdom!"

"That might encourage a lot of our guests to ask about visas," Belvedere said.

Potts said, "Let's look at our histories. The United States was founded by religious fundamentalists. So was the Kingdom."

"Homage to *Jihad*?" suggested No Lips.

Vanna pressed her bright pink fingernails deep into her cheek. Her eyes glowed with malice. Unaware of the impending doom the white-haired, round-bellied information systems manager, dressed in a black leather vest, flannel shirt, and orange suspenders, piped up in an improbably high-pitched voice.

"Ma'am," said Larry Porcas. "I have two words for you."

The burning coals of Vanna's eyes slid slowly across the room. "Mr. Porcas? What are you even doing here?"

"Ma'am. Two words. Harley. Davidson."

"Come again?"

"Harley-Davidson, ma'am."

"Harley-Davidson? Larry, why don't you explain to us what it is you're talking about."

Porcas failed to pick up on Vanna's withering tone. Instead he warmed to his idea. "Picture this." He held up his hands like a movie screen on which to project: "Steppenwolf playing *Born to Be Wild*. Thirty Harleys roar onto the pool deck. The lead bikes flying Old Glory. The bikes go roaring around the pool! The crowd goes – "

"Roaring?" asked Vanna. "It sounds a little *loud*."

"Chrome pipes," said Porcas, eyes popping with delight.

"I don't know what that means," Vanna said.

Porcas nodded. "Big, blasting, loud chrome pipes."

Vanna sat back, arms folded across her chest. She nodded slowly. "Thank you, Larry. Thank you for that ... unusual contribution." She looked around the table at the shocked faces of her team, her glare a challenge for them to contribute something so bold. "I'm not sure we want motorbikes ROARING into my farewell party. Does anybody agree?"

Storp scratched "roaring" from his notes.

Potts whispered to Clements, "How 'bout purring?"

"What was that, Mr. Potts?" Vanna asked. "Was that a suggestion from you?"

"Not a suggestion, ma'am. My suggestion is to not have a theme."

"I thought you had a contribution. Maybe you'd like to share with the rest of us what you just told Mr. Clements."

"I thought the bikes might come "purring" rather than "roaring" into the pool area."

Vanna smiled at Potts' discomfort. "Mr. Storp, please note that the bikes are to be "purring". Mr. Porcas, if we are to proceed with your idea, we'll need more than just the American flag."

"Fly the Kingdom's flag on a second bike."

"We'll need more than just flags to emphasize shared cultural ties between the U.S. and the Kingdom."

"Ma'am." Porcas stood and turned his back to Vanna. The back of his vest was embroidered with the Harley-Davidson bar and shield and large letters above and below the design: "HOG CHAPTER – THE HOLY KINGDOM'S HOLY ROLLERS."

"HOGs," he snarled, victorious. "The Harley-Owners Group. We have a very active chapter here. Over 60 members from the Kingdom, Lebanon, Egypt, the Philippines, Indo. Hell. It's multi-cultural." Porcas stared in open lechery. "Ma'am, if you like you are welcome to sit up on back and ride my hawg."

The team was silent. Only Mutton, a former cop, could suspend his shock long enough to object. "We can't promote an icon of the Hell's Angels and other organized criminals."

"It's a fair point," Vanna said. "Mr. Porcas, are the HOGs involved in community activities? Do they volunteer? Do they do good deeds?"

Porcas stared dumbly.

"Another thing," Storp pointed out. "The Hogs? The pig is not a clean animal in this culture."

Offended, Porcas said, "We're not talking about animals here. We're talking about bikes."

"Not everybody's going to understand that," Storp

said. "They'll think hog. Pork."

"The other white meat," said Potts.

"Deemed by the Prophet to be unclean," No Lips said. "PBUH."

"Unclean!" said Mutton. "Like this place."

"It's not about pork," Porcas said. "It's just pure fun: motorcycles, picnics, rock 'n roll."

"What about the image?" Vanna asked. "Do these HOG friends of yours do any good deeds, or do they just put on 'do rags and ride their bicycles around the city? We need something to counter the negative image that Mr. Mutton has pointed out."

"I can arrange something. Something with the Red Crescent. With the Boy Scouts. Maybe at the Kingdom Hospital next door."

"Get photos," Vanna ordered. "And one other thing. Out of deference to Islam, let's make it FORTY Harleys." She nodded and said, "Forty Harleys come purring into the pool area. I like it. Mr. Storp, please organize a committee to put the plan together."

Chapter 30

The bearded ones returned. The ones with the crazed eyes and wild beards. Clements couldn't see it rationally. In the shroud of fog cast over his judgment by the war on terror, where suspicion and fear superseded evidence and reason, Clements reacted with malice. Where he should have seen a glimmer of hope – if they were terrorists, would they respond to his letter? – Clements preferred to make insinuations that scorched his victims with the knowledge that their visas had been revoked on suspicion of terrorism.

The proud, arched eyebrows collapsed. The clear, black eyes and excited, hopeful looks turned to confusion and sorrow. They did not argue. Their eyes glistened, then fell. The spokesman reached his hand into the slot and felt for their passports as if reaching for unwanted things. The eyes above their beards betrayed hopes dashed, injustice served. The trio slinked away.

Clements saw it immediately, then felt it. He'd let himself down. He'd let America down. He'd handed victory to Terror. "It wasn't good," Clements told Meddler's replacement.

"Why?" Dr. Morrow asked. "It sounded pretty brave to me. Classic. Did you really say, 'That glass isn't there to protect me from you. It's to protect you from me'?"

"Yes."

"Sounds like you stopped the next 9/11."

Clements felt wounded. "I feel cold," he said.

"Sure," said Dr. Morrow. "One cold motherfucker. Stone cold."

Clements missed Ed. Ed would have said the right thing, the comforting thing. "It's ok," Ed would have said.

"It'll be ok."

"One cooooold muthafucka," Dr. Morrow said. "You want some of me?"

The praise demoralized Clements. He felt small. He was being lionized for doing something he despised. He'd suffered for months for issuing visas to Prince Nobody bin Nobody's barber, cook, and cleaner. But with the names confirmed and the revocations made, Clements suffered a deeper regret.

Everything he'd been raised to believe about the United States and about himself, dashed by supreme prejudice. There were a thousand excuses for prejudice: there would always be the Holocaust, and the Holocaust deniers. What difference did either party make to the other? That it had occurred made no difference to the deniers. And denial didn't erase its occurrence.

Clements would suffer the rest of his life for his prejudice. He had saved nobody from nothing. There was his service on the front line. There was his war on terror.

Chapter 31

Mutton trudged through the breezy evening. The black and orange triangles of used car lot streamers crisscrossed the pool area. Hordes of crows flew through the cobweb of plastic flapping on the breeze. A dozen Harleys were parked at angles around the deck: Sportsters, Dynas, Softails, V-Rods, Touring Bikes, Low Riders, Wide-Glides, Electra Glides, bikes as old as 50 years and bikes rolled in fresh from the assembly line, all of them big and clean and shining. Mutton admired the chrome and steel and leather and rubber.

Miss Wellstone stepped off the stool at the far side where she was hanging state flags along the brick wall. She came around to join Mutton.

"Are we celebrating Halloween?" Mutton asked. Orange and black signs for the Harley Owners Group displayed the Harley-Davidson bar and shield. They hung above the bar, near the dance floor, and behind the podium where Vanna would deliver remarks.

Miss Wellstone pursed her lips. "More like the Day of the Dead, I'm afraid."

"Has she seen this yet?"

"At least she can't have me fired for it. This is my last event."

Mutton looked at his watch. "Anyone else coming?"

"They're in the snack bar."

Vanna's golf cart puttered up outside the pool area. She entered accompanied by the Protocol Assistant. She wore a long, brown salwar khamis, embroidered at the cuffs and hems, and held a clump of tissues to her nose. Storp came through the entrance behind her, clutching his stack of papers. The Gunny came out of the snack bar with

Sergeant Decker and Corporal Hunker. Thorner, Clements, and Colonel Windsock appeared behind them.

Miss Wellstone and Mutton joined the semi-circle that formed around Vanna. The breeze whipped the orange and black triangles and the crows circled and wheeled in the dusk.

"So the crows will ruin yet another reception," Vanna said, glowering at Storp, who buried his shame by staring at his stack of paper. "And what are these flags?" Vanna demanded.

"You like them, ma'am?" Miss Wellstone asked.

Vanna's silence and snake-slit eyes indicated otherwise. "Who asked you to hang them? This looks like ..."

"Halloween," Windsock said.

"I was told it was a Harley-Davidson theme," said Miss Wellstone. "Orange and black."

The tension was cut by a loud, deep-throated *brrapp-brrapp-brrapp-brraaaaappp* on the road outside the pool, followed by the appearance of Larry Porcas through the doorway, the Lebanese Harley shop owner just behind, each astride a low, sleek, bike. Porcas lifted a hand off the handlebars, a casual wave. He wore jeans and a black T-shirt, motorcycle boots and shades. The riders turned the bikes in slow, wide arcs, stopped together, and steadied the bikes, half-standing. Then came the big, clean sound of the engines being cut, not quite quitting, the final flutter, then exhausted silence.

"Oh, my," Vanna said, her hand to her heart in false timidity. "They're *loud*."

Storp looked at his stack of paper. "Doesn't sound like purring to me."

Porcas sauntered over.

Vanna said, "I asked for *purring* bikes, Mr. Porcas. *Purring*."

"Heyyy," he said, immune to the tension, "these are hawwwgs. You can't muzzle the hawwwgs."

"Mr. Porcas, you weren't wearing a helmet when you came through that door."

"No, ma'am."

"I certainly hope that tomorrow night you'll be wearing a helmet." Vanna turned to Miss Wellstone. "If we can return to the matter at hand. Isn't this overdoing it? The orange and black? What are these signs? The H.O.G.s? Won't this be a problem with our Muslim guests?"

Porcas, still immune to disapproval, cut in giddily: "Harley Owners' Group, Ma'am." In a low, irreverent pitch he said, "The HAWWWWGS." He curled his lips in rebellion and giggled carelessly. Overhead the crows rode the increasing wind and bludgeoned the air with their cries.

Vanna blew her nose and stuck the tissue up her sleeve. She looked around slowly, spinning on her heel. In a nasal voice she said, "It doesn't look like an American celebration."

Potts cleared his throat.

"What about red, white, and blue?"

"Mom, these flags accentuate the Harley-Davidson theme."

Vanna shook her head. "No," she said. "We cannot have this." She was silent, visibly restraining herself. She fanned her face. "I want red, white and blue. This – this looks like a Halloween party. Or a used car lot. Are these bicycles for sale?"

"Mom. The state flags are hung along the walls."

Potts said, "There are red, white and blue streamers and bunting on the podium. Where you will give the remarks."

"And we'll have red, white, and blue bunting on the gazebo."

Storp was scribbling on his stack. Vanna looked at the black and orange triangles, flapping on the breeze. The number of crows decreased as the sky darkened.

"I like the Statue of Liberty," Vanna offered, pointing at the green, seven foot Styrofoam statue floating in the pool. It floated there, eerily shadowed, bottom lit by the pool lights.

Miss Wellstone took Vanna's elbow and led her forward. "Here – watch your step. I've asked GSO to mark the wires with streamers. The wires anchor the Green Lady."

"Good. We don't want anyone drinking too much and tripping into the pool." Vanna stopped short. "My Goodness!" she said, and brought a hand to her chest. She stared at one of the bikes.

"Mom?" Miss Wellstone, Storp, Colonel Windsock, and Mutton stepped closer and followed Vanna's eyes. Miss Wellstone blushed. Mutton smiled. Storp stepped toward the handlebar and leaned close. He looked up at Vanna shaking his head slowly.

"We can't have this," Vanna said. "Can we get rid of this bicycle?" The handbrake was sculpted in the image of a woman lying on her back, her hands behind her head. She was buck-naked. Mutton found himself staring at the sexy chrome Venus. He couldn't take his eyes off her.

"We must get rid of this bicycle," Vanna demanded.

"I don't know," said Storp. He looked around. "How many of these motorcycles might have this?" He slipped in the word "motorcycle" cautiously. "Larry?"

Mutton inspected the Sportster next to the offending bike. The kickstand bore the same naked image, leaning back seductively and filling Mutton with the same desire he once felt for Vanna. Clements, Windsock, Thorner, the Marines, everyone had joined in looking over the bikes. They found gas cap orgies and pot leaves on mirrors, and a dozen bikes featuring the nude, a pin-up girl, and skeletons on seats, on racks, and engraved into the pipes. One kickstand was shaped as an extended middle finger.

"We can't have these bicycles."

"Motorcycles," Storp said, losing himself for the moment.

Vanna glared, then sneezed. She blew her nose and stuffed the tissue up her sleeve. "My head," she said, taking it gingerly with her fingertips. "My head hurts. We can't do this. We can't do this. The last thing we need is to open *The Green Truth* and find scandalous photos of my farewell soiree. Mr. Storp, can we do the Declaration instead? The Pledge of Allegiance to the war on terror?"

"I don't see how. The event is tomorrow. Maybe we can cover up these things somehow? Larry, can we put duct tape over these – ladies?"

"I'll check. But Harley riders love their accessories," Porcas said.

"Promise me you'll cover every image," Vanna said. "Now, isn't this supposed to be a rehearsal?"

Storp cleared his throat and read from his stack. "At 7:45 I come to the podium and ask the guests to move back. The pushers and pullers help move them out of this space. The Marines march past the bar, turn, do their wheel here. The Gunny calls for the Colors."

"The Marines aren't presenting the Colors?" the Gunny asked.

"The Colors come in on the back of the motorcycles."

The Gunny shook his head.

"When the Marines are in place, we start the music."

"The National Anthem?" Windsock asked.

"We have plenty of time for the Anthem. Afterwards. So, cue the music for the Harleys to enter."

"Purring," Vanna said.

"Yes. The Harleys come purring into the pool area.

Larry, is this enough space for you to turn and park?"

"We've been practicing it all afternoon. We're ready to do it live. With the music."

"The two bikes will enter flying the American and the Kingdom's Colors. The bikes will park here, where we're standing."

"Fine. Then what?"

"Then we cut the music. A moment of silence. The National Anthem. Then your remarks."

Vanna approached the podium. "Where is the carpeting?"

"Do you want carpeting, Ma'am?"

"I need carpeting. My feet will hurt from standing in heels. I want plenty of carpeting by the entrance, too, where we greet the guests."

"Yes, ma'am."

Vanna stood behind the podium and looked up. The floodlights over the bar poured a harsh light down over her.

"How are the lights?"

"They're fine, ma'am."

"Do they make me shiny?"

~ ~ ~

The soft notes of the saxophone drifted over the pool from where the jazz quartet played in the gazebo, gently punctuated now and then by a prayerful warble from the *Muezzins*. The crows flapped and cawed overhead. As the twilight darkened the line to greet Vanna grew and the orange lights threw a jaundiced tint over the party. The lighted water shimmered around the twelve-foot Styrofoam Lady Liberty. A dozen cocktail tables covered with white cloths held unlit candles, toothpick American flags, and bowls of peanuts. Waiters in black tie offered water and soft drinks. Above it all the American flag, high up on its mast, sagged on the dying breeze, the glare of a spotlight pinpointing it against the sky.

Guests unfamiliar with each other met, introduced, moved on. The bikes served as objects of shallow conversation.

"Nice motorcycle."

"Yes, a nice one."

"They are all nice."

"Yes. Are they all Harley-Davidson?"

"I think so. I think the are all Harley-Davidson."

The same conversation between men in thobes, in western suits, ladies in long dresses, a man in a suit meeting a man in a thobe. They asked: "What for?"

Some guessed: "Is it Halloween?"

"Is it the American National Day?"

"No. That is the Fourth of July. Today is Halloween"

"I thought it was a Farewell party."

"Yes, that is it. But, farewell to what?"

"I don't know. To the consulate?"

"Yes, that must be it. They must be leaving. This is perhaps farewell to America."

Passing waiters interrupted: "Beverage?"

"Thank you. They will serve wine?"

"After the prayer."

"I will wait until after prayer."

Portly men in thobes gathered with regal sheikhs wearing white headdresses affixed perfectly, wide, golden agls holding them down. They stood among the shining, low-slung bikes, a glass of soda in hand; bearded men, men with meticulous goatees, clipped mustaches, clean eyebrows over their sharp, dark eyes. They were secretly proud to have been invited but outwardly aloof. Arab spoke to Arab until an American passed by.

"How are you?"

"*Al Hamdu Lilla.*"

"*Al Hamdu Lilla.* It is a pleasant evening."

"Yes. Nice bike."

"It's a Harley."

"They are all Harley-Davidson?"

"Yes. And we are offering rides. Will you take a ride?"

"Maybe later." It is a polite answer: the man in a thobe could not straddle a hog.

Liston sat on the screened porch outside his bungalow next to the pool area. He took his foot off the cooler and passed fresh bottles to Specs and Buzz. They could hear the jazz and the chatter rising from the pool. They watched the façade of the Kingdom Hospital casting a greenish light over the night. Silhouettes and profiles came toward the glass, then stepped back inside. Other figures lingered by the glass.

"*Muttawa.* Looking to make an arrest."

"I hope they do."

Buzz said nothing. He reached for the last of his beer but felt something warm and furry. He didn't flinch. "Mouse."

"I'd think he'd go for the cheese next door," Specs said.

Buzz opened the fresh cold bottle of Heineken. The three communicators, non-diplomatic personnel unwelcome at the reception, sat in the dark watching the façade of the hospital. The hospital watched back.

Thorner waited on the twenty yards of red carpet with Tinker and Clements to make contact with VIPs as they arrived at the pool. Tinker's hands nervously flipping his tie and his pocket flaps while Clements nipped a flask and passed it to Thorner, who took it gratefully, pulled a long drink, and wiped his mouth with the back of his hand like the grizzled rogue that he was.

"We have to be polite to these fucks?" he asked.

"We're pushers," Tinker explained. "Our job is to push

the guests toward the Ambassador-to-Be and introduce them."

"Introduce them? I don't even know them. I didn't invite them. How the hell am I supposed to know these fucks?"

"You're supposed to find out."

"How the hell do I do that?"

"The shuttle drops them off here. When they get out, introduce yourself. Escort them to the reception. And please," Tinker said, laughing in a weak, nervous gasp. "Don't call them 'fucks'."

"These fucks don't give a fuck who the fuck I am. And I don't give a fuck who they are. Foreign terrorist fucks."

Three figures approached from the Marine house: the Gunny, flanked by Decker and Hunker. They wore Dress Blue. The Gunny wore a sword and scabbard. Decker and Hunker each carried a ceremonial rifle. Hunker was smoking.

Tinker asked, "Where are the flags?"

"What flags?" the Gunny asked.

"You're not presenting the Colors?" Thorner asked.

The white Chevy van pulled up in the early evening and the driver came around to open the door. He placed a step stool on the ground and the lone occupant stepped out behind a woody cloud of incense. The large sheikh wore a floor-length white thobe covered by a gauzy, gold-trimmed black meshlis. His moustache was neatly trimmed, and he adjusted his white headdress as Pudge introduced himself and escorted the fat man up the red carpet.

"We're pushers?" Thorner asked. "Does that mean Clements can push that fat fuck over?"

"Our job is to prompt Vanna if she forgets a name. To avoid embarrassment."

"This whole charade is an embarrassment."

Clements returned to where Thorner and Tinker stood and said, "We also have hookers."

"There are hookers inside?" Thorner asked.

"He means the staff who hook onto guests and take them away from the receiving line and bring them to the pullers, who pull them deeper into the party. But the hookers have a hard time because all the guests want to talk to Vanna."

"Why would anyone want to talk to Vanna?"

"Visa problems," Clements said, and nipped his flask.

"Fat foreign fucks," Thorner said.

Windsock sat at a table deep inside the party where Vanna could not see him: it was forbidden to sit during such events. But Windsock detested the shallow chatter between standing guests. He sat with a television anchor, a professor, and a jazz enthusiast tapping his foot to "Take the A Train".

Windsock's eyes followed the floodlight to the American flag. He'd seen to it that a new flag was raised for the event, but it drooped in the humid night. Windsock felt about as patriotic as the drooping flag. He had to work hard to explain that they weren't celebrating Halloween. He worked hard to explain that not all Harley riders were the devil, and that the HOG décor was not an insult to Islam. Windsock struggled to find the patriotic flutter in his chest. He tapped his foot along with his friend.

The flutter Mutton felt in his chest was the sense of foreboding that Vanna would stick him with a VIP. Mutton was sweating heavily, starting from where is Sig clung to his back in its leather holster and harness and emanating outward. His suit trousers were damp. "You need a drink," Thorner told him.

"I've been drinking all night."

"You need a real drink." Thorner handed his plastic cup to Mutton.

Mutton finished the gin and tonic. At the bar Thorner told the waiter, "Two waters."

"I need to rehydrate," Mutton said.

"That lime will replenish your salts."

"You're confused," Mutton told Thorner.

"Speaking of Confusion. Who's Belvedere talking to?"

Mutton followed Thorner's eyes. Belvedere was talking, talking, talking to a short man in a thobe. The man in the thobe managed to interrupt Belvedere' stream-of-consciousness and get a word in. Both men looked down.

"I don't know what it's for," Belvedere said. "They tape them so they don't get scratched on the way in." He said it like a fact he had known all his life. "These machines are worth tens of thousands of dollars. That accessory right there cost over a thousand dollars. They just forgot to take the tape off," he said. He reached out and pulled the tape off the hand brake.

The short man stared at the hand brake. Belvedere followed his gaze. The hand brake was sculpted in the figure of a naked woman. Belvedere excused himself and walked away. One of the paparazzi raised his camera and took a shot of the hand brake.

Vanna asked the head of the Kingdom's delegation, the Minister for Trade and Industry: "Don't you just love our Harley-Davidson theme?"

"Hm? Yes. I like it very much."

"We *had* considered a Pledge of Allegiance to the War On Terror. You and I would have signed parchment."

"Hmmm. Interesting." The Minister looked at his watch. "Well, don't you think it's time we begin?"

"I do," Vanna said. "Yes I do." She signaled Storp.

~ ~ ~

Storp stepped up to the podium in the glare beneath the high, drooping Star-Spangled Banner. The mic rumbled with his throat-clearing. The jazz quartet stopped playing. The pushers and pullers and hookers moved swiftly among the hundreds of guests, directing the crowd into place behind ropes and stanchions. They cleared a space wide enough for the Marines and the motorcycles. Storp counted backwards in a voice that grew fainter and fainter until at two he had achieved a degree of near-silent curiosity. The crowd looked on attentively, waiting for Storp to continue.

"Ladies and gentlemen. Good evening and welcome to the American Consulate. To begin this evening's program, the United States Marine Corps – "

The Gunny led Decker and Hunker onto the deck. They snapped like clockwork, Gunny's commands clear and loud, the slap of gloved hands against rifle and thigh. They turned from the bar toward the open space, wheeled before the podium, lowered their weapons, and assumed parade rest. Silence followed.

Mutton's chest pounded. The mechanical movements of the United States Marine Corps, standing at attention before Old Glory lit up by a single beacon of light, filled him with joy.

Storp said, "Ladies and gentlemen, the colors."

An electric guitar, low and grinding, growled through the sound system. In the distance a low rumble of thunder boiled up, grew louder, belched and brr-appped just outside the pool. The DJ cued up Steppenwolf. *Born to Be Wild.*

The crush of guests, pressed close behind the velvet ropes, gasped. They exchanged puzzled looks as the lead Harley rolled in flying the green flag of the Holy Kingdom. The second bike rolled in flying a large, new Star-Spangled

Banner.

Mutton didn't need an interpreter to read the reaction. Befuddlement, hilarity, condemnation, all registered in the eyes of the hundreds of onlookers, the sum total of shock and awe.

❋　❋　❋

Thank you for reading.
Please review this book. Reviews help others find
Absolutely Amazing eBooks and inspire us to keep
providing these marvelous tales.

If you would like to be put on our email list to receive
updates on new releases, contests, and promotions, please
go to AbsolutelyAmazingEbooks.com and sign up.

Acknowledgments

I enjoyed the benefit of moral and technical support from a lot of people: The guy who laughed with me through childhood and who read this first, my brother John. And Bunky, who hasn't read it yet, because you have to save the finished product for at least one person you hope will like it. My parents, who brought us all together. Barry Leeds and the literary underpinnings of his course catalogue. Michael Strong, who saw promise in early drafts, and Kevin Finch and Brandon Cohen who read later Fulls and offered substantial notes and encouraging feedback. Friends Jan Beiting and Nawaf Marjan found something to laugh about here. And this book would have been nowhere if not for the bonhomie and puzzled sanity of the many, many good friends who did time with me in Jeddah. And the two amigos who tolerated my efforts to describe this book over beers at Sanborns in Mexico City, David Suarez and Gabriel Feddersen.

Finally, to my wife Deepa, who still hasn't taken my name and probably never will. Her forbearance while I write can only be repaid with demands of further forbearance. And for Vikram and Mohan, gamboling away.

I owe thanks and appreciation to Shirrel Rhoades at New Pulp Press for seeing this 10-year endeavor reach the light.

About the Author

B.A. East grew up in Connecticut, studying writing, journalism, and literature at Central Connecticut State University. Prior to that he had some success cutting up his fingers as a deli clerk and reading pulp in the stockroom of the local K-Mart.

After graduation Ben studied education at the University of New Haven while working as a long-term sub in a tough neighborhood where his main duty was to prevent food fights in the cafeteria. Succeeding in this, he joined the Peace Corps and spent two years teaching the eager young students at Providence Girls Secondary School in Malawi, traveling around Africa between terms, usually on the back of a lorry or beside chickens on a bus.

When Ben returned to the U.S. in 1999, he found the whole world had got connected to the Internet while he was gone. He endured a year and a half teaching high school dropouts at an alternative incarceration center in Connecticut and at Brooklyn College Academy in New York, then quickly fled overseas again. He spent two years teaching British and American Literature at the American School of Asuncion in landlocked Paraguay, learning to surf in Brazil between terms.

Ben later joined the State Department's Foreign Service, spent a year studying Arabic, and shipped off to his first assignment adjudicating visas in Saudi Arabia. Subsequent tours have included work in Managua, Nicaragua; Accra, Ghana; Mexico City; and Washington, DC.

Ben's manuscript treating espionage and the West African coke trade was shortlisted in 2014 for the Dundee International Book Prize and the Leapfrog Press Fiction Prize. His short stories and novel reviews have appeared in *The Foreign Service Journal, Atticus Review, Crime Factory Magazine,* and other publications. He's at work on a novel about the lack of a national conversation on gun control.